First published by Beaches and Trails Publishing 2024
Copyright © 2024 by Marie-Hélène Lebeault
All rights reserved.

Editing by Jessica McKenna
Cover by Marie-Hélène Lebeault

BEACHES AND TRAILS
PUBLISHING

# STARS BEYOND REALMS

## THE FIRST JUMP MISSION

# CHAPTER 1

THE MORNING SUN splashed glorious rays of gold over the sleek, metallic surfaces of the Interstellar Academy. Hovering vehicles zipped through the air, and floating holographic displays advertised the latest advancements in space exploration. Alex stood in this bustling atmosphere, a rebellious glint in his eyes as he drank in the towering spires of the academy. The Academy stood as a beaming symbol of human achievements among the stars. Every moment he walked from his quarters to the main campus, he was filled with pride at his position.

Hair tousled with deep-set eyes, Alex was not a typical cadet. His uniform sat slightly askew about his frame, contrasting sharply with the pristine appearance of his peers. His mind, always at work, tossed ideas about parallel universes back and forth as he made his way through the academy's hallways.

He soon arrived at a large lecture hall where his friends Nia, Jaxon, and Yasu sat. Nia looked up from her tablet and gave him a knowing smile. Her intelligent eyes swept over him, and she opened her mouth to say something but thought better of it. They had previously had a conversation about his appearance, and she told him he couldn't change. He recalled the conversation and smiled back at her.

Jaxon, the tech whiz of the group, sat behind them and was

immersed in a holographic display. It looked like something he shouldn't have access to, but Alex didn't want to pry. Yasu, ever the strategist, analyzed a 3D model of a galaxy. In the last few weeks, he had taken it upon himself to devise a plan to theoretically take over the galaxy.

Alex wanted to ask about the rest of the day's schedule. A hole had appeared in his brain, taking something important into its dark space. He turned to Nia, sorry to interrupt her reading. Behind her, he spotted the instructor entering the hall and chose to put it aside.

The instructor walked up to the podium and called everyone to order without hesitation. She was a stern woman known for her no-nonsense approach, and everyone quickly put aside their previous preoccupations to pay attention. The room dimmed as a holographic projection of the Milky Way galaxy filled the space above them. The instructor started the day's lesson on the theoretical aspects of space-time manipulation.

"As future explorers of the cosmos," she began, her voice echoing through the hall, "you must understand the fabric of space-time. But remember, theory is one thing; practical application is another. The universe does not forgive mistakes."

Though Alex tried to listen without judgment, he couldn't help but pulse with questions. He tried to scribble them at the side of his note, but he grew impatient as time passed. As the lecture delved into the complexities of quantum mechanics, his hand shot up, a challenging question forming on his lips.

"Professor, if we were, theoretically, to manipulate space-time, could we not only travel through space, but also explore parallel universes?"

The room had been quiet all along, but a greater hush fell on everyone, all eyes turning to Alex. The professor raised an eyebrow, her lips lifting in a humorless smile. She should have grown accustomed to Alex's interruptions, but they still tired her.

"Mr. Rivera, while your curiosity is commendable, let's focus on mastering our universe before we think about exploring others." Though she sounded amused, her tone carried a hint of caution.

But Alex's question lingered in the air, igniting a spark of wonder in the minds of his fellow cadets. Unknown to them, they were so much closer to the answer than they thought possible.

The lecture concluded, and the instructor left the hall. Alex and his friends gathered up their things, discussing his question with charged animation and exploring all the possibilities of multiverse travel.

Yasu believed that venturing into the multiverse would make his plan to rule the galaxy harder. "What if," he said, slinging his bag over his shoulder, "in the multiverse, there's a version of me who tries to fight me for the position of supreme ruler?" The others looked at him and laughed. Yasu rarely spoke up, but when he did, he occasionally voiced something wild.

They stepped out into the academy grounds, eager to continue the conversation over a meal before their next lecture commenced. Jaxon and Yasu discussed the fate of the multiverse haunted by an evil Yasu, while Nia watched quietly, interjecting to correct assumptions.

Alex listened distractedly, but his thoughts were on the lecture and the actual chance that someone could make a journey through the multiverse. He pulled out his tablet from his bag to check one of his previous notes and saw a notification flash across his screen: 'Briefing with the commander'

"That's what I was forgetting," he said.

His friends looked at him. He held the tablet to their faces. "It seems we forgot we had a briefing this afternoon. We should probably hurry with our meal and head to the briefing room."

They rushed to the cafeteria, selecting the fastest meal and going to an empty table. As they ate, they speculated on why they had been called.

"Maybe they heard Yasu talking about taking over the universe and want to punish us for letting him get away with it," Jaxon said, his mouth full of food.

Nia wrinkled her nose. "I think it might have to do with the Quantum Leap Device. But that's merely a guess. I heard some of the higher-ups discussing it earlier."

Alex tried to recall what the Quantum Leap Device was. Somewhere in his head, he traced a picture from his late-night searches on the Academy's database. He said nothing, but gripped his fork a little tighter and ate a little faster.

The afternoon sun cast long shadows across the Interstellar Academy's main plaza as Alex and his friends made their way to the high-tech briefing room. They entered, slipping in without drawing attention to themselves. The air was laden with whispers of a new, top-secret mission, and the cadets speculated about what it might entail.

High-ranking officials and a few selected cadets sat in the room, all waiting in strained silence. At the front stood the mission commander, a distinguished figure known for leading some of the most daring explorations in the academy's history. His bearing was stiff and straight, like a column that had weathered multiple storms and remained standing.

"Welcome, cadets," the commander began, his voice resonating through the room. "You are here because you represent the best of the Interstellar Academy. Today, we discuss a mission unlike any other – a journey into the unknown, exploring the very edges of our scientific understanding."

The room erupted in exhilarated and curious whispers. Alex exchanged an intrigued look with Nia, who raised her eyebrows in response.

The commander continued, "We have developed an experimental technology that, if successful, could allow us to explore parallel universes. This Quantum Leap Device is the culmination of years of research, but it is untested. The risks are high, but so are the potential rewards."

A holographic display illuminated the room, showing a sleek spacecraft. It was shaped like a long silver bullet, but equipped with thrusters at the sides. The commander switched the view to the interior of the craft, showing the Quantum Leap Device. It was a marvel of clever engineering; complex and polished. The cadets leaned forward, absorbing every glossy detail.

"We need a team of exceptional cadets to undertake this mission. Your stay in this prestigious institution would have prepared you for forays into unknown territory. However, this mission will be unlike any other you've encountered. For this reason, you'll undergo training to navigate the multiverse, to face challenges beyond our current understanding," the commander declared, his gaze sweeping across the room.

Excitement, like a jolt of electricity, surged through Alex. This was the adventure he had been dreaming of; a chance to turn his theories into reality. But he tamped it down as best as he could. They could choose anyone for this mission. He looked at the other cadets around the room; some younger with brilliant intellects, others older with years of experience.

The commander's eyes settled on Alex and his friends. "Alex Rivera, Nia Chen, Jaxon Brooks, and Yasu Garcia – you have been selected for this mission. Your skills and unique perspectives make you the ideal candidates."

Alex exchanged glances with his friends, noting the looks of shock on their faces, and imagining they mirrored the look on his. He had dared to hope, but now that it had happened, it seemed unreal, as though he was floating in a dream.

The briefing ended, and the officials and other cadets shook their hands and offered congratulations and encouragement as they left the room. Now alone with the commander and a few top instructors and officials, the cadets absorbed the reality of their position. They remained in their seats as the head instructor, a man with a fluffy mustache and uncombed hair, gave them an overview of the mission's logistics and the rigorous training that lay ahead.

It was hours before they left the room. Though their bodies and heads ached, they had something novel to look forward to, and that kept permanent smiles plastered on their faces.

Outside, the sun was setting, casting a warm glow over the academy. Alex looked up at the stars, now twinkling in the evening sky. They seemed closer, more real than ever before. He turned to his friends, grinning from ear to ear.

"We're about to make history." Resolve coated his every word. "Let's show them what we're capable of."

Together, they walked back to their quarters, their minds racing with the possibilities of what lay ahead.

⎯⎯▼⎯⎯

The training came first. It was ten weeks of grueling activity, in which the brightest quantum physicists and engineers divulged complex information about their journey. They had the basic drilling the Academy provided for all cadets, and that formed the foundation of their training. They built on it with more in-depth information on astrophysics, quantum mechanics, and ammunition. They rose with the sun and didn't leave the training facility until late at night.

The team worked themselves to the bone during that period, but whenever the tiredness threatened to weaken them, they recalled the journey that lay ahead. They were about to do something nobody else in the academy's history had done, and that propelled them onward.

Over meals, they encouraged themselves, stating what they'd like to be remembered for in the history books. They kept the joke of Yasu's reign over the galaxy alive, hailing him as Yasu the Supreme Overlord. The meals were regulated and specially prepared, providing them necessary nourishment to enrich their bodies and minds. Though nourishing, the food was bland, prepared for necessity, rather than taste. Their conversations helped keep their minds off the tastelessness of each morsel.

In the evenings, as they headed to their quarters, they revised all they had learned, throwing questions back and forth between each other. Alex made a point of ensuring they explored each person's weak point. It was important to him they remained their best.

Eventually, the time for their journey arrived.

The night was clear and star-studded as Alex, Nia, Jaxon, and Yasu made their way to the launch pad. Nervous energy pumped through them, keeping them bouncing on the balls of their feet, but the thrill which had sustained them in the past few weeks remained. Before them stood the spacecraft equipped with the Quantum Leap Device, its lustrous metal surface gleaming under the moonlight.

The technical crew bustled around the spacecraft, performing last-minute checks. The mission commander approached the team. His expression was solemn yet encouraging.

"This is a monumental step for the Interstellar Academy and for humanity." He clasped each cadet's hand firmly. "Remember, you are pioneers on the edge of a new frontier. Stay focused, stay sharp, and trust in your training."

The cadets nodded, each of their faces a mask of determination. They donned their specialized suits, designed to protect and sustain them through the quantum leap. The engineers had custom-built the suits for each of them, and they fit like a second skin. As they boarded the spacecraft, each cadet took a moment to look back at the world they knew, wondering what lay ahead in the uncharted realms of the multiverse.

They got into the spacecraft and assumed their positions, tightening their seatbelts and adjusting their seats for maximum comfort. The atmosphere was tense but focused. Alex took his position at the navigation console, his fingers running over the controls with practiced ease. Nia, Jaxon, and Yasu checked their systems, ensuring everything was in order for the leap.

"Quantum Leap Device is powering up," Alex announced, his voice steady. The spacecraft hummed to life, the core of the device glowing with an otherworldly light.

"Initiating sequence in three, two, one..." Jaxon counted down.

A sudden surge of energy rippled through the spacecraft as it shot into the night sky. The cadets braced themselves, keeping their eyes on their systems to catch any anomalies in time. But they were unprepared for the novelty of this journey. Reality seemed to warp and bend around them. A kaleidoscope of colors and lights enveloped the spacecraft, transporting them through the very fabric of space and time.

The sensation was unlike anything they had ever experienced— a dizzying, exhilarating journey through the unknown. They watched in awe as stars and galaxies blurred past them, each a gateway to a different universe.

And then, as suddenly as it had begun, the tumultuous journey came to an abrupt halt. The spacecraft shuddered, alarms blaring, as it crash-landed on an unknown planet. The force jolted the cadets forward, almost slamming them against their systems.

As the dust settled, they slowly regained their bearings. Alex was the first to come to, his eyes wide with shock. He got out of his seat and went to the others, helping them to their feet. Together, they made their way to the spacecraft's hatch.

With a deep breath, Alex opened the hatch, revealing a world unlike any they had ever seen. The sky was a vibrant shade of violet, and two moons hung low on the horizon. In the distance, towering structures and bright lights hinted at an advanced civilization.

They had done it. They had traveled to a parallel universe.

The cadets stepped out onto the alien terrain, their hearts racing with the realization that their adventure was just beginning. A new world awaited them, full of mysteries to unravel and discoveries to be made.

As they looked up at the unfamiliar sky, they knew one thing for certain: their lives would never be the same.

# CHAPTER 2

DAWN CAME, a large, but distant sun, casting an ethereal glow over the unfamiliar landscape where the cadets stood amidst the wreck of their spacecraft. The crash had left them dazed but, miraculously, unharmed. They found themselves on the outskirts of a sprawling metropolis, its architecture a harmonious blend of nature and advanced technology.

Alex got out first, his eyes drinking in a sky unlike any he had seen before. The sky's violet hue was fading to a pale blue, revealing a city that pulsed as though alive. Skyscrapers of glass and metal soared towards the sky, intertwined with lush greenery that cascaded down their sides.

"Is everyone okay?" he called out, his voice echoing slightly in the still morning air.

One by one, Nia, Jaxon, and Yasu responded, each pushing through the disorientation of their abrupt arrival. They gathered their bearings, their training kicking in as they assessed the situation.

"We're definitely not in Kansas anymore," Jaxon quipped, trying to lighten the mood as he surveyed the alien skyline.

The cadets quickly checked the spacecraft for damage. It was inoperable, and the Quantum Leap Device was visibly damaged. It was a miracle they had made it out mostly unharmed.

"We need to find out where we are, and if there's any way to communicate with the academy." The wheels were already turning in Nia's head, trying to figure out the quickest way out of the mess. Her mind went to the other supplies they had in the craft, but decided against carrying them.

"I wish we could take off our suits." Jaxon lifted his arms up and down. "I feel rather uncomfortable."

The others did too, but they knew keeping the suits on was a protective measure, in case the atmosphere did not agree with them.

The team ventured out of the wreckage, stepping onto the streets of the city. They were met with curious glances from the passersby – beings that were unmistakably human, yet dressed in styles so unfamiliar, they looked like creatures from an unknown race.

As they moved through the city, they were struck by the seamless integration of technology and nature. Holographic displays floated alongside natural waterfalls, lush with greenery. The vehicles glided silently far above it all, leaving no trace of pollution. It was unlike their universe, where nature existed in small clumps in small trees in small parks, surrounded by structures of metal and concrete.

The cadets were cautious, but mesmerized by the sights and sounds of this new world. It was a utopia compared to their Earth.

In another time, in different circumstances, they might have remained immersed in the sights forever. But here and now, their awe was tainted with urgency. They needed to learn more about this place, to find a way back to their universe. First, they had to understand the rules of this world, to blend in without drawing unwanted attention.

As they walked, Yasu noticed a group of individuals who watched them with keen interest. He told his friends about it, and when the group approached, the cadets braced themselves, unsure of the reception they would receive.

"Welcome, travelers," one of them said, a friendly smile on his face. "New faces do not come often. Where are you from?"

The cadets exchanged glances, realizing that their journey had just taken an unexpected turn. They were about to engage with the inhabitants of this alternate Earth, a crucial first step in the mission.

They needed some caution and a lot of tact, or they could lose everything.

The leader, a man with an amiable demeanor, introduced himself as Kael, a local guide. His curiosity about the cadets was evident, but he eyed them with clear suspicion.

"We're... explorers, from a distant place," Alex cautiously replied, aware of the need for discretion.

Kael's eyes sparkled with intrigue. "Explorers, you say? Well, you've certainly come to the right city. Follow me, I'll show you around."

As they walked through the city, the cadets remained astounded by the harmony of advanced technology and nature. The buildings were tall structures of glass and metal covered in lush greenery, and the air was fresh, free of pollution. They walked past a huge glasshouse, full of plants and flowers with purple, pink, and orange leaves, and petals the size of their heads. Nia asked about the building and Kael said it belonged to the Ministry of Ecological Research. "Those are newly developed plants. And the glass structure serves as a controlled environment to aid their growth."

The people they passed seemed content, a stark contrast to the often hectic life on their Earth. Back home, everyone moved so quickly. This was the case for their Academy, where everyone hurried past as if the next stop was the most important in their life.

The tour led them to a serene park filled with exotic plants. These bore similarities to the plants in the glasshouse, but the colors of the leaves and petals were paler. Nia walked forward to a pretty blue-leaved bush, whose flower petals were small and needle-like. She leaned forward to inhale the sweet scent coming from it.

"I wouldn't do that if I were you," a voice said.

Nia looked up and gasped. The speaker stepped back, gasping too. She was the spitting image of her. The only differences lay in her makeup, hair, and choice of attire. Where Nia's was kept out of her face in a tight updo, the girl's hair fell across her face. Her eyelids were also dusted in golden powder, as were her lips.

Nia swiveled to call the attention of the others, but it seemed they had encountered their lookalikes and were studying them with as much curiosity.

For a moment, time seemed to stand still as both groups stared at each other in disbelief, overwhelmed by the realization that they were face-to-face with their alternate selves.

"Is this some kind of joke?" Yasu's alternate asked, breaking the silence.

"No joke," Yasu replied, equally baffled. "We're from... another version of Earth. Another universe."

The revelation sparked a flurry of questions and explanations. Initially, they spoke over themselves, everyone eager to chime in, but they soon gave Alex the lead. He spoke of their journey through time and space, detailing how fast and invigorating it was. The alternate selves were fascinated by the story of the quantum leap and the existence of a parallel universe. Their Alex shared that their Earth was part of a vast Space Federation, a coalition of planets that had achieved peace and technological advancement.

Kael interrupted at a point, confused by the words they were using, but interested in compensation for his troubles. Alex's alternate reached into his pocket, pulled out a handful of coins, and thrust them at him. The man grumbled for a moment, but when Alex threatened to report him to the authorities for illegal extortion, he sauntered off, his lackeys in tow.

Alex and his alternate took charge of the rest of the conversation, their euphoric energy bouncing off one another. This further convinced everyone of how similar their alternate selves were to them.

As they conversed, the cadets learned about the societal structure, the technological advancements, and the political dynamics of this alternate Earth. They were particularly intrigued by the mention of the Quantum Key, a device capable of navigating the multiverse, heavily guarded because of its power.

The encounter with their alternates was a pivotal moment. It provided the cadets with invaluable insights into this universe and a potential ally in their quest to return home. However, it also raised ethical questions about their presence in this alternate world and the impact they might have.

Their alternates led them to a towering structure that balanced on four lone columns, swaying like vines in the wind. Its magnificent design was a testament to the architectural advancement of this universe. Inside, they found interactive displays and virtual reality experiences that offered a deeper understanding of the federation's history, culture, and technological achievements.

Moving through the facility, the cadets learned about the federation's governing structure, its commitment to peace and sustainability, and its exploration endeavors across the galaxy. They were particularly fascinated by the advancements in space travel and integrating diverse alien technologies.

It was during this visit that the cadets learned more about the Quantum Key. Their alternates explained the Key was a closely guarded secret, held in a high-security facility due to its potential to disrupt the fabric of the universe.

The revelation of the Quantum Key ignited a spark of hope in the cadets. It was their best chance to return to their universe. However, they also understood the risks and ethical implications of tampering with such a powerful device.

Sunset arrived a little too fast. The cadets watched the sky deepen to purple again and remembered that they were far from home, with no solid plans for their return. Alex's alternate noticed their demeanor and offered them a place to spend the night. "You can spend the night with us," he said, looking at each of their faces. "We'll figure out a way to sneak in without triggering the alarm systems."

Tired, but less apprehensive now that they had friends, the cadets walked with some more boldness. The streets were alive with people and beings from various planets, each contributing to the vibrant tapestry of the federation. Markets displayed goods from across the galaxy, and holographic screens showcased news from distant worlds. The cadets marveled, absorbing every detail of this thriving Space society.

"This world... it's incredible," Nia said, her voice filled with wonder. "But we can't forget why we're here. Though we were meant to be exploring the very edges of scientific understanding, we still need to find a way back to our universe."

The alternates nodded in agreement, offering their support and assistance. They discussed potential strategies to access the Quantum Key, aware of the challenges that lay ahead.

The evening ended with the cadets and their alternates solidifying their newfound alliance. They were determined to navigate the complexities of this universe together, each step bringing them closer to their goal: returning home.

# CHAPTER 3

Morning arrived, the sun splashing warmth over the eco-structures in the city. Alex, Nia, Jaxon, and Yasu, having spent the night at the guesthouse Alex's alternate suggested, rose early. They gathered at the window in the large room, watching the sun spread its rays over the cityscape.

"This place is so, so gorgeous," Nia said, gaping, storing up every detail for the future. This was a vision to which their world could aspire.

Their alternates arrived soon after, bringing as much food as they could carry. They all sat on the room floor to discuss their plans for the day while munching on bread, bacon, and scrambled eggs. The food surprised them, because it was similar to theirs, but tasted different; more savory and delicious.

When they finished eating, they accompanied their alternate selves to embark on a comprehensive exploration of the federation's capital. Their mission: to gather information and resources for their quest to access the Quantum Key.

The city was a hub of Space activity, with representatives from various planets and species moving about, engaged in trade, diplomacy, and cultural exchanges. The cadets stared in bright-eyed glee at the peaceful coexistence of so many different beings, each contributing to the rich tapestry of the federation.

Their first stop was the Galactic Council, a grand building where leaders from across the galaxy convened. A crowd of citizens flowed in through the three large doors, and the cadets and their alternates joined them. Everyone moved in order, talking politely as they looked at the day's program on their handheld devices. The cadets and their alternates found seats in the higher parts of the chamber and prepared to pay attention to every detail.

Here, they witnessed a council session in progress, observing the democratic process that governed the federation. The discussion was about a new exploratory mission to a distant star system, highlighting the federation's ongoing commitment to discovery and cooperation.

Next, they visited a bustling spaceport, where ships of all shapes and sizes were docked. The cadets gazed, wide-eyed, at the variety of spacecraft, from sleek personal cruisers to massive freighters and elegant diplomatic vessels. Their alternates explained the different ships and their purposes, providing insights into the advanced technology that powered them.

On their journey through the spaceport, they encountered various alien species, each with their unique appearance and customs. The cadets interacted with some of them, learning about their home planets and cultures. These interactions broadened their understanding of the vastness and diversity of the galaxy.

The final stop was a cultural center, a place dedicated to the preservation and celebration of the myriad cultures within the federation. The center was a kaleidoscope of art, music, and traditions from countless worlds. The cadets immersed themselves in the exhibitions, gaining a deeper appreciation for the federation's diverse cultural heritage. Nia took notes about the rich historical tapestry of the world, comparing the information with all she knew from theirs. She believed having an extensive discussion about everything with her alternate self later would Confirm her information.

Throughout their exploration, the cadets gathered valuable information about the federation's structure, technology, and the potential whereabouts of the Quantum Key. They heard the name everywhere, but its location was cloaked in mystery, with people growing reticent or near unfriendly when they brought it up.

They also collected various gadgets and tools that might aid them in their mission, carefully avoiding drawing attention to their true intentions. Jaxon derived the most joy from the variety of new gadgets available. He tinkered with everything he could, alert and attentive when his alternate self explained what each device was for.

The long day slowly came to a close. The group made their way to a quiet café, reflecting on their findings. They ordered pastries and warm, fragrant tea, and took some moments to soak in the gentle ambiance of the decor. In time, the conversation returned to all they had seen throughout the day.

"This federation... It's incredible. The unity, the technology, the diversity." Jaxon's wide eyes were glazed with wonder.

"But remember, we're here for a reason. We need to stay focused on our mission," Nia added, bringing the group back to reality.

Everyone nodded in unison and they brought out their tablets to begin work. They had to formulate a plan to return home, and they had to do it fast. Their people were waiting for them at home, and they needed to let them know they were okay.

The cadets and their alternates were united by a common goal, preparing for the challenges ahead. They knew that accessing the Quantum Key would not be easy, but the cadets were determined to find a way back to their universe.

Later that evening, under the canopy of a starlit sky, the cadets and their alternates gathered in a bustling public square, vibrant with the energy of the city's nightlife. The square was alive with holographic displays and street performers, showcasing the artistic and technological prowess of the federation.

An unexpected occurrence caught their attention as they navigated through the crowd. A series of digital billboards flickered erratically, displaying garbled messages before returning to normal. The crowd murmured in confusion, shocked by the rare sight in a city where technology functioned seamlessly.

"Did we cause that?" Yasu whispered, concern evident in his voice.

"It's possible." Nia's brow furrowed. "Our presence here could create ripples in this universe."

The group moved to a quieter part of the square, discussing the implications of their actions. Yasu recalled their lessons on the delicate fabric of the multiverse from their training period. He reminded them of how one trainer kept emphasizing that even slight disturbances could have unforeseen consequences. The others looked at each other, gulping and realizing how much faster they needed to work now.

Another strange phenomenon interrupted their conversation—a sudden, unseasonal downpour in a city where the weather was precisely controlled. People scrambled for cover, many glaring at the sky with unconcealed disgust.

"This can't be a coincidence," Jaxon said, looking up at the rain-soaked sky. "Our arrival here might be affecting more than we realized."

The cadets' concern grew as they witnessed more anomalies—a temporary gravity fluctuation in a nearby park, causing a momentary sensation of weightlessness and a spontaneous power outage in a section of the city.

With each incident, it became apparent that their presence in this universe was causing a chain reaction of events, disrupting the normal flow of this world. They understood they needed to act responsibly to minimize their impact.

"We need to be more careful," Alex said, his voice tinged with worry. "We can't risk causing any more disturbances. Our mission to find the Quantum Key just got more complicated."

The group retreated to a secluded area, away from the public eye. They sat in a circle under the glow of the city lights, discussing their next steps. They needed to find the Quantum Key quickly and return to their universe before their presence caused more disruptions. They feared things could get worse and lead to full-scale destruction.

They further retreated from the street to the rooftop garden, as the alternate Yasu suggested. High above the bustling streets and beneath the soft glow of bioluminescent plants, the serene environment provided a stark contrast to the chaos they had witnessed earlier. There, they could discuss their situation without the prying eyes of the city.

Alex paced back and forth. Theories raced through his mind and the only way to keep himself from ripping off his skin was to keep moving. "We've learned about the butterfly effect in our training," he began. "Small actions can have significant impacts. I never expected we would witness it so soon." The trainer had emphasized not making any drastic actions that could ripple the balance between their worlds.

Nia, who had been studying a holographic map of the city, looked up. "It's like we're the butterflies in this universe. Our mere presence might cause these anomalies."

Jaxon looked up from his device, where he had displayed his notes from a previous lecture about the butterfly effect. "If we think about the multiverse as an interconnected web, our arrival here could be like a stone thrown into a pond, creating ripples that disturb the existing balance."

Yasu leaned against the railing, looking into the sky, his forehead wrinkled in concentration. "So, every step we take, every decision we make here, might alter something in this world. We need to be extremely cautious."

Their alternate selves listened intently, equally concerned about the implications. Nia's alternate spoke up. "In our studies of the multiverse, we've theorized about such impacts. But we've never had concrete evidence until now. Your presence here could be a valuable case study."

The group discussed the ethical implications of their actions. They agreed that while their primary goal was to return to their universe; they had a responsibility to minimize their impact on this one.

"We need to find the Quantum Key as discreetly as possible," Alex concluded. "No unnecessary interactions, no disturbances. We stick to the plan, and we stay under the radar."

The group solidified their strategy. They would continue their mission with more caution, rejuvenated by new purposefulness, aware that the fate of two universes could hinge on their actions.

As they left the rooftop, the city's lights twinkled below them, a reminder of the delicate balance they had to maintain. The cadets knew that the path ahead would be fraught with challenges, but they were determined to navigate it with care and integrity.

## CHAPTER 4

THE FOLLOWING DAY, the cadets and their alternates went to the ancient library of the federation, a vast repository of knowledge with archives that spanned the galaxy. The library, a magnificent structure of glass and light, housed millions of digital and physical texts from countless civilizations.

They were there in search of any information that could aid them in locating the Quantum Key. As they delved into the archives, their search led them to a secluded section dedicated to ancient prophecies and legends.

It was Nia's alternate who first stumbled upon a curious text, its pages worn by time. "Look at this," she called out, her voice echoing softly in the vast chamber. The group gathered around as she read aloud from the ancient manuscript.

"The Orion Prophecy... it speaks of a Starborne child from the Orion sector who will rise to challenge a great tyranny, bringing about its downfall and ushering in an era of peace." Her eyes widened with intrigue.

The cadets exchanged glances. "Could this be related to us?" Jaxon wondered aloud. "Our arrival here. Could it be part of this prophecy?"

Nia's alternate gave a noncommittal shrug. "Our lives have been peaceful so far. Unless we're counting the Empire." She exchanged a loaded look with Alex's alternate.

"The Empire?" Alex asked. "What Empire?"

The alternate Nia gave them a quick overview of the Empire. At one point, it ruled everything, preventing movement, exploration, and freedom of expression and speech. A long war took over for the current federation to gain an edge over the Empire. It remained, though weakened, and held significant power in certain sectors.

"Could it be possible that the Empire's powers are growing again?" Nia walked towards the bookshelf, itching to read everything in sight.

"We don't know. But if they are, how would you stop them?"

The group pondered the prophecy's implication and its connection to them. The idea that their unexpected journey might be intertwined with a cosmic destiny was both exhilarating and daunting.

A shadowy figure observed their discussion from a distance, hidden among the towering bookshelves. Unseen and unheard, the figure listened intently, their interest piqued by the newcomers and the mention of the prophecy.

The cadets, unaware of the watchful eyes, continued their research. They uncovered more about the prophecy, learning about the tyrannical Empire that had once threatened the peace of the galaxy. A text with worn pages spoke briefly about the Quantum Key, and how the Empire used it in their rule.

"The Empire... they might be the ones guarding the Quantum Key," Yasu said, quietly. "If this prophecy is connected to us, then our path to the Key might also involve confronting this Empire."

The revelation added an additional layer of complexity to their mission. Not only did they need to find the Key, but they might also have to play a role in a larger galactic struggle.

Evening fell, and the group packed up their stuff, their minds wrestling with the new information and trying to come up with the best course of action. The mysterious figure quietly followed them at a distance, their interest in the cadets and their mission growing stronger.

The cadets and their alternates stepped out into the cool night air, the stars above shining brightly. They knew their journey had taken a significant turn, one that could change the course of this universe and their own. But they were unsure of how to proceed. On the one hand, they needed the Quantum Key if they were to return home. However, if the Quantum Key was with the Empire, they would have to confront them to get it. And could they, young and inexperienced as they were, go against an Empire with such vast power?

Under the cloak of night, the cadets and their alternates navigated through the vibrant streets of the city. Now, the lights were dimmer, and it hummed with quieter energy. Their minds were still reeling from the revelations in the library, but they were determined to keep a low profile, aware of the growing complexity of their mission.

As they moved through the market square, now winding down after a bustling day, they couldn't shake off the feeling of being watched. The occasional glance over the shoulder, the fleeting shadows just at the edge of their vision—it was enough to put them on edge.

"Are we being followed?" Nia whispered, her eyes scanning the dwindling crowd.

"It's possible." Alex kept his voice low. "Considering all we have learned in the library, if we are connected to the prophecy, then the Empire would want to keep tabs on us. And even if not the Empire, some other parties involved in the struggle could be interested in our progress."

The group quickened their pace, weaving through the narrow alleys and less-traveled paths, trying to lose any potential tail. But the sense of being pursued persisted, a subtle but constant reminder of the danger they might be in.

Their path took them to a less affluent part of the city, where the bright lights and technological marvels gave way to dimmer streets and a palpable unease. Here, the Empire's influence was more evident—propaganda posters adorned the walls, and the residents moved with a wariness that spoke of fear and oppression.

"This is what the Empire does," alternate Jaxon murmured,

gesturing to the surroundings. "They may no longer be at the height of their power, but their shadow still looms large over many lives."

The people in the streets wore expressions akin to those of grieving patrons, their heads lowered, and their general posture one of subservience. It was a stark contrast to the parts of the city they had seen before, a reminder of the underlying struggles that persisted in this seemingly utopian society.

Though they tried to navigate the area stealthily and avoid apprehension, the inevitable happened—a group of Empire agents, clad in dark uniforms, confronted them. The agents were stern, their eyes cold and calculating.

"We've been monitoring your activities," one agent announced. "You're not from around here. Explain yourselves."

The cadets exchanged quick, nervous glances. Alex stepped forward, his mind racing for a plausible explanation.

"We're travelers, here to study the culture and advancements of your great city," he said, trying to sound confident.

The agent eyed them suspiciously, but before he could respond, a distraction erupted nearby—a group of residents began to protest against the agents, creating a commotion that drew their attention away.

While the guards were distracted, trying to calm the protesters, the cadets and their alternates slipped away, disappearing into a maze of streets. Alex and his alternate kept the lead, running long after they had shaken off their pursuers.

Breathing heavily, they found refuge in an abandoned warehouse, the quiet of the space a stark contrast to the adrenaline of the chase.

"That was too close," Yasu said, his voice tense. "We need to be more careful. The Empire is onto us."

In the dimly lit confines of the abandoned warehouse, the cadets and their alternates regrouped, the weight of their situation pressing heavily upon them. They were not just explorers anymore; they were now entangled in the political machinations of this universe. Their mission to find the Quantum Key had become even more perilous.

The stark contrast between the shadowy interior and the city's vibrant lights outside mirrored the duality of their current predicament.

As they discussed their next move, a soft clattering at the entrance caught their attention. They turned, poised for confrontation, only to see the mysterious figure from the library stepping into the dim light.

"Who are you?" Alex demanded, his stance defensive.

The figure removed their hood, revealing a weathered but determined face. "My name is Rael," he said, his voice tinged with caution. "I've been following your progress. You're not just any travelers, are you?"

The cadets exchanged wary glances, unsure of how much to reveal.

It was Nia's alternate who spoke up. "We can't just tell you who we are. We don't know anything about you."

Rael paused, lifting his hands in a display of surrender. "You need the Quantum Key. That much I know. I'm part of a faction that opposes the Empire's remnants. We seek to dismantle their remaining power structures and bring true freedom to the federation." He paused, eyes sweeping over all of them. "We can work together."

Nia's alternate relaxed visibly at his declaration. "I've heard about your faction."

Rael took the opportunity to reach into his pocket and take out a small device. It had a small screen and a touchpad. He threw it to them and Alex caught it.

The others huddled close, eager to see what it meant. An insignia was at the back, a black shield with a golden sword and banner.

"I recognize it," Alex's alternate said. "I've seen it on the news a few times." He tapped the touchpad, and the screen came to life, showing Rael's face and details. The device served as a means of identification and communication.

"Why help us?" Jaxon asked, still cautious.

"Your mission aligns with our goals," Rael explained. "The

Empire's downfall is long overdue. You spoke about the prophecy in the library, but I don't know how true that is. However, our goals align. The time to act is close and we can work together to get the Quantum Key and cripple the Empire for good."

The cadets realized the depth of their involvement in the affairs of this universe. Their mission had evolved into something much greater than they had anticipated.

"We need to access the facility where the Quantum Key is held," Alex said, his voice firm. "But we can't do it alone. We need your help."

Rael nodded, his expression resolute. "I can provide you with information and resources. But this will be dangerous. The Empire may be weakened, but they are still formidable."

The group agreed to join forces, understanding the risks and the potential impact of their actions. They planned their next steps and had another meeting, in which they would form a strategy to infiltrate the high-security facility where the Quantum Key was kept.

The cadets and their new ally stood together, united by a common cause. The stakes were higher than ever, but so was their determination. They were no longer just explorers caught in an extraordinary situation; they were now active participants in a struggle that could change the fate of two universes.

# CHAPTER 5

IN THE EARLY hours of the morning, before the city awoke, the cadets, their alternates, and Rael, the rebel leader, convened in a hidden base on the outskirts of the city. The base, nestled underground, was a hub of activity, brimming with members of the rebel faction preparing for the day's operations.

Everyone milled about with purpose and urgency. Maps and holographic displays adorned the walls, showing various strategic locations throughout the city. One facility was marked in blinking red. Nia approached it and asked Rael about it. He explained it was where the Empire kept the Quantum Key. "We discovered it was there after we spent years searching for it."

Rael introduced the cadets to key members of the rebel faction, each an expert in their field — from espionage to technology. The rebels welcomed the cadets, recognizing the significance of their mission and the potential impact on their struggle against the Empire.

"We've been fighting the Empire's remnants for years." Though Rael's voice was steady with determination, it held a note of weariness. "The Quantum Key is more than just a tool for navigating the multiverse. It's a symbol of power, one that the Empire has used to maintain control over certain sectors. In the past, it pulsed with such energy that the Empire's warlords could tap from it in their conquest. Though it has weakened over the years, it still makes them a formidable foe. Securing the Key would be a significant blow to their influence. If they aren't checked now, they could grow stronger, entering other universes to subjugate them, too."

The cadets listened intently, realizing the broader implications of their mission. They were no longer just seeking a way back home; they were now part of a larger fight for freedom and justice in this universe, and the rest of the multiverse by proxy.

"Are you the leader here?" Alex asked.

Rael laughed. "No. No. I'm merely the leader of this mission—the Quantum Key heist. Our leader is old and retired, a man of great renown. Few ever encounter him. He has been steady in the fight against the Empire for years, even now, after their powers have weakened. He wants them crushed. As do we."

He drew closer to the table, drawing them with him. "This heist is fundamental to crushing them for good. The Quantum Key is the source of their power, providing energy to their facility and giving their forces the boldness to dominate."

"If you take it, then you cripple them," Nia said.

"Exactly."

"Why now?" Alex wanted to know.

"They recently tried a risky experiment. It failed. The Key is currently at its weakest, and so is the power in their facility. This is the best time to steal it."

"And when we get it, who does the power go to?" This time it was Yasu. The others gave him knowing glances. He looked back at them, raising his eyebrows.

"Nobody," Rael replied. He met their questioning glances with a sharp look. "We destroy it. It's too powerful a tool. If we leave it, it's bound to fall into the wrong hands again. And in case you're worried, don't be. We'll give you enough time to return to your world first before we destroy it."

The meeting shifted to planning the heist. The rebels shared detailed blueprints of the facility, having procured them in a previous heist. The blueprints highlighted its security systems, guard rotations, and potential entry points. The plan was to infiltrate the facility under the cover of night, using a combination of stealth, hacking, and precise coordination.

Rael also informed them they had secured their spacecraft on the day of the crash. "We know it was wrong, but we had to move fast before the Empire caught on."

The cadets shared heavy looks among themselves, but they understood his point. At least, now they had the craft and the Quantum Leap Device available to complete the mission to send them home.

Each cadet was assigned a specific role based on their skills. Alex and Nia would lead the infiltration team because their quick thinking and reflexes gave them an edge in evading capture. Jaxon and Yasu would provide technical and logistical support from the base, coordinating with the infiltration team and ensuring a clear escape route.

The rebels would assist by creating diversions around the city, drawing the Empire's forces away from the facility and providing the cadets with the best chance of success.

The group finalized their plans as the sun rose, casting its golden glow onto the base. They understood the risks involved, but the stakes were too high to back down now.

"We're in this together," Alex said, looking around at the determined faces of his team and their new allies. "Let's make this count."

Rael nodded, wearing a small smile of admiration. They shook hands across the table, sealing their alliance.

The cadets and the rebels checked their equipment and went over the plan one last time. They knew that the night ahead would be one of the most challenging and consequential of their lives.

Afternoon waned, and evening approached. The shadows lengthened, and the sky was awash in orange and purple hues. The cadets, disguised in local attire and makeup, split up to execute the first part of the plan before nightfall. Their mission was to gather essential materials and information for the heist, blending in with the city's inhabitants to avoid drawing attention.

Alex and Nia, their alternates in tow, headed to a bustling tech market, a neon-lit maze of stalls selling various gadgets and components. They moved through the crowd, eyes scanning the shops for specific items on their list. Alex's alternate negotiated with a vendor for a set of micro-cameras, hacking tools, and night-vision goggles while Nia and her alternate secured a compact energy disruptor, essential for neutralizing electronic locks.

Meanwhile, Jaxon, Yasu, and their alternates ventured into a more industrial part of the city. Their task was to acquire blueprints of the facility's power grid and security network. Posing as technicians, they gained access to a local utility hub. Using a combination of charm and subtle hacking, they downloaded the necessary data onto a portable drive.

Throughout their mission, the cadets remained in constant communication with each other and the rebel base, updating on their progress and staying alert for any signs of Empire surveillance.

They regrouped at a predetermined rendezvous point, their nerves frazzled with anxiety, but satisfied with what they had accomplished. They had successfully gathered the required intel and equipment, but the reality of their impending mission weighed heavily on them.

However, their success was not without a close call. As they shared their achievements, Jaxon recounted a moment when he thought they had been spotted by Empire security. Quick thinking and a timely distraction by a resident had allowed them to escape unnoticed.

"This is getting real," Yasu said. "We've got what we need, but we're also getting closer to the Empire's radar."

Everyone nodded, echoing agreement.

Before they returned to the base, the alternates bade them goodbye. They exchanged hugs and shared words of encouragement with themselves. The alternates wished them luck in their journey home and departed, leaving the cadets somewhat hollow but pleased about the time they spent together.

Discreetly, the cadets made their way back to the rebel base, the city's lights reflecting in their determined eyes. Night had come, bringing more exhilaration as their final mission drew nearer. They knew that the next phase of their plan would be the most dangerous yet, but they were ready.

In the quiet before the storm, the cadets and the rebel faction gathered in the underground base for a final briefing. Anticipation hung in the air like a weight about to fall and crush them. The walls of the base, lined with screens and equipment, cast an almost eerie glow over the assembled group.

Rael stood at the front, a holographic model of the high-security facility rotating slowly beside him. "This is it," he began, his large voice charged with emotion. "Tonight, we strike a blow against the Empire and help our friends return to their universe. Remember, precision and stealth are key. We only have one shot at this."

The cadets listened, their gazes focused on Rael. When the briefing ended, Alex and Nia reviewed the layout of the facility, going over their entry and exit strategies. Jaxon and Yasu double-checked their communication and hacking equipment, ensuring everything was in working order.

While they worked, the rebels shared stories of their struggles against the Empire, adding a personal dimension to the mission. Their tales of loss, resilience, and hope resonated with the cadets, strengthening the bond between them.

As the meeting drew to a close, Alex stood up. "We came here by accident, but now we're part of something bigger," he said, looking around at the group. "Whatever happens tonight, we're grateful for your help. Let's do this together!"

The group dispersed to make their final preparations. Equipment was checked and rechecked, disguises were donned, and communication protocols were confirmed. Everyone worked with nervous energy and quiet resolve.

In a private moment, the cadets huddled together. "No matter what happens out there, we stick to the plan and watch each other's backs," Nia said, her voice firm.

"We've trained for this. We can do it," Jaxon added, adjusting his gear.

Yasu looked at each of his friends, wearing a serious expression. "Let's bring that Key home."

The cadets and the rebels moved into position, the cityscape of the alternate Earth sprawling out before them. The stars above seemed to watch in silent anticipation. The night's operation would be a defining moment in their journey, a test of their courage, skill, and the strength of their newfound alliances.

# CHAPTER 6

NIGHT ENVELOPED the city in a cloak of darkness, punctuated only by the occasional glimmer of lights from the towering structures. The cadets, dressed in dark, stealthy attire, approached the perimeter of the high-security facility where the Quantum Key was held. The building loomed ahead, a fortress of technology and guarded secrets.

Alex and Nia led a small infiltration team, moving with practiced precision. They communicated in hushed tones, using earpieces to stay in contact with Jaxon and Yasu, who were stationed in a discreet location nearby, ready to provide technical support.

The first obstacle was the facility's outer security – a series of surveillance cameras and motion sensors. Nia, with her compact energy disruptor, worked with Jaxon and some of the rebels to disable the cameras and sensors. Alex scouted the area with his micro-camera, waiting for Yasu's signal that the area was clear for movement.

They heard a minor explosion somewhere on the other side of the facility; one of the rebel distractions. "Go," Yasu said.

They slipped in, passing through the facility's ventilation hatch. Nia took the lead, as she was better at memorizing and recalling directions. She led them to their drop-off point. "The security systems are disabled," Jaxon said. Nia pulled out the laser blade and cut a hole large enough for them to drop through.

They came down one after the other, Alex standing watch with a couple of other rebels.

Thereafter, they split up into three groups of five, two of the other groups going to their posts to create necessary diversions.

Jaxon kept up communication with their group, feeding real-time information to them. "You've got a patrol coming your way in thirty seconds," Jaxon whispered through the earpiece.

Quickly, Alex, Nia, and the rest of the team concealed themselves in the shadows, allowing the patrol to pass without incident. Once the coast was clear, they continued their advance towards the inner sanctum of the facility, where the Quantum Key was believed to be stored.

The deeper they went, the more fortified the facility became. They worked with Jaxon to disable the security locks and traps laid around the route. Yasu remained in contact with the rebel groups, helping them efficiently take out guards and keep away from Alex and Nia's group.

Finally, they arrived at a heavily secured door, beyond which lay the chamber holding the Quantum Key. Nia deployed a series of hacking tools, working quickly with Jaxon to unlock the door.

The door slid open, revealing the chamber within. Nia stood, panting, staring inside the space filled with sensors, traps, and blinking lights.

"Is it done?" Alex asked, standing close to her shoulder.

"It is." She could almost not believe it. "That was easy. Almost too easy."

As if in response to her remark, alarms around the facility blared. Through the earpiece, Jaxon said, "It seems the chamber has a trip lock. You've been detected. Get in and I'll try to lock you inside."

"Move, now!" Alex urged. Alex, Nia, and the rest of the infiltration team hurried into the chamber holding the Quantum Key. The room was a high-tech vault, illuminated by the soft glow of security lights, with the Key prominently displayed at its center, encased in a protective energy field. The field made the Key a blurry haze, but they could make out the pedestal it sat on, and the metal case housing it. Occasionally, it buzzed with energy and returned to its low hum state.

They approached the Key, the door behind them still open. The sound of heavy footsteps behind them grew louder, signaling the arrival of the facility's security forces.

Nia hurried to bring out the energy disruptor and attached it to the control switch on the base of the Key's pedestal. "Jaxon, I've connected it—"

Behind her, the security forces stood at the door. Alex drew in a sharp breath, recognizing the tall man in front must be important. He exuded power, his gaze shooting bolts of fear through Alex's frame.

"So, the rumors are true," the official said, his voice echoing in the chamber. "Travelers from another universe, meddling in affairs beyond their understanding."

Alex stepped forward, his stance defiant. "We're here for the Quantum Key. We need it to return to our universe."

The official smirked, a hint of amusement in his eyes. "The Key is more than just a tool for travel. It's a symbol of power, a gateway to the multiverse. Do you really think we'd let it fall into the hands of outsiders?"

The tension in the room was palpable as the official continued, revealing his knowledge of their origins and their adventures of the past few days. His tone turned mocking as he arrived at the prophecy. He hinted at a deeper connection between the cadets and the Empire, suggesting that their arrival was no mere coincidence. "You little rascals," he said, his voice deepening with ill-concealed rage. "You stand between us and the rise of our Empire. You threaten all the progress we've struggled to make so far—"

A shot rang from the back, striking one soldier with him in the head. It indicated the arrival of one of the two other rebel groups that joined the infiltration team. The shot triggered the start of a brief skirmish. The team and cadets deployed an energy shield and hid behind it, firing shots at the security forces.

Nia, protected by the shield and further covered by Alex, recalibrated the energy disruptor, adjusting it to the settings of the protective field. Alex covered her, firing at enemies trying to attack while she worked. She yelled in triumph when the field came down. Alex turned and grabbed the metal box housing the Key.

The box was heavy and warm, humming with radiating energy. Alex hesitated for a moment when he grabbed it, because it felt almost alive, like he was holding a sleeping infant in his arm. But he couldn't think about that for too long. He thrust it into the specialized containment unit strapped to his back and turned to observe the chaos. With the Key in their possession and the chamber now a battleground, Alex and Nia were unsure how to escape.

Yasu reached out to them through the earpiece, his voice strained. "Jaxon and I can get you out. But the window is thin."

He seemed to be in communication with the other rebels, too. They created a covering for Nia and Alex, allowing them to make a run for it through the door.

They imagined that the commander and his men would have deployed more personnel to give them chase, but they didn't wait to find out. Their legs grew weary, but they kept running, led by careful directions from Yasu. Alex took the lead, the Quantum Key secured to his back. Nia, right beside him, kept a vigilant eye on their rear, ensuring they weren't ambushed. Two remaining rebels covered their flanks, their familiarity with the facility proving invaluable in navigating the maze of passageways.

As they neared the exit, they encountered a formidable obstacle —a security checkpoint manned by heavily armed guards. The team skidded to a halt, assessing the situation. A confrontation seemed inevitable.

Jaxon's voice crackled through their earpieces. "I've hacked into the facility's security system. I can create a temporary blackout, but you'll have only seconds to move through."

"Do it," Alex responded, bracing for the moment.

The lights flickered and then went out, plunging the corridor into darkness. Using night-vision goggles, the team surged forward, bypassing the disoriented guards. They moved with precision, each member playing their part flawlessly.

As they emerged from the facility into the cool night air, they found themselves in a deserted alleyway. Rael met them there, a couple of armed and kitted rebels flanking him. The sounds of the city seemed distant, muffled by the adrenaline still coursing through their veins.

But their escape was far from over. The facility's lockdown had triggered a city-wide alert, and they could hear the distant whir of approaching security drones.

"We need to split up," Rael said, his expression grim. "It'll be harder for them to track us. Regroup at the secondary safe house."

The team quickly divided, each subgroup taking a different route to shake off pursuit. Alex and Nia, carrying the Quantum Key, darted down a narrow side street, their steps echoing on the cobblestones.

As they navigated the city's back alleys, the reality of their situation set in. They had the Quantum Key, but they were now fugitives in an alien world.

Alex and Nia paused for a moment, hidden in the shadows of an archway. They looked at each other, a mix of triumph and apprehension in their eyes. The hardest part of their mission was still ahead—using the Quantum Key to return to their universe without further destabilizing this one.

## CHAPTER 7

IN THE DIMLY LIT ALLEYWAYS OF the city, Alex and Nia, their senses heightened by the current state of affairs. The city, a labyrinth of light and shadow, seemed to pulse with the rhythm of their pursuit.

The sound of security drones humming in the distance was a constant reminder of the imminent danger. Alex led the way, using a handheld scanner to detect any approaching threats, while Nia kept a vigilant watch behind them.

As they neared the edge of the city, the terrain became more rugged, the urban landscape giving way to the outskirts. Here, the cover was sparse, and the risk of exposure increased.

Suddenly, the scanner beeped a warning – a squadron of drones was closing in on their position. "We need to move faster." Alex's voice was tense.

They broke into a run, darting through narrow passages and overgrown fields. The drones, now visible in the night sky, descended, their searchlights sweeping the ground.

In a desperate move, Nia set off a series of decoy flares, which erupted, illuminating the sky in a dazzling mix of colors. The drones, momentarily confused, veered off course, buying the cadets another chance to evade capture.

As they approached the rendezvous point, a derelict building on the outskirts of the city, their allies from the rebel faction emerged from the shadows. Rael was there, concern and relief clouding his features.

"You made it," he said, ushering them inside. "The others are already here. We need to plan our next move."

Inside the building, the atmosphere was tense. The team knew that the facility's lockdown had put the entire city on high alert. Their escape had been successful, but they were far from safe.

"We can't stay here long," Jaxon said, checking the communication feeds. "Security forces will scour the city. We need to get to the spot fast and use the Key." The spot was the place they had chosen for the last mission. The rebel group kept the spacecraft there, guarded by rebels and solar-powered energy traps.

The group gathered around a makeshift table where a map of the city and its surroundings lay. They discussed various escape routes, each with its own set of risks and challenges.

They split into smaller groups, each taking a different route out of the city to avoid detection. The ultimate goal was to regroup at a remote location, where they would attempt to use the Quantum Key to return to their universe.

As they prepared to leave, they grew more fidgety. They had the Key, but the journey ahead was fraught with uncertainty. The fate of this galaxy and their return home lay in their hands. Alex stood next to Rael for what was the last address. He looked at the faces of his friends and swept his eyes over the rebels present.

"We've had a difficult couple of days, but now it's coming to an end. We've fought hard and we have to complete it by giving this last push. I thank you all for your support and courage. Let's complete this mission together!" Everyone clapped and cheered, oddly strengthened by his words.

They shared quick encouragements and set off into the night.

===✦===

The cadets arrived at the clearing as orange tendrils rose in the eastern sky. Though their current predicament filled them with tension, the thick scent of pine and the tranquility of the surroundings helped to calm them. Here, they prepared to address the unintended consequences of their presence in this universe.

Alex unpacked the Quantum Key, its intricate design glinting in the dappled sunlight. The device, though small, hummed with an energy that belied its size. Around him, the team gathered, wearing identical masks of awe and apprehension. They took the Key into the spacecraft, attaching it to the damaged Quantum Leap Device and a portable console.

"We've caused disturbances in this universe since we arrived," Nia said. "We need to use the Key to rectify these anomalies before we attempt to return home."

This was a task for Jaxon and his technical expertise. He interfaced the Key with a portable console, starting a diagnostic sequence. "The Key is not just a tool for travel; it's a stabilizer for multiverse anomalies. We can recalibrate it to repair the ripples we've caused. I don't think that will destroy it."

The team worked in unison, inputting data and making adjustments to the device. They cross-referenced the anomalies they had witnessed with the Key's capabilities, formulating a plan to restore balance.

As they activated the Key, a wave of energy pulsed from the device, cascading through the surrounding area. The air shimmered as if reality itself was being realigned.

"We're reversing the disturbances," Yasu announced, monitoring the readouts on the console. "It's working. The anomalies are being neutralized."

The process was meticulous, requiring precise adjustments and constant monitoring. The team worked with deliberate care, aware that any misstep could exacerbate the situation.

After what seemed like hours, they made the final adjustments, and the Key's energy pulse reduced. The forest returned to its natural state, the only evidence of their work the soft hum of the now-dormant Quantum Key.

"We've done what we can to repair the damage," Alex said, a hint of relief in his voice. "Now, we need to focus on getting back to our universe."

The team donned their suits. They were ready to embark on the last leg of their journey, their actions having restored a measure of balance to this universe.

They recalibrated the Quantum Key, linking it with information from their universe and planet. As a final touch, they added instructions for the self-destruct sequence to follow. They carried it out of their craft and into the clearing when they were done. If they were going to create a portal, they needed as much space as possible, given their limited knowledge about the portal's size. The rebels assisted them in setting up the Key on a makeshift platform at the center of the airstrip. One of them stayed at the console with Jaxon to manually destroy the Key if any of the processes failed.

Rael and the rest of the rebels stood guard, keeping a watchful eye on the surrounding area. The tension was palpable; they all knew the risks involved in activating the Quantum Key. The potential for unforeseen consequences was high, but the need to return home and destroy the Key was paramount.

As they worked, the cadets reflected on their journey. They had arrived in this universe by accident, but their experiences had changed them. They had formed unexpected alliances, faced formidable challenges, and now stood on the brink of achieving their goal.

"We've come a long way," Nia said, her voice tinged with emotion. "No matter what happens next, I'm proud of what we've accomplished together."

The others nodded in agreement, bound by their shared camaraderie.

With the preparations complete, Alex took a deep breath and addressed the group. "This is it. Once we activate the Key and set up the self-destruct sequence, we should be able to open a portal back to our universe. But we have to be quick. The energy surge will be detected, and we can't risk the Empire closing in on us."

Nia continued, "Also, if we miss this chance, we don't know when we'll get another."

The team took their positions, ready to initiate the sequence. Jaxon, at the console, gave a nod, indicating they were all set. Alex held the Quantum Key, the metal box emitting a soft glow and growing warmer to the touch.

"Activating in three... two... one..." Jaxon counted down.

Alex activated the Key, and a brilliant beam of light shot up into the sky, piercing the darkness. The air around them began to shimmer and warp as if reality itself was bending.

A portal slowly materialized, a swirling vortex of light and energy. The cadets gazed at it in awe, the gateway to their home universe finally within reach.

"Let's go, now!" Yasu yelled as they all moved towards the portal.

They prepared to run through the portal, adjusting their suits and checking the console for any anomalies. Something caught Yasu's eye as he stepped away from the console. A drone hovered a short distance away, training its weapon on them. A rebel fired at the drone, knocking it to the ground. That battle wasn't so easily won. More drones sprung into the air, like bees from a disturbed nest. Rael and his rebels readied themselves, prepared to defend the cadets' escape.

One by one, the cadets rushed into the portal, their figures disappearing into the light. Rael and his team held off the approaching forces, ensuring their new friends made it home safely.

As the last of the cadets vanished into the portal, the Quantum Key deactivated, closing the portal and leaving the clearing in silence once more. For a moment, everyone stood in silence, listening and watching the Key. Then it happened.

The Key exploded with blinding light, causing everyone to turn away from it, shielding their eyes. A high-pitched whine accompanied this explosion. Everyone fell to their knees, bowing their heads and placing their hands over their ears. Several minutes passed before the light and sound faded. The clearing returned to its usual state.

Everyone rose, dazed, looking at the blackened, lifeless metal case where the Key had been. Slowly, the rebels exulted, letting out whoops and cheers. Perhaps the Empire will find another way to rise, but for now, they had cut off their main power source and effectively crippled them in this generation.

## CHAPTER 8

THE CADETS EMERGED from the portal into the familiar surroundings of their universe, the stark contrast immediately evident. They found themselves back at the Interstellar Academy, but it was not quite as they had left it. Subtle changes in the architecture and the technology around them hinted at the ripples their journey had caused.

They took a moment to breathe, hearts pounding. The academy grounds were quiet, bathed in the soft light of the early morning. After their wild adventure, home looked different. The colors were duller, and the air they breathed carried an unnatural weight. Regardless, it was home.

"We did it," Alex said, his voice shaking with disbelief and relief. "We're back."

Nia looked around, noting the differences. "But not exactly the same. Our journey changed things here too, however slightly."

The team walked through the academy, observing the changes. The buildings were cleaner, the metal surfaces more polished. The screens beamed news about the boundless possibilities in the multiverse.

They met a group of academy officials as they approached the main building. The mission commander walked to the fore. The group halted when they saw the cadets. Nia noted the look of surprise on their faces.

"You've returned." The commander's brow was furrowed. "And not without causing a stir. We've monitored anomalies in the fabric of space-time. Care to explain?"

The cadets scrambled to recount their extraordinary journey, describing the alternate universe, the Quantum Key, and the impact of their actions on both universes. The officials listened intently, astonishment and concern slowly bleeding into their expressions. Undoubtedly, the flurry of words from the cadets had jumbled in their heads, leaving them more confused.

"You've ventured into uncharted territory," the commander said after a pause. "Your actions, while unauthorized, have opened our eyes to new possibilities and responsibilities. We'll have to have more meetings about this."

The cadets were escorted to the debriefing room, their future uncertain but their place in the academy's history assured. They had returned as pioneers of multiverse exploration, their experiences a testament to the boundless possibilities of space and time. But the stern expressions on the officials' faces told them they weren't in the clear.

In a stark, utilitarian debriefing room within the Interstellar Academy, the cadets sat across from a panel of high-ranking officials, including the mission commander and representatives from various scientific and exploratory divisions of the academy. The atmosphere was formal, and the gravity of the situation was reflected in the stern faces of the officials.

One by one, Alex, Nia, Jaxon, and Yasu recounted their experiences in the alternate universe. They spoke of the advanced civilization they encountered, the challenges they faced, and the ethical dilemmas they navigated. The officials listened, their expressions shifting from skepticism to intrigue as the cadets detailed their interactions with the Quantum Key, its effects on the multiverse, and subsequent destruction.

"We are sorry to have destroyed it, but it was the only way," Alex said, looking the commander in the eye. "The Empire was threatening the peace of that universe. If they gained the upper hand, there was no telling what else they would have done."

The commander, after a moment of contemplative silence, addressed the team. "Your actions, while reckless, have provided us with invaluable insights into the multiverse. However, we cannot overlook your interference in another universe's politics. Our universe is ours and theirs is theirs."

The room tensed, the cadets exchanging anxious glances. Alex itched to further explain their predicament, emphasizing how pressing it was to act then. A swift look from Nia, her eyes aflame with an unspoken warning, changed his mind.

The commander continued, "Given the extraordinary circumstances and the potential benefits of your findings, the academy has reprimanded but not expelled you. Your experiences will be studied extensively, and you will be required to participate in further research and training."

Relief washed over the cadets. They understood the consequences of their actions and the importance of their newfound knowledge.

The debriefing concluded with the officials emphasizing the need for strict protocols in future explorations of the multiverse. Thereafter, they dismissed the cadets.

The cadets left the debriefing room, all of them nursing their private thoughts on the situation. As they stepped out into the now busy academy grounds, they were met with curious glances and whispers from other cadets and faculty. News of their eventful journey had spread, and they had become a topic of intrigue and speculation.

The team gathered in their favorite spot on the academy grounds, overlooking a valley where a large brass replica of the solar system stood. They reflected on their journey, the lessons learned, and the impact of their adventure.

"We've opened a door we can't close," Nia said, her gaze fixed on the sculpture. "Our understanding of the universe has changed forever."

Alex nodded in agreement. "And so have we. This is just the beginning."

The cadets, once ordinary students, now stood at the forefront of a new era of exploration, their future filled with possibilities and the promise of further adventures in the vast, mysterious multiverse.

Alex, Nia, Jaxon, and Yasu sat in a circle, the silence between them filled with unspoken thoughts and shared experiences. The academy, with its bustling corridors and ambitious projects, felt both familiar and different now.

"It's strange," Yasu broke the silence, "how one journey can change everything—how we see the universe, ourselves, and our place in it."

Nia nodded, her eyes on the horizon. "We crossed boundaries we didn't even know existed. We've seen what's possible, the wonders and the dangers."

Jaxon, always the tech enthusiast, chimed in with a hint of excitement in his voice. "Think about what we could learn, the advancements we could make with this knowledge. If we grow bigger, maybe Yasu will eventually become the supreme overlord he was meant to be."

The others laughed.

Alex, who had been oddly quiet all that time, stirred, and said, "But with that comes responsibility. We've seen the consequences of our actions, and how they ripple across universes. Whatever we do next, we need to be mindful of that."

The conversation shifted to their future at the academy. They speculated about the new research and training they would be involved in, the potential missions, and the inevitable challenges. Anticipation coursed through them, once again leaving them awash with a thrumming anxiety. But this time, after having journeyed across the multiverse and defying an evil Empire to make it back, they were ready for it.

As they talked, the sky darkened, and the first stars of the evening appeared. The vastness of space, with its infinite possibilities, seemed to beckon them.

"We've been given a second chance," Alex said, his gaze fixed on the stars. "Let's make it count. Let's explore, learn, and maybe, one day, help others navigate the multiverse responsibly."

With that, the cadets stood up, their bond strengthened by their shared experiences. They looked out at the stars, each lost in thoughts of future adventures and discoveries. The universe, with all its mysteries and wonders, awaited them, and they were ready to meet it head-on.

## EPILOGUE

IN THE ALTERNATE EARTH, in the same advanced city the cadets had visited, subtle changes reflected the impact of their presence. The cityscape, a blend of futuristic architecture and lush greenery, thrummed with more life and energy.

In a bustling public square, where holographic displays show-cased news from across the galaxy, the alternate versions of Alex, Nia, Jaxon, and Yasu gathered at the edge of the crowd, their expressions thoughtful as they discussed the recent events.

"It's been weeks since they left," Alternate Alex said. "And yet, the changes they brought are still unfolding."

Alternate Nia nodded, her eyes scanning the vibrant crowd. "Their presence sparked something in us, a new way of thinking about the universe and our place in it."

The conversation shifted to the changes they had observed since the cadets' departure. There was a renewed sense of curiosity and exploration among the people, a greater desire to understand the multiverse, its possibilities, and other methods of exploring it. In their academy, they had become mini-celebrities among their peers. People stopped them in the hallway, asking about the cadets from another world.

As they spoke, a news bulletin appeared on a nearby display, announcing a breakthrough in multiverse research, inspired by the accounts of the cadets' journey. Everyone turned to the display at the news, eyes fixed and ears peeled for information. Once the news drifted to other topics, the citizens in the square exploded in conversation.

The alternates reflected on the prophecy they had learned about, wondering about its implications and the role the cadets had played in it. Now that the Key was destroyed, parts of the Empire were collapsing. To them, that meant the cadets had played a role in fulfilling the prophecy.

The alternates looked up at the sky, now darkening as evening set in. The stars above seemed to hold new mysteries, new opportunities for discovery.

"We may never see them again," Alternate Jaxon remarked, "but their legacy here will last for generations."

They left the square, each lost in thoughts of the future, the possibilities that lay beyond their world. The cadets' journey had left an indelible mark, opening doors to new horizons and adventures.

⸺▼⸺

Back at the Interstellar Academy in their own universe, the cadets stood together, gazing out at the vast expanse of space from the observatory deck. The stars twinkled above, each one a symbol of the endless adventures that awaited them.

The academy had changed since their return. There was excitement and curiosity among the students and faculty, fueled by the cadets' extraordinary journey. Their experience had opened up new avenues of research and exploration, and the academy buzzed with preparations for future missions into the multiverse.

As they stood there, the mission commander approached them, a file tucked under his arm. "Cadets," he began, his tone serious but with a hint of excitement. "Your journey has opened our eyes to the possibilities of the multiverse. We're starting a new program dedicated to exploring these alternate universes responsibly. And we want you to be a part of it."

The cadets exchanged glances, eager surprise blazing in their eyes. This was the opportunity they had hoped for, a chance to continue their adventures and apply the lessons they had learned.

"We'd be honored, sir," Alex replied, speaking for the group. "We've seen the risks, but also the potential. We're ready to take on this challenge."

The commander nodded, handing them the file. "This is just the beginning. We have a lot to learn, and your insights will be invaluable. Prepare yourselves; you're about to embark on a new journey."

As the commander left, the cadets opened the file, revealing plans and data for potential multiverse exploration missions. The possibilities were endless, and the excitement among them was palpable.

The cadets looked out at the stars once more, their hearts expectant and resolute. They had returned from one adventure, only to stand on the threshold of another.

In the distance, a shooting star streaked across the sky, a symbol of the uncharted paths and stories that lay ahead. Their journey had taught them the vastness of the universe, the importance of responsibility, and the unending quest for knowledge.

## The End

# SHADOWS OF ORION

## A YA SPACE OPERA

## CHAPTER 1

IT WAS A NEW BRIGHT DAY, and Alex Rivera was running late to his session at the space lab in the main building of the Interstellar Academy. His mind was split between arriving on time and the information he had discovered in his overnight research. He had gotten so carried away, he didn't realize how much time had gone before he headed to bed.

In his deep concentration, he bumped into a few other cadets along the way as he raced down the paved hallways. Some scowled at him, choice words of insult about to sprout from their lips, but he was too far gone. He rushed into the lab with a slice of toast between his lips. Jaxon, his friend, watched him run in and waved him over.

"Have they started?" Alex asked, taking the toast out of his mouth and trying to catch his breath.

Jaxon laughed. "No." He took in Alex's appearance, his tousled hair and disheveled uniform. "What were you doing this time?"

"I overslept."

Alex had a lot of leadership qualities, but he often got absorbed in his work, losing track of time. And sometimes, he overslept, too.

Nia walked over to them, holding her tablet and wearing a slight scowl. "You're late. Again."

Alex tried for a small smile, but Nia wasn't having it. She had argued with him about his lateness, having given up on getting him to look more presentable. He could afford to look like he crawled out of a giant blow dryer, but his lateness was non-negotiable. Their team could get in trouble on account of it.

"I'll do better," Alex offered, but Nia had turned away.

"The technician went out for an emergency meeting. He'll return soon."

Alex was itching to talk to the rest of the group about everything he had learned overnight. There was so much ground to cover in the multiverse and they, in the Interstellar Academy, had merely scratched the surface. He had found some interesting things about planets in the Orion Sector, and making potential contact with other universes. The documents had been in another language, but he spent all night decoding them with a translator until he figured out what they said. What troubled him more, however, was the mention of ripple effects when meeting alternates. The text described localized disruptions—gravitational anomalies, strange time dilations, and shifts in molecular stability. He couldn't help but recall their last mission, wondering what unseen effects they may have already caused. Perhaps if he had Nia's natural aptitude for languages, he would have been able to figure it out faster, but he made significant progress regardless. There was some talk about duplicates, and from what he could glean, meeting duplicates could be a problem when crossing universes.

The technician returned, talking rapidly on his intercom device. The call ended, and he walked past all the other cadets standing around, went to the front of the lab where his podium stood, and said, "Shall we begin?"

The lab session took all morning and afternoon. They were working on improving their spatial abilities in a zero-gravity space.

When the session ended, the cadets headed for the lockerooms, talking about the next experiment on multiverse travel. Everyone had heard a mission might come up soon, but nobody knew who would go this time.

"Maybe it will be the last people," Yasu said. "They didn't have any anomalies this time."

They hadn't been on a mission since their first and last mission to an alternate Earth. It was the first time the Academy had made a successful trip out of their universe. A few other teams of cadets had gone, however, returning with their own stories of adventure and exploration. Previously, the Academy had tried to send the older officers on missions, but were met with more failures. Their scientists continued to work on fixing those anomalies, but the progress came slowly.

The cadets completed their shower and headed to the cafeteria for a late lunch. They heaped healthy servings of the food onto their trays and sat together.

"I found something," Alex said.

The others looked at him, ready to discover what he had learned.

"I have a feeling I know how to stop the anomalies. It seems making trips into universes with alternate versions of ourselves and making contact with said versions leads to a ripple in reality's fabric."

Nia chewed on a piece of meat, expression pensive.

"How would you know that?" Yasu asked.

"I did some digging." Alex placed his tablet on the table, showing them the original document from the Orion Sector. He had to do a lot of hacking to get it, he admitted, saying that Jaxon and Nia's combined abilities might have made it easier to get the information. Next, he showed them the translated version of the file.

They gathered closer, heads pressed together, poring over it. A lot of it was nonsensical jargon, but they could get the gist of it. A space program over there had made links with other universes and the program crashed eventually because the anomalies grew too big. However, getting more detailed information would be difficult with the program closed down.

The cadets' eyes grew wider as they discussed the implications. Their food had grown cold, abandoned in the heat of their findings.

Yasu leaned forward, looking at a section again. "Should we tell someone about this?"

"Who?" Alex asked.

"The commander, maybe." Yasu shrugged.

"What do you want to tell me?" the commander's voice boomed behind them.

The cadets stood, shocked to find him there.

He looked at them, a small smile on his face. Two other high-ranking officials stood behind him, watching with blank and foreboding expressions. "We have a briefing this evening," he said, eyes resting on Alex's face.

Uncomfortable, the others turned to Alex. His snooping on other databases was unauthorized, after all. Perhaps he was in trouble, and by proxy, they were in trouble with him.

"You should have gotten a memo, but it seems you haven't. Perhaps it will come in due time." The commander glanced at his watch. "You have about an hour. Enjoy your meal instead of talking."

The cadets watched him leave, minds grappling with the information. It didn't seem like they were in trouble, but it was hard to tell. Perhaps they were due for another mission?

They finished the rest of their cold food in silence, each privately coming up with potential reasons for their summoning. Sometime before they finished eating, the memos came in with information about the where and when.

They left the cafeteria and headed to the briefing room on the third floor of the main building.

"Jaxon, have you been tinkering with anything you shouldn't have access to?" Yasu asked. About a week ago, he got into trouble for stealing information about new weaponry from the Academy's classified database. He was the group's technological wizard and fond of finding things he shouldn't find. His hacking skills might have gotten him a quick admission into the Academy, but that didn't prevent him from getting into trouble for snooping.

Jaxon scowled, but said nothing.

They arrived early, and the only official present allowed them in, gesturing to the seats around the long table. They sat next to each other at one end.

Accompanied by the two laboratory officials, several other high-ranking officials, and a group of technicians, the commander arrived precisely on time. At the head of the table stood the commander, while the officials and technicians sat. As the lights dimmed, a holographic chart spread out, hovering above the table.

The cadets had seen it before. The chart represented the vast, unknown expanse of the multiverse. A few points were marked on it, showing the universes they had visited, their energy signatures, and the code name chosen for them. If one tapped any of the points, it brought up more information about that universe; the team deployed there, and details on the mission.

"Team Alpha," the commander said, "your first mission set you apart as pioneers in our exploration of the multiverse."

Their mission had set a precedent for multiversal travel. When they returned, they went through several physical and medical evaluations, checking if the travel had affected them in any significant way, the way it had with the older officers. However, they were largely unscathed.

The Academy had proceeded to set up a multiversal exploration program, using the cadets as the leading travelers. So far, there had been no physical ailments recorded amongst them.

Someone selected the point for the universe they visited, Alt-1. Their pictures floated in the corner, with their names beneath them—Alex Rivera, Nia Chen, Yasu Garcia, and Jaxon Brooks. The Academy named them Team Alpha for being the first to venture out of their world successfully.

The mission summary showed that in their visit to that universe, they encountered their alternate versions. It also highlighted their journey back using the Quantum Key, a rich energy source that gave access to the multiverse, and their subsequent destruction of the Key.

The commander continued, "We've made other strides in our work to discover more about the multiverse, sending out other teams, and recording their findings. Now, it's your turn again. We have a new mission, and we've chosen your team."

The cadets bubbled up with excitement. They shot gleeful looks at one another, thrilled at another opportunity to contribute to the research at the Academy. Alex's heart beat so loud that he thought the other people in the room might hear it. This was a new opportunity to explore a new world, and he planned to make the most of it.

## CHAPTER 2

EACH DAY in the next month dawned with the clarity of thought that comes with purpose. The cadets now had something to work towards, and they toiled diligently.

Their days began early, with physical exercise and drills at the space lab. Afternoons found them sitting in the lecture hall, learning more about the findings from the other missions. And they closed out each day with simulated exercises. They had the opportunity to run through their operation of the spacecraft and the updated Quantum Leap Device.

In the course of their training, Alex spoke to some of the officials about his findings. They scolded him for delving into affairs beyond his scope, but they perused the documents with curiosity. One of the older technicians called him into his office a few days later to discuss it.

"We appreciate your thirst for knowledge, Alex," he said, steepling his fingers, "and we would like to research this further."

Alex could hear a "but..." somewhere in there. He leaned forward, widening his eyes.

The technician scratched his chin. "For us to know with certainty that this hypothesis might hold some truth, we would need to make several other trips into other universes. Only then can we say that it has a basis.

Understanding, Alex nodded. "The last cadet team didn't encounter any anomalies," he said. "What happened there?"

The technician looked at Alex with a slight smile. "They didn't meet their alternates."

The cadets were intrigued by Alex's discussion with the technician. It seemed almost too easy that the anomalies could be triggered by running into one's alternate form, but they decided they would find out more about it in subsequent trips into the multiverse.

In other classes, they learned about some of the improvements made on the Quantum Leap Device. The Academy's research enabled them to develop technologies to combat the anomalies. The technologies weren't entirely sound at that point, but they were good enough to prevent drastic ripples like the kind the cadets had encountered in their first trip.

The day for their take-off eventually arrived. They could barely eat that morning because they were bursting with anxiety.

They each carried fresh worries about the success of the mission. Alex worried they might land on a planet similar to the first one they encountered and be unable to learn much else. Nia carried the burden of wanting the mission to be perfect. On their last mission, their actions had led them to destroy a prized artifact. While she had supported its destruction, they had returned to face judgment from the school's authorities. She didn't want to repeat that, desiring a clean record as she left school. Jaxon and Yasu weren't as worried as the other two, but they could sense their low mood, and the feeling rubbed off on them.

"What if we finally meet Yasu's Overlord version in this world?" Jaxon said, trying to lighten the mood.

But the laughter his words elicited was short-lived. Soon, they had to get up and head to the take-off point.

They donned their suits in the dressing room, the mood solemn. Then they walked out to the launchpad at the spaceport for the commander's final briefing. The spaceport was a state-of-the-art multi-tier complex, built of high-strength alloys and transparent composites. Multiple ships were docked there, ranging from small high-speed spacecrafts to colossal cargo haulers. Automated drones drifted about, running small errands and performing mundane tasks. The launchpad sat in the middle of the complex's courtyard, the high-rise building and its watchtowers observing the happenings on the concrete space.

The air was crisp and cool, and the sun shone down on everyone with a fury. The spacecraft stood at the center of the paved landing area, the glossy exterior reflecting the sunlight sharply.

The commander was with several technicians and officials, his eyes hidden behind sunglasses. He left their side to come to where the cadets stood. "You've worked hard, and you'll succeed in this mission. Never fear and remember your training."

The cadets entered the spacecraft, Alex at the helm. He entered the coordinates for the target universe on the Quantum Leap Device, adjusting his mouthpiece. Beyond the glass, the spectators milled around, watching with earnest expressions. "Can you all hear me?" Alex said into his mouthpiece.

They sent back confirmation.

"Preparing for take-off in 3, 2, 1…"

The spacecraft shot off with ease. After their training, the cadets had a better handle on operating it. They broke through the earth's atmosphere, watching the stars get sharper.

"Initializing leap in 3, 2, 1…"

The spacecraft shuddered as it broke through the very fabric of reality into the next. Light and morphed sound rushed past the ship, an exhilarating kaleidoscope of energy. The cadets had seen it once before, but they were still stunned seeing it a second time.

Eventually, they emerged on the other side. But something was wrong. Their arrival wasn't like the previous one. Something was preventing their landing.

"Does anyone else think something is wrong? Or am I simply paranoid?" Jaxon asked, laughing with some nervousness.

"You're not," Nia replied. "It seems the place we should land is… blocked."

Alex was trying to absorb that information on his side. In this universe, a force field heavily shielded the planet and the surrounding systems. The Quantum Leap Device was trying to redirect them to another system in another sector.

"I think we have to go to the Orion Sector if we want to land," he said. The Orion Sector was the closest to theirs, the Gaia Sector. "Or do we return home and report our findings?" He didn't want to return home. This redirection was the perfect opportunity for him to confirm his beliefs about the anomalies in multiverse travel.

It seemed the others shared his views. Jaxon replied with enthusiasm. "This seems like a fantastic opportunity to learn about other planets in the multiverse. Perhaps over there, we can learn more about our planet in this universe. And we'd have a more detailed report for the higher-ups."

"I agree," Nia said. "We can't let this chance slip by us. We couldn't plan the leap to another system in another universe, but now we have been given permission to do it. Let's not waste it."

Yasu seemed hesitant. "The fuel reserves... will they take us there and back?"

Alex and Nia ran calculations on their sides. They needed fuel to make the required light jump to get to the Orion Sector. They would also need extra on their return trip, knowing that the craft could only break into the Orion Sector in their universe. Nia finished first, asking Yasu to crosscheck her findings. He looked through, agreeing that they had enough. Alex's calculations told them the same thing, too.

They worked together on their various consoles to adjust the craft's settings to allow it to make the switch to a light jump. A light jump was a way to cut long space travel distances shorter, taking the ship or spacecraft through a small hole in space at several times the speed of light. The cadets adjusted themselves in their seats and prepared for it.

They broke out on the other side, close enough to a planetary system on the outskirts of the sector to make a landing on one of its planets. The cadets cheered. They had done various simulations on the execution of light jumps, but they had never done an actual one. They looked at the distance covered—several light years — and marveled at the accuracy of the Quantum Leap Device in taking them so far away without a hitch.

"Preparing for landing," Alex said.

They worked together in their various positions to guide the spacecraft towards a planet with signs of oxygen and life. Yasu quickly identified it as Krissia, recalling it from when he was plotting a universal takeover. He couldn't recall any other details beyond a rough estimation of its population and the fact that it was a mining planet. The spacecraft flew there, gliding through the space void but encountering difficulty entering the planet's atmosphere.

"Something isn't right again," Jaxon said, impatiently swiping sweat from his forehead.

The others mumbled agreement. The planet had an ominous force field surrounding it. It would have been ideal to switch the Quantum Leap Device to its original settings and take the ship away from the energy and back to their home universe, but they couldn't move fast enough. The planet sucked the craft in through its hazy atmosphere and downwards to the surface until a crash seemed inevitable.

The cadets scrambled to stabilise the craft, navigating until they had enough control of it to make a safe landing. They landed on a plateau in the middle of what seemed to be a desert, and sat for several minutes, calming their breathing.

## CHAPTER 3

ALEX RECOVERED FIRST and checked on the others. Everyone was unhurt and miraculously, so was the ship. He took a quick read of the amount of fuel they had left and if it was possible to return home with what they had, and it was. As long as they didn't make any other detours, they would get home fine.

"What do we do next?" Jaxon asked.

"Explore, I think." Nia shrugged.

They all took off their belts and navigated around the spacecraft to the exit hatch. Alex opened it and came out first, staring in awe at a bleak reddish orange sky.

A wind blew across the landscape, kicking up dust and dirt and bringing an unearthly chill. No matter which direction they looked, there was nothing: no plants, animals, or structures. The plateau was a flat plain of dirt, rocks, and air, leaving it open for the wind to ravage.

"It's so cold," said Yasu. "If we didn't have these suits, we might be freezing by now." Their suits were designed to withstand extreme temperatures. That meant the suits warmed them in colder climates and cooled them in hotter climates. But that left the parts of them which were uncovered, exposed to the cold.

"We should wear our masks," Alex said, taking his own out of the waist pouch that bore his essentials. The mask would protect their faces from the biting wind and keep dust and dirt out of their respiratory tract. Alex put his own on, effortlessly attaching it to his headpiece and moving his mouthpiece and earpiece into more comfortable positions.

"Is everyone good for some walking?" Alex asked.

They nodded.

They locked the craft, deploying a small force field around it for protection. Then they started out. Alex and Yasu walked in front, Alex with a heat scanner to check for signs of life. Yasu held a geo-scanner to take a reading of the terrain, mapping their coordinates and distance. Jaxon and Nia brought up the rear, holding weapons and goggles.

"There's oxygen here, but no life," Jaxon said, some resignation in his voice.

Nia shook her head, gazing up at the red sky. The sun on this planet was distant, hanging like a far-off yellow ball in the sky. Something about the planet reminded them of Mars, with its distance from the sun and the redness of the soil and surrounding atmosphere. "There has to be life. We got energy readings indicating a significant population when we were in space. Additionally, the planet can't just jam our communication systems like that. It has a similar technology to Earth's alternate in this universe. They protect themselves by scrambling signals on ships and crafts coming to land on them. We'll find people... sooner or later. I see something like a city up ahead, but I think we'll see it better when we get closer."

They kept walking as the sun descended slowly, heading to sleep. The sky grew darker, the burning red color easing to a burnt orange, and then something purplish. They got to what seemed to be the edge of the plateau and found a path amongst scraggly bits of rock. It seemed to lead down from the plateau's height to a lower plane below.

"Could this be..." Alex started, staring intently. The path indicated intelligent life, but his scanner also showed signs of heat in the distance. Like there was a cluster of living creatures ahead.

"Yes, I think it is," Nia said, coming closer to him. She pulled a pair of binoculars from her waist pouch and looked into the darkening distance. From what she could make out, something of a city sat in there, built in and around the hard rocks of a sprawling hill.

"I think I can also see what might be a communication tower…" Jaxon said, squinting through his goggles. "If I can hack into it, perhaps we'll be able to learn a little about the people here."

The others looked at him, nodding in agreement. If anyone could do a hack on unfamiliar technology, it was Jaxon.

They continued their journey, moving with more caution. The cover here was sparse, and now, knowing there was a civilization ahead, they were fearful of being caught. They were all thinking of how perilous their mission had become. What if the people in that city were hostile to outsiders? They all wondered, but none of them said anything out loud. They had collectively agreed to come here, and they had to face the consequences of that decision.

They journeyed down the path to the lower level and began heading for the tower. With each step, weariness set in, reaching into all the limbs in their bodies. This trip had been several hours long, and they all longed for a moment of rest.

They were still a small distance away from the tower when Nia exclaimed, "It seems they're onto us. Look!"

In the sky, a short distance away from them, three aircraft hovered, heading for them. Jaxon also spotted some rovers racing along the ground, moving swiftly towards their position at the tower. The time available was too little for them to make an escape.

The cadets decided it was better to remain where they were and not make any sudden moves. They stood in place under the dark sky, with the wind howling around them, watching the approaching locals of this strange planet.

The closer they got, the better they could observe their technology. The aircraft were noisy, their propellers powered by loud, roaring engines. And the land rovers were huge, moving carefully over the terrain, but kicking up dust and rocks in their approach. The designs of all these vehicles were unpolished and without aesthetic consideration.

"Their technology…" Nia started.

"… is somewhat primitive," Alex concluded, observing through the binoculars. This discovery thrilled him. Already, he could see significant differences between this world and theirs and he itched for the report he would write about it all.

At long last, the vehicles arrived where they were. The crafts landed around the tower, and the rovers drove up to them, parking in front of them. They waited for a few moments as the engines powered down. The vehicles had tinted windows, so no one could see inside.

Eventually, the door of the foremost vehicle opened and two enormous creatures came out. They were thick set with long limbs. Their dress of choice were loose garments with hues of white and shades of gray. They came closer, and the cadets could take in more of their appearance. Their skin was greenish, with hints of red around the neck and nose. They had wrapped their heads in turbans, so the cadets couldn't see if they had hair.

When the locals were close enough, they spoke. Behind them, the other locals had come out of their vehicles, keeping their weapons directed at the cadets.

However, the cadets couldn't understand their speech.

"Who has the universal communicator?" Yasu asked. The universal communicator could translate languages in real-time, helping them adequately communicate in unknown places. Naturally, it was only limited to languages in the ship's database, but it had most of the languages in the sectors surrounding theirs.

Nia stepped forward, holding up her hands. "I just want to bring out my communication device," she said. Nia had extensive knowledge of the popular languages in various sectors around their area. She couldn't speak all of them but could match languages to regions. The creatures looked at each other and narrowed their eyes as she reached into her pouch and pulled out the device. She chose a language from a long list of languages in the Orion Sector and deployed it.

"Hello," she said. "We are explorers from another world. We mean no harm."

The translator took a minute to recalibrate, and then a voice interpreted it for the locals.

They eyed her with suspicion, and the smaller one of the two said, "Welcome. I speak your language. No need for that thing."

# CHAPTER 4

THE CADETS RODE with the indigenes in the back of their rovers. They split them in two, Jaxon and Nia going with the ones who spoke to them, and Alex and Yasu going with another group. The garments and leather seats of the rovers had a fragrant, spicy smell, as if someone had applied perfume to them.

Nia spoke with the man from before. His name was Xev. He was the leader of the security force for their large city. She could glean that he learned their language from his training in the Gaia Sector in that universe. He told her more about why they came out to meet them heavily armed. "We saw a ship from space. We were scared that the Orion Federation might come back.

"Orion Federation?" Nia knew little about the Orion Sector, but she was sure she hadn't heard of the Orion Federation before. She wondered if Yasu had heard about it before in his forays into outer space.

"Yes. They rule here. Watch everything. Take things too. Dangerous people."

His demeanor grew cold, as though the topic brought displeasure to him. Nia decided to shut up. She stared through the windshield at the city, which was getting closer by the minute. The city was lit up with soft yellow lights. Something about the appearance was welcoming, like your family home beckoning you to come in, take off your shoes, and have a warm meal.

This mission was already turning out differently than the last. Here, they had made decisions that differed from their decisions in the last one. They hadn't crash-landed, but they had headed far out of their destination, reaching a planet they knew little about. It was a chance to broaden their knowledge of the multiverse and even their universe, but things could also go horribly wrong.

The rovers entered the city, passing streets made of paved stone, with green indigenes dressed in white, blue, bright orange, red, and gray. The homes were lit with yellow orbs, hanging on the porches and in the doorways. They heard music too, gentle sounds spilling from homes.

Eventually, the rover came to a halt in the courtyard of what appeared to be the barracks. The low-rise buildings had only a single floor. Also, the lighting was different, sharper, and harsher. The cadets came out of their vehicles, drinking in the space. It wasn't like anything they had seen. Compared to their Academy and the last universe they visited, this place could be from the Dark Ages.

"Come with me," Xev said.

He showed them to a place where they could spend the night. It was a small room, and it seemed to be reserved for visiting higher officials. The room had a heating system that hummed in its operation. He told them mealtime was over, but if they came to the cafeteria after freshening up, they would find something small for them to eat.

The cadets sat on the lower bunks, bone-weary and hungry.

"This is quite the adventure, isn't it?" Alex said. Though he was tired, the thrill of the change in events kept his blood pumping. This wasn't a place he would ever have imagined visiting. In his research, he saw some images of people and places in the Orion Sector, and he wondered if he would ever go there. Now, he was and he couldn't be more thrilled.

They stripped off their suits and wore the white and gray garments Xev and the other security official laid out for them.

Beneath the white and gray exterior, they found woolen tunics made with a thick weave, which kept the heat close to their bodies.

Afterward, they followed the directions and went to the cafeteria. The place was heated, but differently. Long energy sticks emitted light and heat at intervals in the ceiling. They sat beneath one of them, huddling close. The food was unfamiliar and served on carved stone plates alongside carved stone cutlery.

Jaxon dug in first, responding with enthusiasm. "It's good!"

The others followed, taking small bites initially, and gulping everything down subsequently. Meal completed, they sat, waiting for Xev, who stood at the other end of the room talking to some personnel. He walked up to them in due time, his expression grim.

"You meet Chieftain tomorrow. He wants to see you."

Something about how he spoke planted a seed of fear in their hearts, but they pushed it aside. They were already here with no mode of escape. It was best to meet the leader and see if they could plead with him to remove the barrier so they could leave.

Before they slept, they quietly discussed the situation. They weren't in any apparent danger, but they could be. Back home, in their universe, Prime, their people would see they had gone somewhere else. Would they send help? None of them had the answers. So far, none of the other cadets had landed in a place they shouldn't.

Sleepily, Yasu said, "We will be in a lot of trouble when we get home." The others agreed, but their eyes were closing already.

---

Morning dawned with a reddish sun flooding the barracks with light and sparse warmth. The cadets arose before then, hearing the -barrack-wide alarm system and the movement of the people within the other buildings. They wore their attire, heading outside to see what was to be done.

Though Xev said they weren't obligated to, they joined the

morning drills with the soldiers. It worked to warm them up and dispel some of the anxiety they felt.

Next came meal time. The cook served everyone hot porridge in stone bowls, and the cadets sat together again, choosing a spot beneath the light. Xev met them and told them what came next. "We go to the Chieftain's home after food. His house... top of the hill. We must walk." They nodded and ate faster.

The walk wasn't so challenging, as they were used to hard exercises from the Academy. They took streets with patrons walking to and fro in their daily business. They wore plain colors, some with turbans wrapped tight around their faces.

"The colors the people wear..." Yasu started, trying to recall if he had seen anything related to that in his research.

"They seem to be coded based on their status, yes?" Nia had been observing the clothing for a while too. Everyone in the barracks had worn white and gray, but beyond the barracks, the people wore other colors.

"They are," Xev said. "White base for everyone. It shows the humility of our beginnings. Then we layer on top. Red for royalty. Blue for servers. Gray for soldiers. Orange for homesteaders." He lapsed into silence.

They arrived at the Chieftain's home, and the guards at the gate saluted Xev. He saluted in return, exchanged a few words with them, and was allowed into the courtyard. He instructed the cadets to take off their shoes in the courtyard before walking on the red carpet leading into the leader's abode.

They padded into his place with socks, walking carefully. Inside, they went through a maze of corridors to arrive at the meeting room. They sat on high-backed leather chairs, awaiting the Chieftain's arrival.

A man walked in soon after, holding an animal horn. He puffed at it, and out came a low rumble, like a bull's call. The Chieftain walked in next, flanked by two guards. On his head was a red turban, tied with expert care and with a gold chain strung around it.

The cadets could tell that the Chieftain was old. His movements were strained, and he took small steps. He looked at them when he sat and they noticed a few wrinkles on his face, and that the red spots on his face were a darker shade than those on the others. He spoke briefly to Xev in his native tongue before addressing them.

"Greeting," he wheezed.

He spoke, and Xev translated. "I hear you come from the stars. But not our stars. Other stars, beyond our universe. That is miraculous. As you come to me, I care for you. But you can help me, too."

Alex stopped them then. "Help you? How?"

The Chieftain chuckled, putting his hand over his mouth. He beckoned one guard standing behind him to come forward. The man came to the table and dropped the large black case he was holding. It turned out to be a computer. He adjusted the screen, which, by the cadets' estimate, was about 12 inches by 18. Then he turned it on. The screen remained black for a time as the computer booted.

When it came on, the guard navigated to a black screen with green grid lines. It looked similar to a map like the chart they had in the Academy that was used for marking off points in the universe. This map was for just the Orion Sector. There were names of planets written in their script, but the cadets vaguely recognized the arrangement from their landing operation.

"There," Xev said, as the Chieftain spoke again. "Something comes from space to destroy us."

The cadets looked at what Xev gestured towards. Somewhere close to their system, a cloud was getting closer. It was detected on the radar as a heat signature that looked like a living creature.

"What is that?" the cadets asked with awed voices.

"We do not know. It has been some months since we saw it. It comes fast. We fear it may consume us."

The cadets rose to get closer looks at it. They hadn't noticed it on their landing. Secretly, they were all thinking that if they had, they might not have landed at all. This unknown entity was far beyond the scope of their training at the Academy. Perhaps more research could uncover what it was, but stranded here, with the primitive technology of this lone planet, there was little they could discover.

"Does it look familiar to anyone?" Alex asked.

They all shook their heads.

"What do you need us to do?" Alex asked, looking straight at the Chieftain. He feared he knew the answer but wanted to hear it by himself.

"We plead with you to protect us," Xev interpreted. "As we know, it is energy. We know we can create a stronger force field to keep our planet safe. What we don't know is how." Xev paused as the Chieftain stared Alex down. "That is where you come in."

The cadets absorbed the information, exchanging glances with one another. They wanted to tell him they didn't know how to help, but something about the hopeful way he looked at them let them know he wouldn't like that.

A new adventure had just begun for them, and they were unsure if they were adequately equipped to handle it.

## CHAPTER 5

THE CHIEFTAIN PROVIDED them with boarding. The chamber had better furnishings; premium wool covered the beds, silken dark blue curtains shielded the windows, and the heating system worked without a sound. They went in with their few belongings, marveling at the detailed architecture in the chamber. The walls were made of bricks with dark-wood paneling covering some portions. A high ceiling leaned on cylindrical columns covered in ornate carvings. From their guess, they could infer that the ceiling was made with plaster, molded into detailed, intricate patterns of fruit, trees, animals, and people.

When they had settled in, they gathered around to discuss their current predicament. The only way to leave the planet was to help the people. Even if that wasn't the case, it didn't seem right to leave without helping them. This moving cloud of energy approaching would most likely wipe out all life on the planet. They were directly in its path.

"We have to help them," Alex said, pacing the room. He was grappling with understanding what could cause such an energy cloud and could not find answers.

"How though?" Jaxon couldn't see how they could save an entire planet from destruction. Their education at the Academy provided them extensive knowledge of space and interstellar travel, but it didn't make them heroes. They couldn't save a planet from a malevolent force, especially when they had no concrete idea of what said force was. "We might have a better chance of destroying their barrier and escaping. I say that's what we should do."

"But we can try at least?" Nia looked from Jaxon to Alex. "We can't just leave these people here with no help."

Jaxon threw his hands up in a huff. "We can't be anyone's savior, Nia. We're just kids. If we're unsuccessful, that cloud will find and kill us, too. We don't know what it is. We need to leave before we're trapped."

"We need to get to our ship," Alex said. "We'll monitor it better from the craft, and we'll be able to tell what it is and, perhaps, infer why it's coming this way."

Nia nodded in agreement. "But what if we can't? I agree with Jaxon that we need a Plan B; an escape plan. These people only think we can save them because we're travelers from the Gaia Sector. And the Gaia Sector has made notable strides in technological development. We might not be able to help them."

Alex wanted to try, regardless. Given the speed and trajectory of the entity, they had some time to make plans. It wasn't a lot of time, but it could be enough.

"This is a prime learning opportunity," he said, looking around at the others. "The information we glean about this thing could aid the Interstellar Academy in future endeavors. We could protect these people and take back useful information for the Academy."

Reluctantly, the others agreed.

They spoke to Xev, telling him about their spacecraft and the systems on board. "We might get more information about this thing if we use our craft, " they said.

Xev agreed to carry them to the spacecraft in one of their aircraft. They went as afternoon waned to evening. The sky was a painting of brilliant oranges, purples, and reds. The wind howled around them, buffeting the aircraft on its journey across the plain. But Xev, used to flying in those conditions, piloted with ease, arriving at their craft in minutes.

The cadets went into the spacecraft and checked their consoles. On their screen, they could see the arrangement of the planets in the system, and close by, the cloud of energy coming closer. It looked like a moving star, but the temperatures were much lower. Something about the movements indicated sentience, as though it were a living creature, seeking life for consumption.

"It's unlike anything we've ever seen," Nia said, her eyes wide. "But doesn't it remind you of something?"

Alex frowned, scrolling through the radar data. "What do you mean?"

Nia gestured to the cloud's erratic movement patterns. "The way it moves, almost like it's searching for something. It's too... deliberate."

Jaxon's fingers hovered over the console. "Are you suggesting it's sentient?"

"I'm suggesting it might be connected to the anomalies we've caused," Nia replied. "Think about it—every jump we've made, every disruption we've triggered... What if this thing is a consequence of our actions?"

"Could something like this exist in our universe?" Jaxon asked.

"Maybe." Yasu shrugged, his brows still furrowed. "If it does, it most likely isn't something seen in the sectors around Earth. That might be why we haven't heard of it before."

"How do we deal with this, then?" Jaxon asked. He didn't like how comfortable the others were just talking about this unknown, dangerous entity. He believed now was the best time to plot an escape if they ever wanted to get out of there.

Alex was watching the screen as the others spoke, trying to comprehend what he was seeing. He recalled their arrival in this universe a few days ago. The planets in the Gaia Sector had rings of energy fields all around them, strong enough that their craft couldn't even make a landing.

"Could we evacuate everyone from the planet?" Yasu asked.

Everyone looked at him. "To where? And with what ships?" Nia asked. "The population of the planet could be in the billions. From what we know so far of their technology here, they most likely don't have enough ships to evacuate the entire population."

Yasu tilted his head. "From what I recall, it's a little less than one billion. But I agree. An alternative plan might be helpful. We don't know if they have the resources to evacuate everyone."

"We could create force fields around the planet," Alex offered. "The Chieftain mentioned something similar when he spoke to us. We could do that instead."

The others sat in silence for a moment after he spoke.

"But they already *have* force fields," Jaxon said. "The communication towers deploy a force field. We can't leave because of them."

Alex nodded. "I remember that. Perhaps malevolent and sentient forces of this sort are common in this universe, and planets protect themselves with force fields. But the planets in the Gaia Sector were impenetrable. We might need to create stronger force fields if we're going to protect this planet from the approaching cloud."

"That could be," Nia said slowly, still trying to find holes in the logic. "But do they have the technology for that?"

Jaxon scratched his chin. "I think we might be able to harness the technology they already have to build a stronger field. I could use my knowledge of our craft's force fields to re-engineer their towers."

As the others dispersed to their tasks, Jaxon caught Nia just before she left. "Hey, about earlier..." His voice wavered, uncharacteristically hesitant. "I didn't mean to undermine you."

Nia paused, her expression softening. "I know, Jaxon. You worry too much. But I need to do this."

He nodded, shoving his hands into his pockets. "Just... don't take any unnecessary risks, okay? We've got enough problems without adding you to the list."

A small smile played at the corners of her lips. "I'll be fine. And besides, someone has to keep Lady Raya in check."

Jaxon watched her leave, his stomach knotting with unease. For the first time, he realized just how much her resolve inspired—and terrified—him.

. . .

They stayed silent for a few moments, but Xev interrupted them by knocking at the hatch. Jaxon went to meet him.

"We are summoned," Xev said with a blank expression.

"Summoned? By the Chieftain?"

"No," Xev said. "By the High Chief. The overall ruler of our planet."

A large craft was resting in the landing area of the barracks. The design was like the aircraft Xev used to take them to their ship, but it had a more streamlined and aerodynamic design, tapering to an almost sharp point at the front. In addition, it had a fresher and newer white paint job, and it seemed to be made of sturdier metals.

"The High Chief's representative comes with that ship," Xev said. "She is in our Chieftain's palace. We go there now."

They took the long climb up to the Chieftain's house, the evening's chill clinging to them. Above, stars blinked cheerily, and the people were closing for the night around them. Once again, there was music in the air. The cadets heard someone singing, the melody mournful.

At the Chieftain's palace, there was music, too. They went into his courtroom, where he sat on his throne next to the representative, watching dancers move with a flourish. Servers moved food around the court on stone platters: roasted tubers, baked flat breads, grilled meats, and sliced fruit.

The representative's dark-lined eyes widened when the cadets came in, and she followed their movements until they sat in the corner.

When the music stopped, the Chieftain rose to speak. Nia set up her universal communicator because Xev wasn't around to interpret for them.

"Comrades, in our midst is an esteemed guest. The Special Advisor to our High Chief, Lady Raya." Everyone in the courtroom cheered. Most of them were in white and red, though some gray and blue garments walked past occasionally. "Let us take care of her and ensure she enjoys our stay in our humble abode."

The dancing and music continued. The cadets watched, mesmerized by the precision and heavy stomping. They ate as they watched, soaking in the distinct flavors of the planet's food. Everything they ate had a full-flavored richness that soothed them.

The cadets oohed and ahhed as they ate, the flavors surprising them after the blandness of the training meals.

Yasu loved the artistry with which the servers presented the food. They reminded him of his home, his people, and their culture of preparing food with flair.

Jaxon enjoyed the spiciness and savoriness of the meats, taking the first bite of each meat dish before the others could. Nia liked the fruits. There was so much variety, and they were served sliced open beside the meats and grains, dusted in spicy powder. She took a special interest in a purple sour fruit with hard flesh. Combined with the fluffy bread and what she called plant butter, it set her senses singing.

Soon, the Chieftain and Lady Raya withdrew to the meeting room, and Xev called for the cadets to follow. They met Lady Raya in the meeting room, eating one of the purple sour fruits Nia liked so much.

"Travelers from Gaia." Her voice was like thunder, rumbling and deep. They also found it surprising to hear her speak their language, but they assumed she might have received an education in the Gaia Sector like Xev. "You meet me in a good mood."

The cadets bowed in greeting, unsure of how to respond. She waved them to their seats with a bejeweled hand.

"We need help," she said once seated. "It will kill us. All of us."

"Do you know what it is?" Alex asked, leaning forward.

Lady Raya waved her hands in front of her face, as though waving the question away. "We see it before. Long before. Our books, histories, talk of it. It eats entire planet. Kill all life. Very bad."

The cadets exchanged scared glances.

"How did you protect yourselves?" Alex asked.

"Then, it was not big. Small, very small. They use some force and redirect it. It go to another planet and kill them. Very bad. We were lucky. Our planet was small. Not many people. And the demon, it was small, too. It looked for big life. Now, we are not lucky. We try redirect methods and they don't work. Our planet has many people now. The demon is bigger too. It comes to us."

"So, we should redirect it for you?" The wheels were turning in Alex's head, trying to imagine how much energy such an endeavor would cost.

She shook her head. "It is close. We need other method."

"Like an energy force field?" Jaxon asked.

Lady Raya nodded, smiling as though impressed by the answer. "The others in Orion Federation... they use force field too."

The Orion Federation!

The cadets all latched onto that information.

"The rest of the planets, too," the woman continued. "Outside the Federation. Outside the sector. Plenty of things are in space. We need protection. Our force field might not hold against this thing."

Nia chewed on her lower lip and sat up. "Have you asked the Federation for help?" If the Federation was protecting themselves with force fields, surely they could protect these people, too.

Lady Raya's eyes darkened, and she turned to the Chieftain. She said something to him in their tongue, and he replied in kind. They seemed to argue about something, but the cadets' communicator was off, and so they couldn't understand the exchange. Xev sat there, watching with an unreadable expression.

Shifting in her seat, Lady Raya reached for another sour fruit on the table. "The High Chief and the Federation do not mix. They fought some years ago. Listen, I'll tell you about it."

She told them about the Federation's government. It was set up hundreds of years ago to spread peace, prosperity, and technological advancement in the Sector. The Federation built up a strong military force and made great strides in agriculture, medicine, and science. Initially heralded as a beacon of progress, the Federation's structure began to crack under the weight of its expansion. Many of the advances in technology and engineering used by the Federation, including energy systems and transportation, were shared with all member planets, including Krissia, during the early years of its existence."

Lady Raya hesitated before continuing, her voice tinged with both pride and regret. "Even after our departure, the legacy of Federation technology lingered in our systems. The tools we use today, especially in energy management and force field construction, are adapted from what they once gave us. But without access to the newest updates or materials, we've been forced to innovate using what little we have left. It's why our systems look similar, yet struggle to keep up with modern Federation standards."

She gestured to the schematic of Krissia's current force fields displayed on the table. "This is why we need their engineers, their materials. We've stretched the remnants of Federation design as far as they can go, but without external aid, we can't hold this thing off."

The last president was that way. He ruled with an iron fist, greed blurring his vision. He changed laws to increase the levies on the planets in the Sector. The High Chief hated the terms, and went to the Council to demand fairer levies. His people were overworked and the rewards for their obeisance met with little to no benefits. He stood before all the other representatives and leaders across the Federation, pleading for more lenient taxes.

The Federation's president refused to budge. He sat on his seat, a leg slung languidly over the arm, and told the High Chief he could sever ties with the Federation if he wanted. Incensed by the man's insolence, the High Chief agreed.

"We are not part of Federation anymore," Lady Raya concluded. "But we are part of Orion Sector. Hence, we pay tax. But it is small, and it does not allow us rights to protection by Federation. We lost many rights when we left the Federation. Even our trade of ores and energy sources end bad."

The cadets let out deep breaths as one. The story explained why the planet was so desperate for outsider help.

"Would it be possible to appeal to him one more time?" Nia asked.

Lady Raya studied her face for a moment. "Who?"

"The President. This is a life-or-death situation. Surely, it's worth a try."

Lady Raya sighed, her voice heavy. "The High Chief is proud, yes. But he carries the weight of our people's suffering. When he severed ties with the Federation, he thought he was saving us. Every loss since then... it haunts him."

Lady Raya laughed, tilting her head backwards. The cadets watched in quietness. Eventually, she said, "The President is dead. A new one took his place. But our High Chief, he is proud. "The High Chief feels trapped by his own choices," Lady Raya explained. "He fears that rejoining the Federation would betray the memory of those who fought to free us from its grip. But pride alone cannot save a planet." Her voice softened. "Perhaps you can persuade him where I cannot."

Die? And so many people with him? The cadets felt a chill run down their spines at such resoluteness and pride.

"You see our position?" Lady Raya spread her arms wide. "We appeal to you because we have no choice. But you also stand to gain."

Alex's ears twitched at that revelation. "How?"

"We are a mining planet. Our land has rich energy resources. You save our people and we give you a lot. Enough to make you more rich than all people you know."

She waved at the servers standing behind her. They left the meeting room and returned with a chest between them. They dropped it on the table, and Lady Raya leaned forward to open the chest. Inside the box sat three cylinders filled with a glowing yellow liquid.

The cadets instantly recognized it as Molten Star, a rich radioactive energy source for fueling entire power plants. Something of this quantity could power the Academy for months.

The appearance of this incentive should have been a game changer, but it wasn't. Lady Raya hadn't told them anything about letting them leave if they didn't agree to help. If they didn't come up with a plan fast, the demon would consume the planet, with the proud High Chief, the cadets, and their gift.

# CHAPTER 6

THE CADETS SLEPT long and deep, arising late in the morning, rejuvenated. They sat around their beds, discussing what they knew so far.

"We don't have a choice," Jaxon said, his voice unusually harsh. "This is one of the worst decisions we've made since we entered the Academy. If we fail, we all die." He ran a hand through his hair, avoiding the others' gazes. "We should stick together, Nia. If anything happens—"

Nia's expression hardened. "I can handle myself, Jaxon. You don't have to keep saying it like I need protecting."

Jaxon's hand fell to his side, his words stuck on the edge of his tongue. He wanted to say more, to explain why her plan unsettled him so much, but he only managed, "I know you can. That's not the point."

Alex's frown deepened as he observed the exchange, sensing an undercurrent he hadn't noticed before. He decided to keep his thoughts to himself for now, focusing instead on the logistics of their mission.

"Don't be so negative. I'm sure Alex has a plan." Nia glanced in Alex's direction. She was afraid, too, inwardly fidgety and outwardly searching for a straightforward way out. "Right?"

Alex adjusted his posture on the bed, drawing his legs closer to himself. "I think we should give it a shot. We have some technology on the spacecraft that we can harness in creating stronger force fields, especially given the energy resources they have."

"We can also use the towers, I suppose," Jaxon said. "I think if I can get to one, I can tinker with it and figure out how it works."

"And what if all this doesn't work?" Yasu asked. He had been quiet for a long time, carefully translating the reports about the entity from times past. Though the information was arranged unfamiliarly, making him re-read various sections multiple times, he could gather that they had tried to use the same methods from the past, and it hadn't worked. "What if this thing is now too strong? Especially since we have no experience with it?"

"I think someone needs to go to the Federation," Nia said.

"Someone?" Alex gave her a sharp look.

"I volunteer. I can speak to Xev and Lady Raya, and we'll go together to the Federation and plead with them for help. The stakes are too high. We can't base all our actions on the hope that we successfully set up force fields here. We need to make other proactive decisions."

Jaxon shifted uncomfortably, arms crossed tightly over his chest. He fixed his gaze on the floor, his voice quieter than usual as he spoke.

"Let Yasu go instead."

The others turned to him, surprised. Jaxon's usual confidence seemed to falter, his hesitation uncharacteristic. He ran a hand through his hair and added, "It just makes more sense. Yasu has the experience with political briefs."

Nia's jaw tightened. She studied him for a moment before replying, "And I have the knowledge of Federation customs. You're worried about me, aren't you?"

Jaxon's eyes flicked up, then away. "I'm just saying it doesn't have to be you."

"But it is me, Jaxon." Her tone softened, though her stance remained firm. "This is about more than just who goes. It's about making sure we're doing everything we can to help these people. You understand that, don't you?"

Jaxon hesitated for a beat, then gave a small nod, his expression guarded.

Now, the three others stared at him in silent confusion. Nia broke through the quietness. "I think I can handle myself, Jaxon. I want to go, partially because the Federation could really help them out, but mostly because I would love to learn more about the rest of the politics in this sector."

To that, Jaxon had no reply. He didn't want to lose any of his friends, but the thought of losing Nia hurt much more. She was the first friend he made in the Academy, sitting next to her in the orientation hall and following her from there on out. Though he wished he could stop her from going, her independence of thought and curiosity about governments was what he liked about her most. He knew she would enjoy this trip and shouldn't stop her from going.

They agreed before the afternoon, deciding to do their best to set up the force fields around the planet. They also agreed that Nia should appeal to the Federation for reinforcements.

They left the room and met one guard at the door for help. Using the communicator, they explained where they wanted to go and who they wanted to see. The boys went with one soldier to look for Xev, while Nia went to look for Lady Raya to explain her point.

Their work began in earnest. Xev directed them to other technicians and engineers in the city, explaining the background of what needed to be done. Alex and Jaxon broke down what they hoped to achieve with the towers and the energy from the abundant Molten Star resource on the planet. Yasu also added that they would need a plan to relocate most people to regions with more agriculture and wildlife. That way, they could keep the field's focus on those areas.

On the other side of the Chieftain's palace, Nia met Lady Raya eating fruit in a makeshift garden. The plants there looked like desert crops, hardy and used to limited moisture. She explained how she and the rest of the cadets had helped, but also needed backup. "We have advanced technology, but this force is unfamiliar. We might lose. I don't want that to be the case. We should contact the Federation now and appeal for assistance, or we might be too late and lose everything."

Lady Raya agreed with her. For weeks, she had been thinking the same thing. Every time she met with the High Chief, he remained unflinching in his conviction that they would stay without any external help. But she believed that with the previous President in the grave, the Federation had changed in some ways. This was an excellent time to approach them and appeal for fairer terms and a better alliance. "We go together, you and me."

"Would you meet the High Chief for permission to leave?" Nia asked.

Peeling the pastel pink skin off another fruit, Lady Raya laughed. "No. Appeals have made no difference. We go without his blessing. I tell him we go for supplies on Teros, and we meet the Council instead." Teros was a planet on the inner part of the Sector known for its numerous factories and engineering products.

"And what if the High Chief finds out?"

Lady Raya shrugged. "He may kill me. But better I die doing right than die with the whole planet."

Nia had more questions. "If you're so resolved to die, why did you wait until now to take action?"

Lady Raya took a bite of the fruit in her hand, and looked at Nia. "Inquisitive child." She dropped the fruit on a tray as though disgusted by it. "I should have gone since. I waited for the right time. Your appearance here is the right time."

Unsatisfied but unwilling to press the issue, Nia let it drop. She was pleased to be included in the journey. "I'm a child and a stranger on this planet. Is it really okay for me to come to such an important affair with you?"

Lady Raya scoffed. "Your presence might benefit me. The Federation might think you are an important dignitary from the Gaia Sector. And they will be more kind to us, believing outsiders are watching."

That evening, the cadets met with the Chieftain, Xev, and a few other officials to finalize their plans. The cadets were to go to the capital continent with Xev the following day. While there, they would be better equipped to reach the people with greater influence and receive help.

The cadets thanked the Chieftain for his hospitality, emphasizing that they would do their best to protect the planet with all they had in them.

The stars shone like pinpricks of light shining through a dark cloth that night. The cadets sat outside watching them, wrapped in blankets. Jaxon leaned closer to Alex, breaking the comfortable silence. "I don't get how she's so fearless. It's like she doesn't think anything can touch her." He sighed, running a hand through his hair. "It's not that I don't trust her. I just… don't want to see her get hurt." Alex placed a hand on his shoulder, his gaze steady. "That's why we're a team, Jaxon. We watch each other's backs." Unfamiliar constellations dotted the sky. They talked about the things to come after. They were apprehensive about the separation they would face along the way, but they knew it was inevitable. The mission must be completed, and they were determined to face it with courage and resolve.

## CHAPTER 7

Morning came with gray skies and no hint of sunlight. A gale swept through the city, sending a dry, bone-aching chill through their layers. The servers brought leather tunics lined in fur for the cadets to wear. They splashed warm water on their hands and faces from the faucet and headed outdoors.

They met Xev and the Chieftain and offered their final thanks and goodbyes before heading to the landing strip, where there was a craft to take them to the capital continent. The aircraft was bigger than the others on the landing strip and had an even coat of white paint on it. The pilot was new. He spoke to them in their language, stumbling around the words. However, they could pick up that he was sent from the capital to escort them safely to the High Chief's palace.

They sat in comfortable, leather-wrapped seats and belted themselves in. The craft ascended with some difficulty because of the harshness of the surrounding winds. Soon, they were in the air; the aircraft swaying slightly due to the turbulence.

The flight lasted a couple of hours. They flew above the clouds and saw nothing but more clouds. For a time, the cadets went over their plans, but eventually, they lapsed into silence. Yasu read more about the planet's geography, still thinking of the best course of action for evacuation. Nia researched the Federation, learning more about the planets involved and which planets held the most power. Jaxon and Alex studied the energy systems in place, deciphering how they could integrate their technology with these people's.

As the plane descended through the clouds, the cadets pressed their noses to the window to observe the Capital's layout. It was different from the city they came from, way bigger, and more developed. A few buildings stood out, made of metal and concrete and reaching up into the sky. But in general, the city didn't have the technological advancement of the other places they had been before reaching this universe.

Two black hovercars were on the landing strip to pick them up. The drivers and security detail wore white leather tunics, layered with gray and blue wool. They bowed and said greetings in their language and then in the language of the cadets. The cadets piled into the cars, offering their thanks.

The ride to the High Chief's palace was bumpy, but they couldn't complain. They watched the world outside, seeing people moving with quick steps along the streets. They soon arrived at the palace, ready to meet the people who would aid them in saving this world.

Nia fidgeted with the hem of her ceremonial robes as they passed through the gates, her apprehension growing with every checkpoint. The palace loomed ahead, its towering spires casting long shadows across the courtyard. The processes to get them into the palace were lengthy, with the security at the gates making checks and asking a lot of questions. Xev reassured them it was mere protocol; the High Chief was important and they couldn't be lackadaisical about his wellbeing.

They were ushered into the High Chief's courtroom when they got through the final checkpoint. It was a long hall made of dark stone and concrete pillars. Tall, stained glass windows let in the weak sunlight, painting the paved floor in pretty colors. They walked in, heading to the foot of his throne.

The High Chief sat on the ornately carved seat of white stone, bent over with age. Through eyes tinged white with cataracts, he stared at the cadets. "Thin," he said, uttering the word as though it were something dirty. "Small. Children."

Lady Raya waltzed to their side, a big smile plastered on her face. She said something in their language, which the communicator interpreted as, "Though they are young, they are capable. These are geniuses, some of the brightest minds in their world. They will help us to the best of their abilities."

The High Chief leaned back on his throne as though worn out. A sigh escaped his lips, echoing all around the courtroom.

"My blessing," he said, furrowing his brows. "Have."

Lady Raya smiled bright and wide.

She escorted them out of the courtroom and to a briefing room on the same floor. "He give blessing. We proceed."

The cadets nodded, filled with energy and ready to begin.

"Nia, you come with me." Lady Raya fixed Nia with a hard stare. "We must begin our journey to *Teros*. Your friends remain and work with our engineers. We all have different battles in this war."

Before the cadets dispersed to their various points of action, they met in a deserted hallway to speak one last time.

"Could this be goodbye?" Yasu said, biting his finger.

"Never!" Alex said, shaking his head violently. "We can do this. Despite facing a tyrannical empire, we stayed alive. We will come out of this alive, too."

"Make sure you return safely," Jaxon said, awkwardly tapping her shoulder.

She laughed a bit, trying to dispel her general lingering apprehension, but it remained.

They huddled together in a group hug and promised to come together and make the journey home safe.

Nia went to the spaceship that would take her, Lady Raya, two other high-ranking officials, and a small crew to the Federation's capital on the planet Eolu. Lady Raya had selected everyone on-board carefully, ensuring nobody would speak to the High Chief before they left. They went into the ship, belting in and preparing for takeoff. Nia watched the stars get closer through thick windows, a small coil of dread sitting in the pit of her stomach. But she pushed it aside. This opportunity to learn more about the Federation and the governing processes involved was a good one, and she couldn't waste it.

The journey was as smooth as space travel got. The ship's radar monitored the entity's approach in the distance, and they discussed its speed and motion. It looked like a rolling cloud and a traveling sun all at once, but mostly, it struck terror into them.

They slept and ate and watched the stars. They kept up communication with their planet, Krissia, finding out how they were navigating the preparations. Things were proceeding slowly, but they were developing. Krissian engineers had worked with the cadets to determine the best points to deploy the force fields. They were also working out the best mode of evacuation.

At some point, Lady Raya had to tell the High Chief where they had gone. Their spaceship had passed Teros by then and they still had a journey ahead of them to arrive at Eolu. The High Chief was requesting progress reports and she had to come clean. Everyone in the ship watched her from their various stations. Nia noted how confident the woman looked, wishing she could grow up to make such brave decisions herself.

The High Chief was livid. He demanded that they return immediately, but Lady Raya told him they wouldn't. "We have to save our people," the universal communicator said in translation. "And we cannot rely on only one method. We have to make peace with the Federation."

On the other side of the line, the High Chief went on and on a little bit more. Lady Raya watched a blank space with an unreadable expression. Eventually when she ended the conversation, she replied to the questioning look in Nia's gaze with a "Success, yes."

---

Nia spoke to Alex a few days later, her voice laced with frustration.

"The Federation has every reason to help them. They know what's at stake, but they're too caught up in their own politics to act."

Alex's voice crackled over the comm. "And the High Chief isn't making it any easier. Between his pride and the Federation's bureaucracy, it feels like we're trying to balance a star on a needle."

"Then we have to push harder," Nia insisted. "They won't act unless we make them see the cost of inaction."

Alex hesitated before replying. "Just be careful. If you push too hard, you might end up breaking something instead."

The closer they got to Eolu, the more Nia's fear grew. Away from her friends, in this strange world where everyone spoke a different language, her confidence was waning. She knew so much about the planets in the Federation, their customs and traditions, but she was still so young.

"What if we fail?" she asked Alex.

"We won't." His voice was low, strained from a day of hard work, but it held a note of confidence. As always, Alex believed that he could accomplish anything with his friends. "We can't. We'll all go home together and face the consequences of this decision, whatever those consequences may be."

They talked more about the progress made on Krissia. They had found a way to reconfigure the towers to get a stronger force field. "The cloud's movements aren't random," Jaxon said, gesturing to a pulsing red line on the display. "It's tracking the residual energy from our leap. It's like it's following our breadcrumbs." Jaxon sat cross-legged on the floor, surrounded by holographic projections of the Krissian tower schematics. The energy pathways glowed faintly, pulsing like veins on an alien creature. His brow furrowed in concentration as he traced their flow with his finger. "If we reroute the auxiliary energy from these nodes," he muttered, "we might stabilise the field long enough to hold off the cloud."

Alex crouched beside him, studying the schematic. "And what happens if the nodes can't handle the load?"

"They'll overload," Jaxon replied bluntly. "Best-case scenario, the towers short-circuit. Worst case..." He trailed off, letting the unspoken consequences linger.

Nia leaned against the console, her arms crossed. "Worst case, we blow the entire system and leave them completely vulnerable." Her tone was calm, but her eyes betrayed her unease.

Jaxon glanced at her, his jaw tightening. "We don't have a choice. If we don't try, that thing wipes out everything here—and us along with it."

"The Quantum Key worked because it stabilized dimensional anomalies," he muttered. "If we can figure out how to replicate that principle, we might be able to amplify the towers' range and strength."

Alex leaned over his shoulder, studying the projection. "But the Key wasn't just a stabilizer. It created a balance between forces that were fundamentally opposed. Do you think the towers can handle that level of stress?"

"They don't have to," Jaxon replied, his voice tinged with a mix of confidence and caution. "We're not recreating the Key; we're just borrowing its principles. If we reconfigure these nodes to handle the energy flow, it should hold—at least long enough to protect the planet."

Nia, seated nearby, nodded thoughtfully. "It's risky, but it might be our best shot. Let's get to work."

They had to move major components across continents to reconstruct the towers, but they were working fast.

He also told her about the High Chief's wrath. "He was so unimpressed by Lady Raya's deceit. We met him two days ago. He remembered you used to be with us, and asked where you had gone. When he heard you left with her, he flung a stone goblet at the wall and it shattered into pieces. He says he prays for your failure."

Nia gasped. "That's extreme."

"Truly. But his pride is at stake. I doubt his prayers go deep. He might inwardly wish for your success."

Nia didn't know how to feel anymore. She told Alex she was afraid, but he encouraged her to believe in Lady Raya's confidence. That helped her calm down.

They arrived at a landing port in Eolu. The workers at the spaceport guided them to land in the correct position using glow sticks and reflective signs. They proceeded out of the ship, Lady Raya at the head of the line, striding fast, as though she owned the place. They had dressed Nia in the ceremonial garments of their planet; thick white brocade with blood-red silk layers over it. They tied a turban on her head, tucking her hair in, and stringing long brass chains over it. Next to Lady Raya, she looked like the more important guest.

As the craft cut through the clouds, Lady Raya turned to Nia. "The Federation Council will not be kind. They remember betrayals better than kindness. They will test you—try to humiliate us. Be ready to stay firm." Lady Raya spoke in another language to the people at the port, explaining who they were and why they were there. The people confusedly glanced at Nia, evidently wondering why a Gaia Sector native was in their procession. But Lady Raya explained she was a princess from a Gaian royal family interested in learning more about their government.

They boarded an aircraft to Eolu's capital, the headquarters and heart of the Federation. The craft was of a sleeker build than anything Nia had encountered on Krissia. The metal was a highly polished gray and the body was shaped like a bullet. They boarded the craft, belting themselves into their seats.

As the craft cut through the clouds, Nia's apprehension returned. She wished to speak with the others, for a chance to explain her fears to them and have them calm her down in return, but it was impossible. Communication channels out of Eolu were well-guarded and majorly restricted to those allowed by the Federation. Thus, Nia focused on the novelty of the experience. She imagined she might never witness another council session in the Orion Federation.

From her reading and discussions with Lady Raya, Nia discovered that sessions could go on for several days, discussing various issues and attending to them one after the other. Customarily, the sessions came with breaks of several hours in between for the officials and senators to rest before the next issue was brought forth.

Nia dozed on the flight and awoke with a shudder when Lady Raya shook her shoulder. They exited the ship and went into hovercars waiting beside the landing strip. The hovercar moved through tarred streets fringed with two-storeyed concrete buildings. Occasionally, Nia saw taller structures constructed with a mix of stone, concrete, and steel.

They arrived at the Council House in due time. It was the most prominent structure Nia had seen since her arrival in this universe: a monumental building with gray concrete, a steel frame, and tempered glass. Lady Raya checked her pocket device where she was monitoring the council schedule, and she announced their slot was still ahead. They hurried in, running up the stone stairs in front, and through security checks, and followed an escort into the Council Theatre.

Here, Nia held her breath in awe, marveling at a theatre bigger than any she had seen in her life. The stage and podium sat at the bottom, with over twelve thousand rows of seats on increasing levels leading up and away from it. A red-skinned man with horns and a tusk was speaking at the bottom when they entered and walked to their assigned seat. Close to their seat was a screen where they could select the interpretation they wanted and receive a written translation of the speaker's speech.

For the next few hours, various people from different planets came forward to speak. Attendants came in, bearing finger foods and drinks, and Nia ate with enthusiasm, observing the processes and taking notes. When their scheduled slot arrived, Lady Raya went down the stairs to the stage alone.

She stood at the microphone and greeted the spectators from all over the Federation in several languages. Lady Raya began telling a Krissian folk story with an elegant flourish, and she segued into pleading the case for their planet, giving details on their former interactions with the Federation.

When she was done, the moderator gave space to the Federation representatives to ask questions. Several questions were flung down, each coming with a malicious bite, expected to derail and fluster her. Lady Raya explained Krissia was ready to discuss new terms for a more favorable alliance. She referenced the gifts they had brought as a token of goodwill; a chest filled with Molten Star and some metal ores native to their planet.

One representative, white as a blank sheet with a bulbous head and black attire, said, "You turned your back on us. Now we turn our back on you. You left us when it was favorable, and now try to return when you're about to die?" His laughter croaked through the loudspeakers and other representatives joined in.

Nia couldn't hold in her thoughts. She turned on the microphone close to her seat on and said, in a rush. "But that isn't fair. Your Federation guards the Sector. You can't just abandon some planets because they don't pay you as much as other planets." She caught the look of surprise on Lady Raya's face, but plowed on in desperation. "These people will die. They need your help. They're willing to give a gift as a token of their goodwill and pay to transport the engineers and materials to Krissia. And yet you spit in their faces."

For a moment, there was silence. Nia turned off the microphone, her gaze finding the expression of pride on Lady Raya's face, and lowering to the ground. She wasn't a real delegate, and she had just done something the Academy had demanded the traveling cadets never do— interfere in foreign politics. Perhaps her presence at the Council did count as interference, but she believed as long as she didn't make any actions, it didn't count. Now she had crossed a clear line. But the pressure had been too great; she couldn't help herself. She sat back in her chair, bubbling with indignation at the flippancy of the delegates from the other planets.

Murmurs filled the hall, eyes resting on Nia and the rest of the Krissian delegation occasionally. Nia also noted the disapproving glances the other members of their delegation threw at her, evidently irritated by her interruption. Lady Raya answered a few more questions and returned to her seat before the voting began.

"You interfere," she said when she had arranged herself in her seat.

Nia was about to apologize, but Lady Raya held up a hand, turning away. "I like that," she said.

Though the applause reassured her, a gnawing fear crept in. She had violated one of the Academy's core directives. When Alex called later, she hesitated to admit the full extent of her actions, unsure if pride or guilt weighed heavier on her heart.

Nia sat back, adjusting her garments, pride swelling in her belly. She liked Lady Raya; the woman's poise, grace, and confidence. If the woman liked her interruption, that was the only thing she would care about.

## CHAPTER 8

EVERY MORNING during the month of their preparation, the cadets checked the radar and estimated how much time they had left. The hours and the days slipped through their fingers. As they finished one task and headed to another, more sprung up. And every day, slowly and surely, the energy cloud of doom drew closer and closer. It had gone over two planets in the system already. But as those planets were lifeless rocks, uninhabited, except by a few rovers and research equipment, no harm came to them.

In the duration of Nia's trip, they had successfully created an evacuation plan for the Krissian natives, re-engineered the design of the towers to create force fields with more protective power, and began the testing.

The language barrier made the processes even more difficult. Xev couldn't work everywhere with them. Only a handful of workers spoke their language, and they had only one universal communicator, as Nia had taken the other. Nonetheless, they strived each day, working around the limitations, and pushing their fears aside.

They found joy and entertainment in various forms. They picked up some of the language in their interaction with the natives, learning how to say a few helpful phrases. With this minor understanding, they could take part in the popular games and dances in their culture.

Yasu took a particular interest in the wide variety of board games they had on the planet. When he wasn't working, he played with a native, losing and learning from his losses until he registered his first win.

Jaxon and Alex absorbed themselves with more work after hours. Alex read about Earth in this universe, making translations with painstaking slowness and consulting Yasu for help when needed. He learned that most planets in this universe used force fields to restrict unwanted visitors, but they also served as protection from other space phenomena.

Frequently, while Alex tinkered with the information, Jaxon worked with some equipment in the corner of the room, dismantling it and rebuilding it for a better understanding of their functions.

After Nia arrived in Eolu, they could not reach her and Lady Raya. That threw up a note of fear in their hearts. Jaxon spent two days pestering Alex, saying, "What if this was a big ploy to trap us here? If they've taken Nia, we won't be able to return home. We should've just hacked the control towers and escaped while we could."

Eventually, weighed down by Jaxon's worries, Alex met Xev for answers. Xev assured them that things were fine. Eolu had strict policies against unauthorized communication going in and out of the planet. All communication had to pass through their channels. An additional barrier to their ease of communication was the High Chief's disconnect with Eolu. If the two planets had a cordial relationship, easy communication would have passed through the High Chief's palace. "We will hear from them soon," he said, confident, tapping Alex on his shoulder. "And we will hear that they are successful."

The energy cloud drew closer, unbothered by their lack of preparedness. Before the day's activities began, the lead engineers and technicians monitored its approach. The closer it got, the better they could understand its composition. Jaxon frowned at the readings. "The energy signature here—it's faint but familiar. Could this be a byproduct of multiversal travel? What if every jump we make leaves behind fragments, like breadcrumbs, that something out there follows?" His voice trembled as he stared at the hologram. It had a dense core and exerted a gravitational pull on the environment. So far, they could also notice a haze of crushed rocks and dense gases billowing around it.

They also observed the planets it had gone over, noting the effects on the surfaces. The research equipment left on their surfaces were damaged in varying degrees. Some equipment was so badly battered that they couldn't communicate with them anymore. Others had scrapes and bumps and worked to send some signals back to their space program. They had limited visuals from the cloud's passage, only noting that the cloud subjected the planets to an impenetrable darkness full of electromagnetic forces akin to those of their system's star.

One thing they could all agree on was that, though the cloud moved like it was alive, it wasn't. An entity that large couldn't come to being and exist in the void of space with no oxygen. Nobody could conclude what it was, but there was a consensus among the Krissians that it was a demon.

In all this, the cadets were recording their experiences on this strange planet in this alternative universe. For one, they observed there were no anomalies, giving them hope that Alex's findings might be true. They had been there, going around the planet for several weeks, but the Quantum Leap Device hadn't recorded a single anomaly. For another, they were learning more about energy conservation from the Krissians. Though Krissia was blessed with vast stores of Molten Star, they were conservative in their use of it. Their equipment might be large and somewhat outdated, but they were efficient, with few energy losses.

The cadets discussed their fate on arrival at home. None of the other cadets had gone on a mission for this long. They joked about some of their technicians back home, imagining they might be much older and perhaps married by the time they returned to the Academy. But all their jokes couldn't keep away the apprehension of the consequences of their detour. Coming to this planet hadn't been a necessity, but a journey born of curiosity.

"We're bringing back lots of information," Yasu said, looking through his notes. He had never written this many notes in a single semester at the Academy. He hoped that, somehow, this information would be enough. Sending cadets out to explore the multiverse was risky business. Hence, they had to show themselves to be invaluable, good at exploration and discovery. He hoped they had discovered enough.

"And Molten Star. Don't forget the Molten Star," Jaxon added with a shaky grin.

"But would it be enough? What if they stop us from future trips into the multiverse?" Yasu glanced at each of them, aware of what such a fate would mean. "They can't do that. Can they?"

The others had answers, but didn't want to say them. So, they sat by their food in silence.

<hr />

On the evening the cadets finally successfully set up a force field strong enough to deflect the blasters in their spacecraft, they received a summon from the High Chief. The force field covered the city they had landed next to when they first arrived. They had previously evacuated the people to the nearest agriculturally rich region, as those were the priority for protection.

The cadets joined the engineers, soldiers, and technicians to cheer. They had reconfigured the blasters on the craft to match the energy signatures and forces observed from the cloud. They were certain the cloud's influence would be different, but the knowledge that the force field was now so strong was enough for the time being.

A soldier rushed to the tower where they were celebrating, singing merry tunes, and dancing in a circle. He shouted in their language, perhaps hoping they would understand, but they needed an interpreter.

An older engineer interpreted the soldier's words slowly. "The High Chief. He wants to see you."

The soldier escorted the cadets to an aircraft, moving briskly. The wind billowed around them, blowing the rest of the soldier's words into the sky. They strapped into their seats, looking out of the window, their hearts pumping at breakneck speed, and wide smiles on their faces. Outside the leather and metal of the craft, the sun descended to its bed and darkness drank up the sky.

They went from the aircraft to the High Chief's palace in darkness, looking through the windows at the lit-up streets and the people in them. Waving their hands in the air and playing music, they were jubilating. They seemed to recognize the hovercar as belonging to the High Chief and waved at it as it went past.

At the palace, they sat in the meeting room for a few minutes, waiting for the High Chief. Servers came in with platters of food and drink, wearing bright smiles and speaking excitedly. Their communicator translated their words as thanks and praises. They responded with demure smiles, wondering if it was too much.

The High Chief came out, carried into the room on a large, wooden chair. He reclined, watching the cadets wipe crumbs and oil from their lips.

"Your work," he said, closing his eyes as he tried to recall the translation of the next thing he wanted to say. "... good." He seemed to give up on trying to speak in their language and launched into a speech in his tongue about how their efforts had granted their planet a fighting chance. For a time, they had all been panicking, with some richer indigenes fleeing in ships to other planets in the Federation.

He told them of his displeasure with the Federation, despising the loathsome way they preyed on their planets, forcing everyone to bow to their every whim. He hated that Lady Raya had to go to them with gifts and an outsider to plead for their aid. "I gave that woman too much power."

Alex asked the question he knew the others had. "Have you received any word from Lady Raya's party?"

Jaxon and Yasu leaned forward with eager expressions.

The High Chief closed his eyes, his wrinkled face growing pensive as he listened to the translation. He replied, speaking with deliberate slowness, as if to add some drama to his words. "They succeeded."

The cadets almost leaped out of their seats in excitement. They hadn't imagined the evening could get better, but it had. Their friend's mission had been a success and they would all return home happy.

"They return now with the Federation's forces. When your friend is here, you can all return to your world before the cloud comes. We thank you for your aid. Our planet will never forget you."

Pride swelled in the cadets' hearts. The fear of their return home remained, but the knowledge that they had faced additional responsibilities head-on and succeeded gave them respite.

# CHAPTER 9

As NIA and Lady Raya's ship got closer, the cadets and people of Krissia made final touches to the force field designs. They knew that more engineers with more outstanding expertise on force fields were coming in the delegation from Eolu, but they wanted to put their best feet forward.

However, the closer the delegation got, the more perilous their journey became. The cloud's approach had blocked their usual trajectory, forcing them to take a longer route on the other side of the system. This longer route put them at a higher risk of not setting up in time before the cloud swept over Krissia.

The cadets spoke to Nia, learning what the mood on the ship was like. "Everyone is more upbeat and happy," she said, beaming, "but we also fear we might not make it in time."

Another thing that worried the cadets was their return trip to their universe. If the cloud got to Krissia before Nia's party did, they would be forced to remain on Krissia the entire time the cloud moved over the planet. And that movement could be a few weeks long.

"We have accomplished a lot in the time we've been here," Alex said. "Most of the things we've done are things we never imagined we would do. Our journey cannot end here. We will succeed, save these people, and return home in time."

What Alex didn't tell the others was that he did calculations every night, checking how slim the landing and takeoff windows were. From his calculations, given the cloud's velocity and the distance and speed of the delegation from Eolu, there was a small window of a few days. His knowledge made him believe that something could go wrong. Calculations were occasionally imperfect. Every night, his findings differed and that weighed on him.

Alex pushed his concerns aside by throwing himself into work. They were running tests on the integrity of the force fields daily, using their spacecraft's blasters. Focusing on the work kept him from remaining preoccupied with his thoughts about the doom cloud and his friend's arrival.

At long last, the delegation was close enough that they could land. Alex, Jaxon, Yasu, and Xev flew to the planet's capital on the day of the landing, staring into the sky, watching the spaceships lower into the planet's atmosphere and navigate to their landing spots. A small crowd had gathered to watch the landing, the High Chief in their midst, sitting on his wooden chair and wearing a displeased expression. Everyone clapped and rejoiced, happy for the timely arrival.

The palace prepared a welcome party with musicians, dancers, and food. The delegates from the Federation initially balked at the reception, but soon, they were dancing too, infected by the high energy of the indigenes.

The other cadets swooped on Nia, stealing a moment amid the chaos. Jaxon threw his arms around her in a bear hug, and the others huddled close, surrounding them. They released her from the hug, but told her stories of their adventures. Jaxon and Yasu hadn't spoken to her as much as Alex had during her return trip, so they told her everything they had wanted to tell her while she'd been away. Though Nia had her own stories, she stayed quiet, watching her friends' high energy and animation.

The High Chief called everyone to order, rising with support from a guard and another royal. He spoke of the progress made so far and the work left to be done. Emphasizing the presence and technological knowledge of the cadets, he referred to their efforts, which brought much-needed aid in their time of need. He welcomed the Federation agents with a cold wave, saying, "We hope that this time, our alliance will be fruitful, peaceful, and prosperous!"

Lady Raya applauded along with everyone else, but when the High Chief turned a cold gaze upon her, she dropped her hands to her sides. Nia made a not to plead for mercy on her behalf before they left.

The crowd exploded with fresh cheers. The merriment continued late into the night, with music and drinks flowing in a never-ending torrent.

None of it could sway the cadets. With their job completed, they had to return home. They met in a quiet portion of the palace courtyard to discuss their departure plans. Alex revealed his calculations then, showing them the math that had plagued him all that time.

"I fear if we don't move quick enough, we might get caught by the cloud's gravitational pull as we attempt to make a light jump. We have enough fuel for the journey home, but not enough to fire up the thrusters and get us away from the cloud if we get caught by it."

The others, though not as thorough in their calculations, had similar worries. They sat for some minutes, sharing ideas.

"Why don't we go straight into the multiverse then?" Yasu offered. He was staring at his notes, recalling their trip there. "The force of the break through the fabric of time and space will be enough to save us from the gravitational effects of the cloud."

The others nodded, Nia adding, "We can do that and make a jump on the other side!"

Alex mused, wondering if it was a viable solution. As though reading his thoughts, Jaxon said, "We'd need more speed and precision than ever before for this trip. But I believe we can do it." He thumped Alex on the shoulder. "We have a good leader. Even though he often persuades us to get into awkward situations."

They had found a solution that comforted them so they could enjoy the rest of the night's activities.

The cadets had one last meeting with the High Chief before they boarded their spacecraft. He sat in his chair and beckoned each of them forward, placing a hand on their heads in blessing. As he held Alex's hands in his wrinkled ones, he thanked them once more for their help. The Federation's technicians had gone over the work they had done with the Krissians, noting that their input, though not completely effective, might have saved much of the planet from annihilation. "Travel safe," he said, in closing, "and come again."

The cadets boarded their spacecraft, accompanied by cheers from an exuberant Krissian crowd, and with the Molten Star in a lead box placed in a guarded containment of the ship.

They sat at their consoles, observing the approaching cloud through the windows and its proximity to their planet, making calculations on the best take-off route. Out in space, the entity looked like an enraged storm cloud; a turbulent spread of darkness with a fiery core.

"We've got it," Alex announced, seeing the calculations from the other cadets.

They could begin their flight.

They shot into the air, applying the thrusters to break them out of Krissia's gravitational zone, and aiming away from the cloud. Their spacecraft wavered, buffeted by the powerful forces at play in the vicinity, but they worked together to initialize the Quantum Leap Device.

Alex counted down, and the cadets braced themselves, hoping it would work. The spacecraft lurched, as though pulled by the cloud, but it broke through the barrier and zipped into the world between worlds, where all that existed was light and sound, and the pure exhilaration of doing something that would've been fiction several years ago.

They crashed through the other side, reemerging close to a planet that looked very much like Krissia. Alex checked the

Quantum Leap Device and let out a loud cheer. The others, hearing his excitement, let out whoops of their own.

Their adventure had taken them to lands they never imagined they would go, and now they had returned safe, to the world familiar to them. They embarked on the last leg of their journey, full of determination and a replenished desire to explore.

## CHAPTER 10

THE SPACECRAFT FLEW into Earth's atmosphere; the cadets signaling the attendants at the landing dock. They were shocked to hear from them, asking repeatedly, "Team Alpha?" The cadets laughed, guessing where the shock came from. They had been gone for roughly three months. It was expected that the Academy would think they had been lost forever.

They navigated to the landing area, easily manipulating the spacecraft's controls. Several moments passed after they landed, and they remained in their seats, soaking in the realization that they had done it. They had gone to another planet, in another system, in another universe, and despite the challenges, they had made it out alive.

When they came down from the spacecraft, they met the stunned looks on the faces of the attendants.

"You're alive!" Disbelief was evident in their expressions. "What happened?"

Excited though they were, the cadets couldn't spill the story so soon. They needed to meet the commander to explain why they had gone somewhere out of scope, and what had happened on the trip.

They walked to the commander's office in the main building, keeping their heads high, Alex in front. Other cadets and officials who saw them stared in ill-concealed surprise. Some called questions after them, asking if they were ghosts or what trouble they ran into on their adventure. But the cadets, driven by a desire to face the repercussions of their actions as quickly as possible, ignored everyone.

Alex knocked on the door, waiting for the commander's voice to beckon them in. When his voice rang out, deep and with a tinge of disgruntlement, they turned the knob and walked in.

The commander gazed at them as though he half-expected they would disappear. A long minute stretched in which they all stared at each other, and a scowl appeared on the man's face, deepening slowly.

"You have a lot of explaining to do, Team Alpha. We noticed your spacecraft re-entered our universe some days ago but couldn't believe it was possible."

They had their notes ready, passing them over the table to him, and talking over one another. They all collectively decided to leave out the part where Nia interrupted a senate meeting, painting her as a passive spectator. Eventually, the others fell silent, leaving Alex to lead the interaction. Alex, bursting with nervous energy, chronicled their adventure, explaining why they took a detour and headed to another planet in the first place, and giving a detailed summary of what they found there.

Several hours passed, and evening had come by the time Alex concluded the story. The commander sat in his seat, looking at Nia's notes. She had drawings of the garments of the people, drawings of the vehicles, drawings of the buildings, and even sketches of some systems in the Sector. He gave no reply for a long time, observing what they wrote about the people, cultures, technological advancements, development, and politics.

The commander grunted, eventually pushing the notes aside. "Truly, your findings are monumental. Once again, you have set yourselves apart as geniuses eager for knowledge." He was silent again. "However, no part of this mission was authorized." He held Alex's gaze, his brow furrowed. "Your only mission was to make contact with Earth in that universe. On finding you couldn't reach

Earth, your next action would have been making a return journey. Not embarking on another."

The cadets nodded, lowering their eyes in penitence.

"Will we be sanctioned?" Alex asked.

"Naturally. Your actions have consequences. But given the nature of your findings, you might find that the sanction, whatever it may be, will be a light one. You disobeyed orders but brought a treasure of knowledge our way. That is what this Academy is for; finding knowledge against all odds."

The cadets left the commander's office with a little lightness. The weight they had carried on their shoulders throughout their trip was gone.

They headed to the cafeteria to find the meal for the day and discuss everything about school as they ate. They collected the metal trays from the shelf, missing the stone trays in Krissia. The food was mashed potatoes and some greens, and the cadets stared at their trays, missing the Krissian cuisine.

"Does it feel like the more we venture into the multiverse, the less real home feels?" Jaxon remarked, glaring at the plate of food before him.

The others chuckled, understanding the sentiment perfectly. They nursed thoughts of what other universes and planets they would go to, and what new people they would meet. The thoughts were exhilarating, and though they had some fear that their punishment might prevent them from venturing into the multiverse again soon, they were positive they'd get another chance in the future.

## EPILOGUE

Far away, across the boundaries of the multiverse, the people of Krissia watched their clear skies. Now that they were free of the demon, the people of Krissia felt a great sense of relief, which brought them even more happiness. They sang with more fervor, danced with more energy, and ate with more gusto.

The High Chief and Lady Raya sat in the meeting room in his palace.

After the cadets left and the Federation agents began the work with the force field, the High Chief had proceeded to scold Lady Raya. For a time, his silence had tricked her into thinking he had forgiven her act of insubordination, but it wasn't so. "If you weren't my child, I would put you in chains and have you locked up permanently," he said, quaking in his chair. Something about the way he said it elicited laughter from Lady Raya. She threw her head back and guffawed long and hard, until her father joined in with some reluctance.

"Do not do that again," he warned.

"If I have to, Father," she said, "I would do it again. Over and over. For the well-being of the people."

Now, they reminisced about the cadets' stay, recalling the vigor with which the people had worked having foreigners in their midst.

"They were young, but they were intelligent and inspirational," the High Chief said.

Lady Raya couldn't agree more. The people constantly talked about them, calling them Gaians with reverence, remarking on their willingness to help a people they had no prior dealings with. It mattered little to her that they had blackmailed them initially. There seemed to be no other way to get them to help. If the cadets had flown away, they would have been at the mercy of the Federation, driven to more extreme measures to gain their attention.

She also recalled Nia's boldness at the council. Perhaps the Federation would have aided them without Nia, but Nia's words might have cut deep into the hearts of everyone there.

"Do you wonder where they'll go next?" asked the High Chief.

"Occasionally. They spoke of being travelers. I wonder where their journey will lead them next."

The two had no answers to their questions. They reclined on their stone chairs, listening to the music spilling in through the windows from the streets, confident that no matter where the cadets went, they were bound to succeed.

**The End**

# ECHOES OF THE VOID

## A YA SPACE OPERA

# CHAPTER 1

RAIN FELL in a constant torrent from a slate gray sky onto the shiny walls of the Interstellar Academy. Four bright cadets, minds buzzing with thoughts of how many other versions of them were watching the rain in their worlds, sat by a large window eating ice-creams.

"The one version of Yasu who has finally achieved world domination is angry because he wanted to throw a party today," Jaxon Brooks said.

Alex and Nia laughed in response, but Yasu looked unamused.

A few months ago, Yasu Garcia had undertaken a project to see how a villain could dominate and take over the universe. He did it for fun, interested in exploring all the areas that a criminal mastermind would cover to make his plan flawless. He had long since given up on the project, turning his attention to other things, but his friends brought it up occasionally to tease him.

The cadets lapsed into silence, and their thoughts drifted away.

Alex Rivera's mind went to multiple places as it always did. He was constantly questioning the multiverse and the possibilities tied to its existence. In their last lecture, the instructor expounded on unexplained cosmic phenomena. They had experienced one such phenomenon in their last mission into another universe. It had been a billowing cloud of energy and dust, which roamed over planets in the Orion Sector, consuming all life in its wake. They couldn't destroy it, but they helped in protecting the planet from its influence.

In her teaching, their instructor said, "The universe is boundless, filled with cosmic storms and celestial events we have scant knowledge of. As we venture further, breaking through the fabrics of the multiverse, we discover more happenings we know even less about."

Alex raised his hand to ask a question, and she gave him her usual tired look. His questions, while intelligent, often interrupted her workflow. He merely referenced their last mission, asking if such anomalies might have existed only in other universes. So far, in their universe, they encountered planetary collisions, novae, and cosmic storms. "What if other universes have the perfect environment for the creation of events that differ from those in ours?"

The instructor stared back at him, the classroom falling more silent around them. One cadet coughed, and in embarrassment, quickly mumbled an apology.

"Our understanding of the multiverse is limited," the instructor said, looking away from him. "We have only enough resources to make a few trips out of ours. When the time comes and we have built sufficient resources for constant travel and research, we will have a more rounded knowledge of the other worlds. But for now…" She wore a small smile, tight with a warning against further interruptions.

Presently, Nia Chen let out a small gasp. "A memo. Did any of you get one?" She was often the one to keep tabs on their schedule. Knowing she could have missed something bothered her.

The other cadets pulled out their tablets – Alex extricating himself from his deep thoughts – and checked for the memo. The commander was requesting to see them in the briefing room again.

"Has anyone done anything wrong?" Nia asked.

Jaxon wore an expression of guilt, and though he tried to hide it, Nia caught on.

"What did you do, Jaxon?" she asked, her tone firm.

Jaxon held his hands up as if surrendering. "I returned it. I promise."

"What was *it*?" the others asked in unison.

"There was a power tool in the space lab. I saw it during our last session, and I borrowed it. But I returned it. I promise!"

They let out mild laughter, but Nia still shot him a death glare. He got into trouble for breaking into classified documents about all the missions into the multiverse a couple of weeks ago. He mostly did it to prove a point to Alex, but it still got the entire group in trouble.

They couldn't afford any more mishaps. They hadn't been on a mission in ages because they were sanctioned for unauthorized travel on their last mission. On arrival in the other universe, they discovered that the Earth and other planets there were covered in protective force fields. Rather than return home, they unanimously decided to explore other planets in that universe. Though they returned with useful information, the commander and the Academy's disciplinary body deemed their actions insubordinate and unruly.

"The meeting is in an hour. Do we need to do anything else?" Alex asked.

They all shook their heads.

Free for the next hour, they got to the briefing room in time. The rain had eased to a slight shower by then, and they walked from the lecture building to the main building under a drizzle.

An older attendant was preparing the briefing room and arranging the documents for the meeting. He gave them a knowing look as he waved them to their seats and the cadets took that as a good sign.

Several minutes passed, and the cadets preoccupied themselves with their devices, reading their lecture notes and checking schedules for the following day. The commander came in, flanked by higher officials, technicians, and physicists. Observing the expressions of the higher-ups who came in, the cadets each felt a jolt of excitement.

It looked like good news.

"I'll go straight to why we're all here," the commander said. "Team Gamma was scheduled for the next outing. However, Tom broke his wrist in training yesterday."

The cadets knew Tom. He was older than them and had a brain that computed complex equations with ridiculous speed. He was also the team leader for Team Gamma and was pretty good at his job. From their interactions with his team, the cadets could tell he held them together like glue.

"Their team cannot function without a leader. Hence, we need a replacement for this mission." The commander held Alex's shiny-eyed gaze momentarily as though allowing the words to sink in. "We've chosen to let you take their place."

The lights in the room dimmed, and the multiverse chart hovered above the table, glowing with a green light. It showed some marked points, indicative of universes the Academy's cadets had explored. Whenever someone selected a point, it showed more details about the mission and the team of cadets deployed.

"Though in your past missions, you have taken drastic decisions leading you out of the mission's scope, you have also exhibited qualities we at the Academy commend: curiosity and a thirst for justice."

They nodded, their hearts swelling with pride.

In their last interaction with many of these officials, they had received a severe scolding. Their mission was laid out and dissected before everyone, and some officials had been scathing in their review. But here, they heard words of praise, which made them think that they were indeed contributing to the growth of the Academy.

"As yet, we cannot find out more about other universes from here. Until we've reached that level of advancement in our field, we will send you out into the multiverse.

"We've been monitoring the energy signatures from one of the universes on our radar. It's close to ours, or as close as it could be where universes are concerned. Our discoveries lead us to believe that the universe has interesting information that could advance our knowledge here at the Academy."

The commander paused for effect as the universe in question was pulled up. The cadets could immediately see why he was concerned about it, noting the low numbers on the energy reads.

But more than anything, the revelation gave them the thrill of exploration once more.

"As always, your training begins in earnest. You must work hard and make the Academy proud."

The cadets beamed, absorbing the goodwill of this opportunity. Here was another chance to see new worlds and discover something new about unexplained phenomena in the multiverse. They were going to grab it with determination and make the best of it.

## CHAPTER 2

THE NEW TRAINING lasted three weeks. The engineers and physicists had changed the Quantum Leap Device, making up the basis of the cadet's new training. They had to get acclimatized to the different operations to better prepare for the new dive into the multiverse.

Their diet changed during the training, as usual, switching them over to nutrient-dense meals which often tasted bland. They ate together, their devices beside them as they reviewed new information about their next mission.

"What do you infer makes this universe so different?" Alex asked, chewing a lump that might have been chicken, but didn't taste like it.

"Perhaps the stars are smaller?" Jaxon offered. He was the only one among them who seemed to like the food, shoveling spoonfuls into his mouth with few breaths in between.

Alex pondered on it, his food abandoned. From across the cafeteria, the cook yelled, "Mr. Rivera, clean up your plate!"

"Smaller stars and smaller planets too," Yasu said, laughing at the flash of irritation tearing across Alex's features.

"Smaller planets why?" Alex asked.

"We're all making guesses, aren't we?" Yasu looked at the other two, raising his brows. "Smaller planets, smaller people, smaller energy signatures. It was merely a hunch."

Nia swallowed some food and joined in the conversation, flashing Yasu a smile. "Hunches are fine. I just think a universe of miniature proportions wouldn't be so close to ours. Something else is at play here. We will find it soon enough. Let's eat, even though the food tastes like boiled socks."

The three weeks went by quickly, and their departure day arrived. They met the commander and some other officials for a final briefing. They recognized one of them, sitting with a glass of dark brown liquid at the back of the room, as the man who had antagonized them bitterly during their disciplinary hearing. His presence struck fear into them, but the warm look on the commander's face made them a little calmer.

"The day of your journey has now arrived, and you will make your third trip into the multiverse," he said. "You have undergone rigorous training, testing your physical, mental, and psychological abilities, and have faced adequate preparation for the travels ahead."

He looked around the room as he paused, as though considering how best to say what needed to be said. "Nevertheless, your actions in the past lead us to believe your team is capable of much good but much destruction as well. We do *not* want that to be the case with this mission. Your strict orders are to investigate and document the anomalies we've observed on our side. We do not want you engaging in any actions pertaining to the politics of the region or interfering with said politics."

Alex lifted a hand, and the commander nodded in response. "And what if we find Earth isn't available for a landing? Do we have permission to visit other planets and sectors?"

The commander smiled. "You have permission to visit other planets and sectors for this mission, yes."

The other cadets exchanged thrilled looks with each other, but Alex was overjoyed. If they had permission to engage with other sectors, they could explore more during their journey.

The briefing session closed with more warnings and the officials wished them a safe trip. The cadets returned to their rooms sleepy, and with renewed determination and a sense of adventure.

The next morning arrived, the sun shining weakly through swollen clouds. The cadets assembled at the landing strips, donning their spacesuits. The commander and other officials were there, watching the proceedings with pride.

The cadets got into the spacecraft and adjusted their seats at their consoles. Once again, Alex had the lead control of the Quantum Leap Device.

"Are we all in position?" he asked, checking the coordinates on the Quantum Leap Device.

Everyone responded in the affirmative.

"All right!" He gave a thumbs-up to the technicians in the control tower. "Preparing for take-off in 3, 2, 1…"

With a rumble, the thrusters shot the spacecraft through the clouds. Alex switched the Quantum Leap Device on, calling, "Initializing leap in 3, 2, 1…"

The Quantum Leap Device powered up, allowing the spacecraft to cross into a new universe. As it had been the first two times, it still was an exhilarating experience, breaking the craft into a new space. The cadets braced themselves as the craft tore through a tunnel of brilliant light and sound. Eventually, the energy swooshing around them vanished and they reemerged in a quiet place in space.

"We've made it!" Alex raised an arm in a cheer.

"Does this place look odd to you?" Nia asked. They could see this universe's version of Earth hovering in the distance, a vision of greens, blues, and white swirling clouds.

Beyond the Earth though, they could spot something wrong, something missing. The sky was almost spotless, as though the stars had taken a break.

"It looks incredibly odd," Jaxon replied. "Could this be the reason for the low energy signatures?"

"Possibly," Alex said, narrowing his eyes. This was much different than he was expecting. He gave the sky a once over, drinking in the lack of familiar constellations.

The cadets passed stunned looks around the craft, certain this mission would be the perfect blend of challenging and exciting.

# CHAPTER 3

"WE SHOULD TRY TO LAND," Nia said into the silence. "We can't find much about this *situation* from up here. Perhaps we'll have extensive discussions with the people on this planet."

Ever wary, Jaxon said, "What if we can't? What if these people are hostile?"

The others cast furtive glances his way. Jaxon was often the most pessimistic in the group. The others attributed it to his rough upbringing. After bouncing around several foster homes, he came into the Academy through a scholarship program. He knew his way around machines and everything powered by electronics, but he was wary of strangers.

"Let's be positive," Alex said.

"Last time we landed on a planet, we were trapped until we helped them out. What if the same thing happens here?"

Yasu considered it. "Good point. We'll just have to be wary as we land."

They moved the spacecraft and searched the planet's surface for a viable landing spot. Upon finding one, Alex signaled them to initiate the landing procedure, and they proceeded.

As they entered the planet's atmosphere, messages bleeped on their consoles. It came through in different languages, with different scripts. "Identify yourselves," it read in their language.

"Can everyone see that, or am I going mad?" Jaxon said.

Nia laughed. "Someone wants to know who we are. I say we tell him we're the extraordinary Team Alpha, who have saved planets from tyranny and, well, a more subtle form of tyranny."

"I suppose it's from a control tower in their space program or something," Alex said, laughter coating his words. "We should let them know we are travelers and come in peace."

"What if they're hostile?" Nia asked, and the others murmured in agreement with her question.

"I believe they aren't." Alex typed a message to the program, explaining who they were. It simply read: *We are travelers from another world. We've come here searching for knowledge about space, and the unknown universe surrounding us.*

They waited a few moments and a message returned, asking them for the craft's identification and some identification from their institution. The others searched for the documents on the database, and when they found them, they sent them across.

They waited again, holding their breaths.

In a quiet, anarchy-hungry part of Alex's brain, he wished he could shake things up on the planet and go in straight for the landing. A tussle would ensue, but he would...

A message came in, welcoming them as visitors to the planet, but stating that they would need to follow the strict specifications for landing. There was a long list of instructions to follow and they read through them, intrigued. They deliberated amongst themselves, deciding that the best thing to do was to follow the instructions.

They went in for the landing, easily finding the landing strip with its flashing lights. The city surrounding it got clearer as they descended lower, showing them the solid layout of identical cream-colored houses, with identical porches and identical gardens a short distance away from the space station. There was something quaint and peaceful about it.

Alex checked on the other cadets after the landing, ensuring they were unhurt and couldn't see any anomalies on their consoles. Everyone replied in the affirmative, indicating their enthusiasm to explore the new planet.

Outside the spacecraft, a few people had gathered around the landing strip, observing the craft, and waiting for the inhabitants to come out.

Alex got out first, inhaling the planet's crisp air deeply. Above his head, the sky was dark and somewhat cloudless. A single starglowed in the expanse, twinkling down on everything, somewhat lonely in its appearance.

"There's an unearthly beauty to it," Nia remarked, looking up at the sky.

The people standing around the ship approached, wearing cautious expressions. One stood in front, burly and stern.

"Greetings, travelers," he said, his voice coming out like a cracking whip. "From which parts do you come?"

Alex stepped forward. "We're travelers coming from another universe. Another version of your planet, Earth."

Murmurs rose among them, their cautious expressions morphing into confusion. The man in front sent a stern look back, and everyone lapsed into silence.

"How did you come to achieve that, this jumping universe? It almost sounds like magic."

A crooked smile tilted Alex's lips. "Yes. But then, every great scientific discovery has at one point caused others to question if it was real or magic."

The man stared at him, folding his arms against his broad chest. He seemed to like Alex's reply, because a smile spread across his face, adjusting the foreboding aura attached to him. "A man of great words. I like you."

Though he was friendlier now, the man seemed like a sharp blade. He told the cadets that he and his companions would need to search them and their craft for potential weapons that might harm them and the planet.

"You seem trustworthy," he said, taking turns to look each of them in the eye with a piercing gaze. "But we can never be too careful. You could be terrorists from another sector. We must be vigilant."

The cadets consented to the search, letting the man and his

comrades enter the spacecraft with blinking sensors. They asked several questions about their universe, and reason for coming, and the cadets answered with sincerity, letting them know their Interstellar Academy was in the business of uncovering the mysteries of the universe and using the knowledge to improve their world.

"We learn new things in each mission and those help us to learn more about our place in this world and our own," Alex said.

The man didn't reply, merely grunting and beckoning them to follow him into the premises.

As they walked, the cadets noticed the return of his foreboding aura. He introduced them to where they were, explaining that it was Earth's Universal Space Station. "We welcome all visitors through here. And also send more visitors out of here."

"It's beautiful," Nia remarked. "We saw this lovely city nearby. It had multiple identical houses in a grid pattern." She had found the city's layout pleasing, reminding her of the cities she built with her brother as a kid.

The man grunted again. "That's where the staff live. But recently, we've had to make changes."

"What changes?" Alex and Jaxon asked in unison. They glanced at themselves with pleasant surprise, but they got no answer from the man. Having no other choice, they decided to let it go, believing they would find the answer in due time.

In a stark white office with brilliant lights, the officials asked the cadets to sit around a metal table and await briefing. They waited there, talking to themselves about what could be happening.

"Could we be arrested?" Jaxon asked, worry flashing across his features.

"They seemed hostile," Nia said, "but not hostile enough to arrest us. Perhaps they might send us away. And we'd have to go exploring alone." She wrinkled her nose. "How fun."

"It seems there's some political strife in this universe, too," Alex said. "They might be wary because they have a history of travelers coming in to cause problems. We can't blame them."

The others murmured in agreement, deciding they would have to show the officials their mission statement for the briefing.

A few people walked in a few minutes later, carrying clipboards and wearing stern expressions. The cadets promptly recognized one of them as the −

"Commander!" they yelled, surprised but happy to see him.

He and the other officials flinched but recovered gracefully. They sat next to each other, schooling their expressions into grim blankness.

The cadets also recognized one of the other officials as the man from their world who had antagonized them during their hearing, Colonel Klaus. They stared from the commander to Colonel Klaus, noticing how similar they looked to their alternates from home.

They introduced themselves as officials from the Interstellar Academy of Earth, a prestigious institution tasked with researching the boundless expanse of the universe. They were there to interrogate the cadets, curious about what knowledge they brought from their world.

The commander's alternate introduced himself. "I'm Harold S., the commander of the Interstellar Academy…"

The cadets gasped again.

He cocked an eyebrow, watching them with an apparent lack of amusement. "What about this is shocking?"

"Our commander in our Interstellar Academy is called Harold too," Alex said, eyes shining. "You're his alternate."

The commander and the other officials drank in that information. Colonel Klaus moved in his seat, craning his neck to observe the expressions on the faces of the other officials.

"Surely, we can't believe these *children.*"

"Hold on, Colonel," the commander said. "We have research proving the potential existence of other universes. This could be our first contact with another world. I'm sure we can find out more about them."

He requested some means of identification, and they handed him their mission statement, signed by their commander. He stared at it for several minutes, his brows furrowing deeper, while the other officials looked from one to the other.

Eventually, he passed the statement to the official next to him with a sigh. "They aren't lying," he said, his voice tinged with wonder. "They are from another universe. A universe where *I* am their commander and sent them on this mission."

━━☰✦☰━━

The cadets went to the Interstellar Academy with the officials. They got into a hovercar with designs very similar to the ones on their home planet and rode next to silent guards. They attempted to ask some questions about the planet, the absence of stars, but they got nothing. The guards instructed them to wait until the following day for the briefing with the commander in the morning.

They were given rooms in an unoccupied section of the Academy's dormitory. As they passed by the other cadets in the Academy, they noticed the bright-eyed stares they got and wondered about them.

"Could they know our versions in this world?" Jaxon asked when they got into their allocated room.

Alex shrugged. "It's possible."

"Or maybe it's just our suits?" Jaxon said, beginning to undo the velcro catches on his. "I told you these feel weird. But they also look rather weird as well."

Alex shot him a tired look. "We should all get some sleep. Tomorrow might be a long day. We have a briefing with the commander, and we all know how information-packed those are."

The cadets didn't need a second invitation. They took off their suits in silence, dressed in the pajamas in the locker, and went to sleep.

Dawn came with rain, falling in a blinding sheet against the glass. They looked through the window together.

"I can't believe the rain followed us here," Nia said.

Yasu chuckled. "I think it's more like the weather on both planets is similar."

Nia wrinkled her nose as she stepped away from the window. "I prefer my version better."

They changed into the cadet uniforms provided in the locker and went to the cafeteria to eat. They took their trays to the service area using provisional passes from the commander. All the other cadets in the hall followed their movements with their eyes, murmuring amongst themselves.

Yasu twisted uncomfortably in his seat when he sat down. "All these eyes on us…"

"I'm uncomfortable too," Jaxon said. "I want to eat, but I feel uncomfortable with everyone watching us."

"Just eat as you normally do," Nia said. "You eat fine when we're at home."

"I don't know these people!"

"Just –"

"Yasu!" A girl stood beside their table, her olive skin tinged with an unnatural red hue and her black hair streaming to her waist. Her gaze rested only on Yasu, carrying an intensity that made the four cadets halt. Her lips trembled, eyes filling up with water, and then she flung herself on him, throwing her arms around his neck. "I feared I'd never see you again. Everyone thought you died, but I kept hoping it wasn't true." She pulled back, brushing his hair from his forehead.

Then, as if recalling the others were there, she looked at them, suddenly self-conscious. "We thought you died too. It's so good to see you again."

## CHAPTER 4

THEIR ALTERNATES WERE DEAD!

The information registered slowly, adding to all the other reactions they had been getting since they met the officials from the Academy. They must have thought the cadets were revenants, coming from the grave to haunt them.

The cadets wanted to ask the girl more questions, but a stony-faced official came and dragged her off. He returned to tell the cadets to hurry up with their meal and stood next to them: a deterrent to other cadets.

They ate as quickly as possible, spurred by the potential information they had to learn. Though they wished to talk some more, the official's presence forbade any conversation.

The official escorted them to the briefing room at the end of the meal. A small crowd sat around the table, their expressions perfectly composed.

"A girl jumped on Yasu in the cafeteria," Alex said. "She said you all thought we were dead. We're assuming it's our alternates."

The commander nodded, a grim smile on his face. "Well, saying they died is very definitive, and nothing we know is definite. We have a hunch that they may yet return."

The cadets didn't understand and cast confused glances between themselves.

"I know you must have many questions," the commander continued, scratching his chin through his salt-and-pepper beard, "and we'll answer them in due time. Their ship was taken by something we call the Void. It's a dark blankness bearing similarities to a black hole. It drinks up light, life, stars, and planets, moving across sectors and planets."

He gestured, and someone dimmed the lights. Over the table, a spinning 3-D holographic image of the universe appeared. Unlike the version the cadets had seen in their world, this one was without many stars; entire systems were gone!

"Incredible," Alex mumbled under his breath.

"Truly incredible," the commander said. "But truly dangerous as well. The Academy and Universal Protection Commission are committed to discovering and stopping what it is. Or else, we risk losing our entire universe to this blight."

He further explained their progress in their research on the Void. They had to halt other research programs and focus on the Void, sending cadets and officers to sectors where the Void had taken stars and systems, to find out what people knew about it. However, their knowledge was still lacking, though a few years had passed.

"We sent *our* Alex, Nia, Yasu, and Jaxon to one such sector, and we found that the Void might have origins in the Lyra Sector." Someone zoomed in on the Lyra Sector. "So far, it's one of seven sectors where nothing has been removed. But that's not all. We analyzed images of the sector from several years ago and found traces of the Void. It seems it was the first place the Void appeared in as well, several millennia in the past."

"That's suspicious," Nia said.

"Indeed. We believe the Lyra Sector might hold knowledge about the origins of the Void. We're sending a team there to investigate further and uncover more secrets about the Void."

Thoughts floated in the cadets' heads as they left the briefing room. The thought of a void drinking matter and energy in the universe's vastness was frightening and exhilarating. Alex specifically found it interesting. Here, again, in another universe, he was encountering something unexplained and different from everything in his world.

"We should request to be members of this mission," Alex said when they returned to their room.

"What?" Jaxon wore a wary expression. "We just went up against an evil space cloud and barely survived. Now you want us to go on a mission about a disappearing and reappearing black hole?"

Alex turned to him with an excited stare. "It will be a fantastic learning opportunity."

"Yes. But also an opportunity to die. Our alternates in this universe might be dead."

"But by joining the mission, we could also get a chance to save them. The commander didn't say it, but they most likely believe that destroying the Void could bring back everything it has taken away."

Jaxon threw his hands up. "If this was a mission to fight a big bad guy with a twirly mustache, I might have jumped at it. Humans are easy to fight because they *die*. How do you fight something so amorphous that nobody knows what it is? Instead of saving these guys, this could be our last mission. I never get to invent anything cool. Yasu never gets to rule the universe –"

Yasu cried, "I don't want to rule the universe!"

"And Nia never discovers the planet with a perfectly diplomatic government."

"That's not what I want," Nia said.

Upset by Jaxon's lack of enthusiasm, Alex faced the other two.

Yasu held his hands up immediately. "I fear I'm on Jaxon's side here." The mission was so overwhelming to him. He usually loved discovering new things, but this was taking him out of his quiet comfort zone. They had barely survived their last bout.

Nia rubbed her arms, looking through the window at the swollen clouds. "I'm on the fence. On the one hand, I want to learn more about this *void* thing. But on the other, I fear it might be much bigger than us."

Alex's shoulders slumped. "So we came all this way for nothing?"

The others didn't have time to say anything else. There was a knock at the door, and they paused, swiveling to it.

Alex opened the door, revealing the girl from the cafeteria and Tom. Or Tom's alternate.

"Tom?" The cadets stared at him in disbelief, noticing how good as new he looked. Rather unlike the Team Leader from their world who was wearing a cast around his wrist.

The boy's eyes narrowed, and he entered the room with the girl. "So, I suppose I'm in your world too," he said, folding his enormous arms across his chest.

"Yes, you are," said Alex.

The girl waved. "And I suppose in your world, I'm not there. And I'm not dating Yasu." She grimaced at the look of discomfort on Yasu's face. "I'm Safira. And I'm sorry for climbing on you this morning. I just never expected to see you again."

Yasu mumbled a reply.

Stepping forward and squaring his shoulders, Tom said, "Let's cut to the chase. We want you on our mission."

"Why?" Jaxon asked, his brow furrowed.

Tom fixed him with a death stare. The cadets found it equally funny and surprising. In their world, he was fond of doing that, too. He always looked ready to get into a fight, and he saved his deepest scowls for Alex. Beyond the looks, he and Alex shared a cordial relationship, exchanging information where necessary and ignoring one another at other times. "Because the Alex, Nia, Yasu, and Jaxon we knew were smart, courageous, and curious about the world around them. We assume you are, too. And we need the sharpest minds on this mission. You couldn't have been selected for multiversal travel if you weren't among the brightest minds in your Academy."

Safira nodded next to him, her black eyes glittering. "We know it's such short notice, but the fate of our world hangs in the balance. We could lose everything. We have to head to the Lyra Sector and find out what we can as quickly as possible. And we could use as much help as we can get."

"But why us?" Jaxon asked, ignoring the looks of caution the other three shot at him. "We're strangers. We could be dangerous."

The two newcomers exchanged a look, communicating silently. "We trust you," Safira said eventually. "It's definitely ridiculous, but I looked into Yasu's eyes, and I believed I could trust him. Even though I was a stranger, he held no malice. I'm a good judge of character."

Jaxon didn't like the response. He went to his bunk and flopped on the mattress. While he enjoyed these trips into the multiverse, he hated every part where he had to face something life-threatening. It seemed every new step brought him against something bigger and more skilled at taking his life.

Tom took over from Safira. "We also believe ending the Void can reset everything. We have no evidence that everything that went into it is completely lost for good. Some days after our friends were taken, we got signals from their ship. It was short-lived, but it gave us hope they are still alive."

"We want to save them, and we need your help," Safira said finally, wearing a thin smile. "We'll give you some time, but we need an answer by tomorrow."

When no one spoke, they left the room.

Alex shut the door behind them and stood with his back to it. "So, what do you think we should do now?"

Nia looked contemplative. "It's worth a shot. It could be risky, but if we can potentially save all that has been taken in this world and our alternates, too, we should try."

"I agree," Yasu said. "The only alternative is heading home –"

"Which we should do!" Jaxon shouted. "Why isn't anyone seeing how that's the best way out of this?"

"Okay, Jaxon," Alex said, his tone terse, "if that's what you want to do, go ahead. We'll leave you here with the Quantum Leap Device and our spacecraft. If we're taken by the Void, you'll go home and tell them what happened."

Jaxon rose from the bed, brow furrowed. "You know that's not fair. We have to stick together."

"Then stick with us," Alex said, coming closer. Nia patted his arm trying to calm him. "We've made it out twice now. We can do it again. I have a good feeling about this."

Jaxon knew most of Alex's good feelings about anything were tied to his curiosity. If he was curious about something, he always had a good feeling about dipping his toes into it. Though Jaxon was terrified, he was curious as well. He decided to believe in Alex's conviction.

"All right then. I'm in."

# CHAPTER 5

TOM AND SAFIRA were thrilled to hear of the cadets' desire to participate in the mission. They told the commander about it, explaining how outside aid from skilled cadets may give them a fresh perspective and an extra push to success.

The commander deliberated on it. Safira and Tom had been chosen for the mission because Safira had some ancestral links to the Lyra Sector, and Tom was older and more experienced in space travel. Two other members were in the mission, and they were older and more experienced. The commander was unsure if sending the cadets alongside them was a good plan, especially as the last time they sent Alex, Nia, Yasu, and Jaxon, they didn't return.

He discussed his views with the other officials, explaining the advantages and disadvantages of sending travelers from another world on this mission. The other officials deliberated on it for over an hour. Colonel Klaus was especially against it, citing the disappearance of the last cadets they sent on this mission.

"We need more experienced hands for this," Colonel Klaus said. "We all agree that the cadets are intelligent, brilliant, and physically superior because of their upbringing, but we can't keep throwing them into tough missions. Some of our older pilots and fighters can go, too. If we kill all the children, who will do important missions in the future?"

Their Academy had a knack for sending cadets on missions. They had noticed cadets were more eager to engage, curious, and had sharper learning curves. Naturally, cadets were also prone to reckless decision-making. Still, their successes in previous missions made them ideal candidates for every new mission.

"I have a hunch this time we'll succeed," the commander reiterated. "Their Academy tasked them with a journey through the fabric of space to come to our world. Surely, they must be among the brightest minds in their world."

The officials were split, many supporting the commander's vision, and still many others taking Colonel Klaus' side. They eventually went the way of democracy, casting a vote to decide.

With a clear margin of ten votes, the commander's position won.

He promptly sent the cadets a message requesting they meet with him in his office.

They got there just as he was returning from the meeting. He stared at their faces, recalling the faces of the versions of them he knew.

"We've chosen to allow you to go on this mission with the other cadets and veterans. It will be a perilous one, facing something we have limited knowledge of, but I believe you are equipped to handle it. We have studied the Void and mapped out its operation pattern, making a rough prediction of where it will be. From our predictions, your pathway to the Lyra Sector is clear."

The cadets nodded, the seriousness of the mission syncing in.

Preparations came next, everything moving in a hurry. They were to take part in rigorous training, breaking down the operation of the spaceship and the protocols involved in the journey. They met the other members of the mission, Mario and Lucille. They were much older and had made multiple journeys into space throughout their service at the Academy. They both looked very familiar, indicating they too existed in the world from which the cadets came.

Mario and Lucille had also lost friends to the Void. Three of their friends were on the ship that the alternate versions of Alex, Nia, Yasu, and Jaxon had been on.

Though Mario looked slightly grumpy, Lucille was happy to have them on board. "I've always known your alternates to be some of the most intelligent cadets in the Academy. Let's work together and bring our friends home."

In their discussions with Mario, Lucille, and the other higher-ups, Alex suggested taking their spacecraft with them on the ship. The ship was big enough to house smaller crafts for smaller missions. "We might also find that the Quantum Leap Device could come in handy in a crucial part of the mission."

The commander stroked his chin, deep in thought. "What crucial part?"

Alex shrugged. "Something about the Void's disappearance and reappearance makes me think it might switch between universes. At some point, we might figure out where it goes, and that might bring us closer to solving the mystery."

The higher-ups discussed Alex's proposition a little more in a private meeting. They had a detailed guide of the Device's operation and capacities. The meeting concluded with a unanimous decision that the Device could come in handy on the mission.

The day for their take-off arrived. The cadets were suited up and went to the ship with their comrades. Safira wore a strained smile, her eyes fixed on the sky. Tom asked her if she was all right as they got into the ship.

"I'm frightened," she said. "I get dreams where I hear the Void speaking to me, telling me it'll come for me like it came for Yasu."

Tom patted her back and gave her a reassuring smile. "We won't let it take you. Don't worry."

The cadets were used to running everything on their ship alone, but they had more minor roles this time. Mario was the ship's leader and gave all the instructions, delegating tasks based on their expertise. Alex was his co-pilot, given his exceptional skills in piloting smaller spacecrafts. Tom, Nia, and Yasu worked on navigation, selecting the best routes through the systems and calculating the right places to make light jumps. Safira, Jaxon, and Lucille were in tech support.

They took off smoothly, heading into the abyss with their hearts in their mouths, and plotted a journey to the Lyra Sector, selecting the quickest path. They swung into action, taking their first light jump and breaking into space closer to their destination. It was difficult to make more than one light jump at a time, so they set the ship on auto-pilot, allowing it to go at a constant velocity toward the sector.

"We have to be vigilant all the time," Mario said. "The Void is wily, strains of it appearing in various sectors, licking up planets and stars. Whenever we see anything of the sort, we must make a jump as quickly as we can to avoid it."

"Won't that put a strain on the ship?" Nia asked. "I know getting caught by the Void is the worst thing that could happen to us. But so is getting spliced mid-jump."

"It won't strain it." Jaxon had been reading about all the known ways out of the Void's reach. "The ship can handle two consecutive jumps at once. We just don't let it do that because there could be an emergency on the other side. You always want to have the power for one extra jump in front of you."

There wasn't much to do in the ship except watch the navigating consoles, monitor the fuel level and integrity of the ship's parts, and steer the ship around large floating obstacles. In their downtime, Yasu taught them the game he learned on their trip to the Orion Sector. They didn't have the set they used on that trip, so he made do with marked pieces of paper.

While on navigator watch duty one day, Nia heard Safira gasping in the common area. She went to her, patting her back and trying to calm her down, but the girl turned, grabbing her wrist with a steely grip. Her eyes had rolled back in her head, showing plain whites. Her voice rang out, clear with a soft grit to it. "The world shall fall. The world *must* fall."

Nia was terrified, horrified by the girl's tightening grip and the hatred stark in her features. She squirmed, trying to pull away, but was unwilling to make too much noise and draw more attention to the situation.

Lucille seemed to hear, however. She came to them, prying Safira's hands away, and shook her firmly. "Snap out of it!"

The girl was unresponsive, repeating her grim warning repeatedly. She only stopped when Lucille smacked her face.

Safira, now back to her senses, held her face and wept silently. She muttered an apology with her head bowed.

Mario called a meeting to address the situation later. He sat at the edge, looking grumpier than usual, his legs crossed and arms folded. "Explain yourself."

Safira told them she had been having strange dreams about the Void calling to her. She said they had gotten worse the more she planned for the trip, and now, on the trip, they sought to overwhelm her.

"We should've left you behind," Mario said. "Some of your ancestry is linked to the Lyra Sector, right? And your *boyfriend* was on the last mission, too. Perhaps you're too close to the mission."

Alex didn't like the disdain in the man's tone. "You can't say that with certainty. She might be afraid, but she's done her work well so far."

"As she should. But she's becoming a nuisance. She cannot keep entering into this strange trance-like state. If she does that at the wrong time, she could jeopardize the mission."

"I see your meaning, but —"

"But nothing, fake Alex." Mario fixed him with a grim stare. "We're running a mission with high risks here. The entire board might be fooled by your successes in past missions, but I see you all for what you are: children. You all have to pull yourselves together. And she does too, or I'll restrain her myself —"

"I'll keep an eye on her," Yasu said. He shifted with discomfort. He had felt uncomfortable around her since their first meeting, but he felt some personal responsibility to care for her. He had a small belief his alternate in this world would want him to do that.

Mario gave him a dirty look and proceeded out of the common area.

When Yasu looked at her, still wary, she gave him a weak but thankful smile.

═╾╲╱╾═

They made two more light jumps before arriving at the Sector. One jump came immediately after the other, following the sight of strains of the Void along their path. The cadets gazed out of the ship's glass windows at the darkness drinking all light ahead of them. It was drifting, but they knew it could move quickly, overtaking the ship and swallowing them whole.

They sped through the calculations, finding the best trajectory for the jump and initiating the sequence.

They broke out of the jump in the Lyra Sector, unscathed and safe from the Void.

"We're headed to the planet Gilrai in the sector's outer ring," Mario informed them. He had selected it after deliberating with Nia, Yasu, and Tom. The planet was the closest place to begin some investigation and recuperate before they began another trip.

"Why Gilrai? We won't find anything there," Safira said. "From what I recall, it's a small farming planet and mostly deserted."

"We might find useful information there regardless," Mario said. "Get some rest. With our velocity, we should be able to make a landing in the next forty-eight hours."

The cadets made necessary checks over the next several hours to prepare for their landing. At that time, Safira was on her best behavior, sleeping only a few hours at a time, and rising early. Yasu tried to speak to her, letting her know he wouldn't allow Mario to do anything to hurt her, but she brushed him aside, assuring him that she was fine.

They landed safely in an extensive field in the most densely populated part of the planet. A city was close by. It wasn't as well-developed as any city on their planet, but it seemed like the best place to go to find answers.

They went to the city, still dressed in their spacesuits. They walked through semi-deserted streets, meeting only people who ran the moment they attempted to speak with them. The people had reddish, scaly skin, large black eyes, and slight horns protruding from their foreheads.

"How will we ever get any information out of these people?" Jaxon complained. A bright sun beat down on them and, stuck in the suit, he was drenched with sweat.

"We'll keep trying," Nia said, giving him a reassuring pat. "We'll probably encounter the security forces soon."

She was right. They rounded a corner, and ten security personnel were waiting there. They wore dark gray outfits and held laser guns. The one in front seemed to swear at them. "Humans!" What came next was a bunch of undecipherable words, but they could glean some of it with the universal communicator. The gist of it was that they had lived peacefully all this time and didn't want any disturbance from strangers.

The native security people stood there, brandishing their guns. Nia attempted to speak their language to them and failed. Impatient and realizing she wouldn't be getting it right anytime soon, Mario stepped forward with the communicator.

"The whole universe is in danger," he said. "Our research has led us here, to your sector, to find what we can about the end of this world as we know it."

"Go away!" they said. "The world ends, the world ends."

Mario made efforts to try again, but this time, they were more adamant. Yasu and Tom, who brought up the rear, alerted Mario about the other personnel watching them from the windows of the surrounding buildings.

"If we don't leave now," Yasu said, "they'll kill us. And our journey will end."

Mario, reluctant, called for a retreat. They told the people they were leaving, and they headed back to the ship in defeat.

## CHAPTER 6

"WHERE ELSE CAN WE GO?" Mario asked, looking over Nia and Tom's shoulder at the navigation console.

"The Andorg," Safira said behind him.

Mario spun around to look at her. "What?"

"That's where I wanted us to go before. The Andorg."

"What is that?"

"From what I'm reading here," Nia said, "it's a planet on the inner ring of the Lyra Sector. An ancient religion in this region used to regard it as the ancestral seat of their god."

Tom backed her up and read a brief passage from *The Bite-Sized Guide to Touring the Galaxy* that said the planet was largely occupied by priests and other believers in the Angoo faith. The planet was once the center of the sector at the height of the religion's influence, with many rulers in the planetary council being baptized into and ordained by the faith.

"Every step we take further into this whole thing, the more exhausted I am," Jaxon said. "Now we have to do research at a temple?"

Nia cocked an eyebrow at him. "What's wrong with a temple? Religions might be largely out of fashion in our part of the universe, but in many other parts, they were the backbone of their technological rise. Temples can still be a helpful guide by providing information and knowledge."

Mario was reading more about the Andorg over her shoulder. "And I suppose you know about it because you've been there, right?" he asked Safira.

"No," Safira replied. "I heard about it when I went to my distant home planet, Ixis. It's on the other side of the sector, in the middle ring."

Mario huffed. "Set a course for the Andorg then. We have no other leads. Let's hope this takes us where we need to go."

Nia and Tom worked to chart a course to their destination, and Alex adjusted the ship's settings to aid their arrival there.

Time moved slowly on the ship and they entertained themselves by playing the games Yasu taught them and sharing stories about their lost colleagues. The cadets also narrated tales about their world and their journeys to other worlds. Their comrades wondered about the anomalies.

"So you're saying if *your* Tom came on this mission instead of you, there'd be anomalies here?" Tom asked, brow furrowing in disbelief.

"It's still a hypothesis," Alex said. "We haven't done enough trips into other worlds to know if meeting our alternates always causes anomalies." Though the scientists at the Academy were working with that assumption, encouraging their travelers to avoid their alternate selves, there wasn't a concrete conclusion on whether it was true.

"But if it does, that means *your* Tom would've caused anomalies with ours," Lucille said, mesmerized. "That isn't a good thing."

Jaxon pulled Alex to the side before they arrived on the planet. "What if we don't find anything there?" he asked. "What if we journeyed all this way for nothing?"

"You seem more negative than usual," Alex remarked, wearing a thin smile. "You weren't this bad even when we went up against the space *demon*."

"That was different. It was a cloud."

"And this is a Void." Alex frowned at him.

"Exactly. It's scarier."

Alex doubled over in laughter, but when he stopped laughing, he reassured Jaxon he had a good feeling about the mission. "I believe we'll learn a lot on this new planet. And you will be happy you came along."

They landed on Andorg in due time. From space, they could see a planet full of greenery and buildings of yellow and brown-colored stone. Safira didn't have enough information about the planet to give them any solid guidance, so they landed on an upraised slab in a portion of the planet where they sensed the most people lived.

From the sky, they saw the slab was close to a city, built in a concentric circular pattern around what they believed was the Temple of the Great God Tarrhus. Their view from the air corresponded with images they had seen of it in the guides.

Their landing drew out a bunch of people, who gathered around the slab wearing expressions of awe. They were of different species; some looked close to humans, others had green skin like those of the Orion Sector, and others looked similar to those they met in Gilrai.

The travelers stood outside the ship, looking at the indigenes gazing up at them. One by one, the natives pointed, chanting in their language, "Harga, Harga." The universal communicator picked the word up and interpreted it as "goddess."

"Who are they referring to?" Alex asked, staring back at the reverent expressions with a hint of fear.

"Maybe Nia," Jaxon offered, "because she looks otherworldly."

Nia gave him a pointed look. "I think it might be Safira."

As if in response, Safira stepped forward, her heart pounding in her chest. She said something to the locals in their tongue; the words rolling off her tongue as if she had spoken the language all her life.

The communicator picked her monologue up. "Friends, the end of the world approaches. My comrades and I seek answers. Our search has led us here, to your home, to find the origins of this blight threatening the fate of our worlds. Guide us. Help us. Please."

The people pointed down a long road. It led through the city to the heart of it, where the huge temple sat, towering above all the other buildings. "You'll find answers there," one of the older men said. "The temple holds secrets for eons. Search well, goddess."

Safira bowed and the people bowed too, their heads touching the ground.

Unwilling to waste time, she beckoned to her friends and they hurried into the city and down the street the people had pointed out to them.

"How did you know that language, Safira?" Mario asked.

"I don't know," she said. "Perhaps my mother spoke it to me in infancy? Hearing them chanting unlocked a hidden memory. This place seems more familiar. I believe we're close to our answers now."

<br>

They moved fast, though the sun warmed them through their suits.

They found the temple to be deserted, weeds growing over the slabs and the walls. At the front of it, there was a large bronze statue of a man with three heads and six arms. One of his faces wore a glare, the other a smile, the last a passive expression.

"The great god, Tarrhus," Safira said, gazing at the glaring figure.

"We should hurry up," Mario said. "I'm getting some information from home. It's unclear on this device, but I think we can look around here, and when we get back to the ship, we'll check it out."

"What if it's urgent?" Lucille asked.

"Nothing is more urgent than getting the answers we need," Mario said, pocketing his device.

The temple doors were large, without any clear way of unlocking them. They were made of bronze as well and covered with intricate carvings. They fiddled with the wooden bars for a time, moving parts with discord until Jaxon and Lucille figured it out. It was a puzzle, involving four moving parts.

Jaxon and Lucille passed instructions around, assigning each person a role. The team struggled with the heavy mechanism, the sound of grinding metal echoing through the cavern. As the doors groaned open, they revealed rows of memory columns glinting faintly in the dim light. These ancient devices, lined with inscriptions and pulsing faintly with energy, seemed to hold the answers they sought—answers that could explain the Void's origins and its connection to their multiverse. Now inside, they collectively breathed a heavy sigh. The place smelled frozen in time, musty and ancient. They turned on their torches, casting bright rays over the plants that had grown over the place.

"We should split up," Mario said. "This place is huge. We'll cover more ground if we're split. We meet up back here in an hour."

Mario went with Yasu, Safira, and Jaxon, while Lucille took Alex, Nia, and Tom.

Lucille's group headed to the upper levels, flashing their lights around. The stairs were crumbling in parts, but they still held their weight. There was a story on the walls, told with a bright-colored mural. Some people chased others, brandishing sharp weapons. Some people gathered around a hole in the ground filled with green liquid. Hands held a naked baby up to the sky.

"Look at this!" Nia said, staring intently at one of the walls. "Isn't this the Void?"

The others huddled around her, looking at the painting she was referring to. Three naked men stood in front of a darkness, their bodies unnaturally bright in contrast.

"What do you think it means?" Tom asked.

"No idea," Nia said, moving forward to observe some of the finer details. "But it tells us one thing: we're closer to the truth. This place *does* have memories and information about the start of the Void."

They got to the second level and found a cold room filled with rows and rows of shelves stacked with books, scrolls, and –

"What are these?" Tom asked, holding one of the big cylinders in his hand. In it was a slimmer cylinder in a gloopy liquid.

"Memory columns," Nia said, without missing a beat.

Lucille came closer, taking the one in Tom's hand from him. "I've heard about these before. I didn't think I was ever going to see one in my life. They went out of fashion centuries ago."

Tom walked to another shelf lined with them. "How will we read the information in them?"

Alex looked around, standing close to a stacked shelf in awe. "There should be a memory reader somewhere close by. I can see a large system with a monitor."

Lucille followed his gaze, her eyes landing on the system to which he referred. It was the size of a cow, built of metal and surrounded by cool gray stone. She hadn't seen anything like it since she was a kid and got her first book on the history of computers. "Yes. That's so ancient. But I think I can figure out its operation."

Tom peered at one of the containers he held, sniffing it. "But the language?" There was a label on this column, but the language was unclear.

"I can try to scan it with the universal communicator," Nia offered. She hurried to his side and held out the communicator. It took a while to get it going, as it was struggling to tap into the ship's language database from that distance, but eventually, she did.

"The burning of the red tree," she read, confusion evident on her face. "That doesn't help us much. Let's find others."

After much searching, they held several columns, bearing labels like *destruction of death, the fire at the end of the world, the origin of god, the great war of Ludwik,* and *creating the apocalypse.*

All that time, Lucille had been tinkering with the system, trying to get it to power up. She was finally successful, sweat beading on her brow. Nothing on the system was in any language she knew, adding to her frustration.

"Everything about this leads us to a dead-end," she said, wiping sweat from her forehead. "We should check the upper levels and then go to the rendezvous point," she said. "An hour is almost up."

Nia was reluctant to go with her. She pointed at a book she had stumbled across bearing the title *The Birth of Ends.* "I'm just really curious about what might be inside," she said. "It will be slow going making the translations, but I want to look through it and see what I might find about the Void."

Lucille didn't have a problem with it. She asked Alex to stay with Nia, to help her with the translations and to provide any other assistance she might require.

They sat cross-legged on the ground, Nia getting into business. The book was large, the pages made from a material similar to linen. Though the print should have faded, the sealed conditions of the chamber kept the books safe. Lots of illustrations peppered the pages, showing warriors kitting up for battle, details on their weaponry and armory, and descriptions of their home planet.

Nia translated a short passage. "Ixis. That's where Safira's fore-bears are from, right?"

Alex recalled the name from their previous conversation. "Yes. I believe so."

"These warriors are from that planet. They held significant strength in the area, using organic computers to augment their abilities."

Alex cocked an eyebrow. "Organic computers?"

The name sounded familiar, but Nia couldn't identify when or where she first heard it. "It seems they're computers made with organisms." She flipped to the back of the book where the index lay and searched for organic computers. A few other pages were refer-enced. She chose one at random, confounding Alex with her speed. "A very strange thought crossed my mind," she said. "What if the Void is a corrupt organic computer?"

Alex considered it. "But it operates like a black hole. At least, that's what everyone said about it."

"Maybe. But what if?" she asked with a shrug.

Nia worked with an efficiency Alex struggled to keep up with. The twenty minutes they spent with the book while Lucille and Tom investigated upstairs felt like over an hour. She flipped between pages, letting Alex know what to write down in places, browsed over the images, picking up information about the Ixian warrior tribe, the Angoo religion, and the civil unrest in the Lyra Sector that happened a couple of millennia ago.

By the time Lucille and Tom returned from the upper levels, Nia had a hunch she knew what caused the Void. Alex had a sensation he knew, too, but they needed further investigation. They bubbled with excitement, looking forward to sharing their findings.

Meanwhile, Mario's group was investigating the basements of the temple. They, too, found a cold chamber filled with rows and rows of memory stores. Jaxon rushed to the memory columns, finding many longer than his arm and with circumferences bigger than his head.

"Incredible," he cried. "I thought these no longer existed."

Yasu grinned at him, taking in the expanse of knowledge sitting on shelves. "Nia would love to sink her teeth into this."

Jaxon nodded, going around the shelves to look at more shelves.

"How much can we do with what we have here?" Mario said with a touch of irritation.

"Calm down, Mario," Jaxon said.

"Calm down? Our world is about to end!"

Safira wandered about the chamber, looking at the systems installed in various nooks around the room. They were probably their only way of uncovering the information in the memory columns.

Something about this place was familiar, but she was unable to place her finger on it. She arrived at the back of the chamber and found a large door with a small stone tray in its middle. There was a carving of a demon on the door, red gemstones marking the place where its five eyes should've sat on its face.

She stared at the creature's face and sensed her consciousness slipping away. A flicker of recognition struck her as the Void loomed in her vision, its swirling black tendrils entwined with faint, glowing traces of energy. She realized that the patterns mirrored the distortions they had seen after each multiverse jump. Her heart pounded as a chilling thought emerged—was the Void a consequence of their tampering? The disembodied voice echoed again, its tone resolute yet haunting, as if it were not merely a warning but a verdict. The Void loomed before her again, a disembodied voice emanating from it, saying, in the language of these people, "The end shall come.

The world must end." That vision faded, and a memory flooded her, filling a hole she never knew existed. The memory was fragmented but vivid. She saw glimpses of a burning sky and twisted shapes crawling out of the Void, their forms shifting and unstable. A voice—deep, resonant, and eerily familiar—spoke within her mind, *"This is not the first time. The Void has always waited, growing stronger with every breach."* She staggered, the weight of the revelation pressing down on her. She must've gasped loudly because Yasu was at her side in a moment.

"Are you all right?" he asked, holding her arm.

"Yes," she said, though her voice was strained. Her eyes lingered on the door for a moment longer, her mind racing with fragmented thoughts of the Void and its cryptic message. She followed Yasu to join the others. Jaxon was struggling to switch on the system, using intuitive knowledge about how he believed such devices worked. The screen came on soon, a message displayed in white script on a dark background.

"Safira," Jaxon called, "can you understand this?"

She drew closer, gazing at the words. "It seems to be locked," she said, slowly. "Only those with authority can get in."

Mario swore under his breath. "What authority? Why is every part of this mission impossible to penetrate?"

Safira stepped closer, pushing her palms against the keyboard, unlocking the device.

"How did you know to do that?" Jaxon asked, his mouth agape.

Safira stepped back, her heart pounding. "No idea."

Yasu touched the small of her back. "Are you okay?"

She looked at him, her eyes full of guilt. "Yes. I am. Just a little surprised. It seemed intuitive. I figure Jaxon could have cracked the mystery without my help."

Jaxon was already busy on the system. The screen showed a detailed language selection, and though he didn't understand the default language, he knew a language selection window when he saw one. He found their language somewhere in the middle of the list and selected it.

*Welcome!* was displayed on the screen in glowing letters.

"We're in!" Jaxon said, whooping. "All hail me! And the goddess, Safira."

Mario wheeled on her, his gaze darkening. "What exactly did they mean by that?"

"What?" Safira's eyes widened.

"What did they mean by 'goddess?'"

Jaxon took one of the cylinders and slotted it in the vacant hole on the side of the system. A window popped up on the screen, requesting for input about what to do next. Jaxon selected "read memory," and the system began to whirr, sparing Safira the burden of answering Mario's pointed question.

"What is that noise?" Mario asked, stepping towards Jaxon.

"It's reading the memory cylinder," Jaxon said matter-of-factly. A video began to play, showing the temple's construction. The narration was in a different language, and Jaxon groaned. "Is there a way to get subtitles on this thing?" He tinkered with the settings, cursing the ancient nature of the technology here.

Safira showed up at his shoulder again to direct him, easily finding a subtitle file and converting it to their language. Jaxon looked at her in awe again, impressed at the ease with which she navigated this technology.

"We should start heading back to the rendezvous point," Mario said. He was glaring at his pocket device, unable to focus anymore.

"But we've barely seen anything," Jaxon said.

"We can return later. For now, we need to go to the ship. Come on!"

They filed out of the chamber, going to the rendezvous point. Safira lagged, her eyes scanning the chamber and finding the sealed door at the back again. She waited until the others were out of sight and went back into the chamber, shutting the door behind her and running towards the door.

They met the others close to the door, Alex, Nia, and Tom standing with a couple of cylinders in hand.

"You're late," Lucille remarked.

"There's a problem at home," Mario said.

Lucille's face turned ashen, her breathing coming out in short bursts.

Mario wore a grim expression, running a shaky hand over his face. "A message came in on the device. It seems the Void reappeared in our sector, in a system close to ours. It's only a matter of time before it gets home."

Lucille let out a bone-chilling screech.

═══╤═══

Safira sliced her finger, allowing the blood to flow out. Bracing herself, she placed her finger down on the stone tray, pressing it down so that the blood could flow into the tray. The door groaned, the gemstone eyes of the creature glowing.

The others watched in tense silence, their unease growing with every passing second. Jaxon leaned toward Alex, his voice low but sharp. "How does she even know what to do? This whole thing feels too convenient."

Alex frowned but didn't respond, his eyes fixed on Safira. She turned to face them, her expression unreadable. "I don't know how I know," she said, her voice steady but carrying an edge of defensiveness. "But if you don't trust me now, then why are we here?"

Yasu stepped forward, placing a hand on Jaxon's shoulder. "Let her finish. If this works, we'll have our answers. If not... we'll deal with it then."

Then, with a loud, grating sound, the door began to open, mist pouring out of the chamber within.

# CHAPTER 7

A FIGHT ENSUED.

Forgetting his previous excitement at encountering such ancient technology, Jaxon spun to Alex to attack him. "*You* told us this will work out. What part of this is working out?"

Alex tried to calm him, holding his shoulder. "We haven't finished here. There's so much to learn in this —"

"Memory columns!" Jaxon cried. "They use memory columns. We can only learn so much in so little time. Now that thing is going to *eat* our alternate home. And we won't be able to return to our real home."

Alex stepped closer to him, imploring him to be patient.

Mario, on the other hand, was making plans to return to the ship with Tom. He wanted to attempt to reach Earth and get a bigger picture of the situation back there. "The rest of you can stay here, look through the canisters or cylinders, and find what you can. We'll be back in no time."

"Where are Yasu and Safira?"

Jaxon looked doubly distressed. "Don't tell me that, with everything happening here, those two —" He couldn't finish the thought. He let out a loud shout, the sound echoing around the room. "They may be in the basement. Perhaps they had a lead. Safira is good with the computers."

Yasu noticed Safira slowing her pace and leaving the group. He followed the rest of his group to the rendezvous point but only stayed until he heard Mario's announcement. He returned to the basement and the chamber in which they had been just in time to see her open the door and enter another secret chamber.

Unwilling to startle her, he crept behind, moving with practiced stealth. A chilling mist spilled from the chamber, pooling on the floor around the door.

He got to the door and found Safira standing in front of a large organism. It was shaped like a cauliflower or cabbage, bulbous and flesh-colored. Vines protruded from the bottom and around it, surrounding the room. The name of the organism existed somewhere in his mind, but he couldn't access it.

Safira was close to the thing, touching its body with a bloody hand. He wanted to rush to her, but something about the moment seemed private, intimate.

The organism slowly came alive at her touch, extending its vines around the room, connecting to her head, limbs, and torso.

The memory of what the organism was returned to him. He couldn't recall the name, but he could recall its function as a memory store from ancient times. They had gone extinct because the storage got corrupted easily, corrupting the users in turn.

At this point, Yasu was terrified, but he still couldn't go inside. He thought, *What if this process is like loading a memory device? What if I touch her and I corrupt something?*

He watched for several minutes, which felt like hours. The vines lifted Safira, holding her in place mid-air, unmoving. Time stretched around him, and when he considered running to her, the others showed up, calling their names.

The organism shuddered, the vines releasing and dropping Safira onto the hard stone floor. Yasu winced and rushed to her side.

She blinked, her gaze unfocused. "Yasu." Her fingers grazed his right cheekbone. "Don't hate me for what I have to do," she said. "Bear with me just a little longer. I'll save us all, but don't hate me."

Jaxon's voice was the loudest. He rushed into the inner chamber, pulled by the mist pouring out. "What is this place?" He pointed at the now dormant large organism. "Is that what…"

Safira got to her feet with Yasu's help. "I know how to stop the Void."

The others had clustered around the door and looked at her with concern and surprise. She looked pale and unstable.

She pushed past them. "We must hurry. Every minute we delay is a minute in which the Void gets closer to destroying everything. We can discuss more extensively on the ship."

As she spoke, fragmented memories surged in her mind—her mother's voice weaving tales of ancient warriors who fought against an all-consuming shadow, of lives sacrificed to keep the darkness at bay. Safira stumbled, clutching her head as a vision overtook her: a great temple engulfed in swirling blackness, and a voice—deep and resonant—whispering her name. She steadied herself, the echoes fading but leaving behind a chilling certainty. "This isn't the first time," she murmured. "The Void has always been here, waiting."

They rushed out of the chamber and up to the higher level. On their way, they met Mario and Tom returning from the ship. Gone was the usual grumpy look on Mario's face; he now wore a mask of anguish.

"That message was from a few days ago," he said, squeezing his pocket device. "I don't know how we didn't receive it all that time. But there has been no further communication."

An unsettled silence fell over them as they pondered the implications of the lack of communication. Everyone could be okay, but the Void's presence had them scrambling to make preparations and they had neglected to send another message. Or it could be that it had already taken Earth's system, with all its planets and its star.

"It's not too late," Safira said, her voice ringing small and tremulous. "There's still time to save us and I know how."

"How?" Mario's eyes blazed with something akin to hatred. "I have a gnawing feeling that you're part of the whole thing."

Safira recoiled as if struck. She was part of it, but not in the way he thought. But then, how could she explain that? "There's no time to explain. We must hurry."

"You have to at least try to give us an explanation," Jaxon said. "Everything as we know it is crumbling fast. We don't have the luxury of just trusting you."

The others murmured in agreement.

As much as Alex and Nia would've enjoyed going through every tome and memory cylinder in the vaults, moving quickly was more important. But they needed a reason to move so swiftly. They didn't know this girl well and what they knew of her linked her to a tribe who might have been responsible for the Void. For all they knew, she could be tapping into her roots right there and stalling until the Void took everything.

Yasu had similar thoughts but was more inclined to trust her blindly. Perhaps it was intuition based on the fact that his alternate had trusted her enough to date her, but he believed she had the group's best interest at heart.

Jaxon and Tom simply wanted to return home safely. Much of their findings on this temple planet hadn't led anywhere, but they could stay here as long as was necessary to find it.

Tom had known Safira since his first few days in the Academy, and he trusted her more than the others. He knew her mum descended from a long line of warriors in Ixis, here in the Lyra Sector, but that was where his knowledge of her history ended. If indeed she knew something about how to stop the Void and the Void *had* originated in this sector, he believed she must be telling the truth.

Safira took a deep breath, knowing she had to tell the truth now. "We all know my origins, don't we?"

Everyone exchanged glances.

"That you're from the Lyra Sector?" Mario asked, stepping forward. "We know that much, but nothing else."

"My mum was from planet Ixis. The Gante tribe, consisting of a long line of warriors. They protected the systems in their region, using ships and complex weaponry that ran mostly on organic technology. They were *good* at what they did. So good, the priests on the Andorg grew frightened that they'd overthrow them."

Nia and Alex exchanged a glance. They had seen something about that in the book. The author detailed the civil unrest in what had been known as the Myrass Confederation. The squabble was about ownership of territories with organisms bearing useful organic resources. The Angoo priests took one side in the squabble, while the Gante tribe warriors took the other.

"Was the plan to destroy them?" Nia asked. "The Gante tribe, I mean. Did they want to destroy the priests?"

Safira shook her head, her hair flying about. "No. At least, not exclusively. It was a war. And everyone wants to win the war. The Gante tribe might have had years of warfare experience on their side, but the Angoo priests had numbers. Most of the people were faithful to the priests and their god. And so, they joined the priests and fought on their side.

"They battled for a couple hundred years, destroying organic weaponry and corrupting computers. It was dreadful on both sides. Many people fled the region, going to nearby sectors like Gaia, Eos, and occasionally, Orion. My ancestors fled, too. They were a mixed family, part Gante and part natives of the Andorg. They moved first to the Eos Sector and then to the Gaia Sector."

There was a moment of silence, and in his impatience, Mario broke it. "How does this relate to everything else?"

"It explains how I can access the information on the giant computer in the basement. I'm not only related on my mother's side. My father's family descended from the Andorg too. My blood opened the door in the basement. Nobody else's blood could've done that. I could also unlock the computer in the underground chamber." She glanced at Jaxon, her gaze apologetic. "The message said that only the chosen ones were allowed in, only those whose sweat held the key. I tried it, and it worked."

Jaxon looked tired. "But how does this help us?"

"I'm getting there!" Safira's breaths came out rapidly. "I connected to the computer because I was chosen. I'm a descendant of the Andorg priests on my father's side. I also got access to the computer behind the door. I saw what happened at the end of the war. It's like the memories in the computer are memories placed there from the minds of everyone who participated.

"The Angoo priests wanted a quick fix. They sought to run an experiment on an organic supercomputer that could wipe out the Gante tribe simultaneously. The plan was to link their genetic data and lick them all up one by one. But they underestimated the powers of organic computers.

"They experimented on a near-deserted planet and harnessed the energies of the sun and the planet's molten core. The computer was too powerful. They didn't have the technical abilities to shut it off. It went rogue, creating a small black portal with significant gravitational pull and collapsing the planet's core. Everything was going in, and they tried, over and over, to shut it off. But it was doing its best to take what it wanted too.

"Eventually, it seemed to them that they succeeded. The portal vanished with the computer. They returned home, to the Andorg, and found they had won the war. The last members of the Gante tribe had been sucked into large, black portals. The Angoo priests, unwilling to divulge the secrets of their win, sealed the stories in this computer."

"So, the Void is the mouth hole of an organic supercomputer?" Nia asked, her tone skeptical.

"Yes. It is."

Jaxon let out harsh laughter. "Once again, *how* does this help us?"

"Your Quantum Leap Device," she said, staring at Yasu because he felt the safest. "The supercomputer disappeared from this plane, but I have a hunch it went to an alternate universe it created. If we can find it –"

Alex nodded, recalling his former proposition to the commander. Another of his hunches had ended up being right.

Jaxon coughed. "I say we hurry. Time is of the essence. If the Void is this giant, self-sustaining being, then it might have some sentience."

"And could sense us poking around in its birthplace," Nia said, shuddering.

"Yes!" Jaxon said.

Mario was contemplating the story, his hand on his chin. He looked world-weary, bearing the weight of all this information on his shoulders. "We don't have much of a choice now, do we?" he said eventually, with a heavy sigh. "Tell us where we need to go, Safira."

## CHAPTER 8

THEIR FINAL DESTINATION was the Void's birthplace, Uz, an abandoned planet on the sector's edge. It was in a deserted system with multiple surrounding gas planets. Safira helped them locate it on the navigation console, and she aided Tom and Yasu in setting the fastest course over there.

Yasu met her in private as they embarked on the last leg of the trip. "Are you frightened?"

She put on a thin smile. "Oddly, no. It seems this is my destiny. I was having these strange dreams before we got here, but now, I feel at peace."

He patted her arm and drew back quickly at the surprise on her face.

On their journey, they worked on the Quantum Leap Device to find potential alternate universes the Void could be in. If it was one the Void created, it might have energy signatures similar to theirs.

They found a few other universes with similar energy signatures: unnaturally low. Alex, Jaxon, and Tom worked on this together, their faces similar masks of confusion.

"We have to get this," Tom said. "We're so close. If we knew this before, we might have fueled up and explored all the nearby planets."

But that wasn't the case. They drew closer to Uz, still trying to reach home and failing. Lucille had a dull stare on most days, gazing out the window with a device in hand. They sought to offer her what comfort they could, but eventually, they realized that the only comfort to be had would come from destroying the Void.

They arrived on Uz in good time.

The planet looked like what it was: the deserted home of a failed experiment. It was a cluster of large rocks floating together, held together by their gravitational pull on each other. From space, they looked at the planet's ruins and sought to find where the experiment could have taken place.

"There," Nia said as their search grew several hours long. "That looks like a potential place."

They observed the image on the telescope, identifying the charred husk of an industrial city. Mario agreed it could be the location. "It doesn't hurt to land and check," he said.

They went down to the planet, observing a thin atmosphere surrounding it. They suited up in silence, attaching their earpieces and mouthpieces for communication and topping off with the oxygen supply.

They opened the hatch and exited the ship, heading for land.

"It's so cold," Jaxon said.

"You complain when it's cold. You complain when it's hot. When are you ever pleased?" Nia said, rolling her eyes.

"When the temperature is just right," Jaxon retorted.

Mario shushed them. "Now is a good time to be quiet, you two. We must pick up information that could link us to the Void's super-computer host. Less speaking, more action."

They hopped across the broken planet's surface, heading towards a large building in the distance. The sky was black nothing-ness above them, less stars gracing the expanse in these parts.

Safira hopped ahead of everyone, widening the gap suddenly.

"Safira," Mario said, "You're moving fast. Care to explain?"

"This place," she said, "I've seen it before. In the memories I uncovered. That building is where it happened."

The others hurried behind her without hesitation. They arrived at the building, sweat dripping down their backs and faces. The giant door opened with little resistance when they pushed it. They gasped when they saw the enormous stone portal inside. Vines wrapped around it, still green and luscious despite the lack of atmospheric support.

"Everything about this place astounds me," Jaxon said, his voice awed.

The others couldn't say anything, understanding just how he felt.

Safira's voice came out of thin air. "Here's how we're going to do this. We need to awaken the supercomputer. It'll show a signal leading to its host across the portal. Someone needs to link the signals to the energy frequencies of the other universe. And we can track it back home."

"Then what?" Alex asked.

"I'll go there," she said.

"What?" Everyone exclaimed.

Safira's back was to most of them, so they couldn't see the anguished look on her face. "If I get the energy signature from any of you, I can sync it to the computer here and create a portal."

"What are you talking about, Safira?" Yasu asked, his heart beating fast. He recalled her sadness when she dropped from the vines in the Andorg. "What do you mean by you'll go there?"

She faced them, her expression resolute. "I have to do it alone. I'm the only one here who is chosen. I'm the only one who can stop it. I'm the one who has to do this."

"No. No. We can do it with you, Safira," Yasu said, stepping towards her.

"I left a letter for Yasu," she said, softly. "I detailed everything in it for his benefit. But you can read it too. This is the only way. If I destroy the supercomputer, the world it created might go, too. I can't let anyone else get trapped there. I'll access the computer and shut down everything."

A tense silence ensued, everyone considering the weight of Safira's proposition. It was risky and they would have to sacrifice her, but it seemed to be the only way. Mario stepped forward and shook her hand, commending her for her bravery.

"I've been hard on you all this time. But you've proven yourself. Let's make this last push and secure victory."

Safira said a rushed goodbye to everyone, embracing them as they came to her. Yasu gave her a silent hug, feeling the smallness of her body. He felt envious of his alternate, for having met and fallen in love with a woman with her spirit. But behind the envy hid a shred of shame. He had met her and he had been unable to save her.

The group split up with determination in their steps. Safira, Mario, Tom, and Yasu stayed at the portal while the others returned to the ship.

Safira took out a blood sample and poured it into a small slot at the base of the vine. Light spread out from the portal's perimeter, suffusing the area with unnatural warmth.

"Have you gotten a signal?" Safira asked.

Sitting next to the Quantum Leap Device, Alex and Nia watched the readouts on the screen. They got a lot of garbled signals, but nothing was clear. It seemed the computer was trying to slip away from them, knowing it was about to be shut down.

"Jaxon," Alex called. "A little help here."

Jaxon headed to their side, staring at the jumbled-up figures on the Quantum Leap Device. He sat next to Nia and began to fiddle with some settings. "Is it possible to get a quick genetic scan of the vines?" he asked eventually.

"Sure," Yasu said reactively. "Sure?" He looked at Safira.

Safira nodded and went to one of the vines, slashing it with a small blade. She dropped the sample on Yasu's portable scanner and he sent the information to the others.

"All right," Jaxon said, heart hammering fast. "I've got it."

The last moments Safira was with them were laden with deep emotion. Yasu watched her from his side of the portal with his heart beating in his mouth. "She looked almost ethereal walking through the portal," he said later. "I was so devastated to see her go." The others couldn't make fun of him for feeling that way.

When she disappeared, the air felt a little colder, and the lights surrounding the portal disappeared too. Yasu, Mario, and Tom stood there for a few minutes, watching the minutes tick past. They had no way of knowing if their mission was successful. For all they knew, they could've lost –

With a thunderous noise, the vines began to harden and crack. From the ship, the others listened in a state of panic, knowing only that their friends were fleeing from the sight of this collapsing monument.

They rushed out of the building, their blood pumping so much faster.

"Could that be it?" Jaxon asked nobody in particular.

"Could be," Mario retorted. "Only one way to find out. We wait it out and see if we hear from home."

They received word from Earth a few days later. They had been traveling back to the Andorg. They believed even if they were unsuccessful, they could find out more by translating the books available there. But it was unnecessary.

The commander spoke to them that day. "We got a signal from the ship with your alternates," he said. "They're alive. Fairly disgruntled, but alive."

The news elicited shouts of joy around the ship. For a few minutes, they allowed themselves to exult in their success, pushing aside the grief of the price they had to pay for the victory. It was one person's life against the lives of myriad others, and though the sacrifice had been great, the rewards far outweighed them.

They did a small memorial for Safira that day. Tom told stories about her that sent everyone into laughing fits, and they drank some fruit juice from the ship's stores.

"What comes next?" Yasu asked, already itching for home to escape the melancholy.

"We go home, I suppose." Nia shrugged. "If we return to their

Earth, we risk running into our alternates and triggering the anomalies."

Alex agreed. "We have to leave while we can. Of course, this gives us quite the journey to arrive at our Earth, but it can't be helped."

They spoke to the others about their plans, detailing why it was pertinent to leave as soon as possible. Lucille turned away, as though she wanted to cry. Tom's eyes welled up, but he took it with grace. Mario, ever the grump, merely grunted.

They chose a day for their takeoff, communicating with the commander beforehand. He took the news sadly, having expected to introduce them to their alternates and investigate the anomalies with them.

"We're sad to see you leave," he said, "but we're forever grateful for your assistance. This mission would have been impossible without your input. Thank you."

The cadets made preparations for their return home. They adjusted the Quantum Leap Device's settings and began to prepare their reports for their commander. The others helped them where they could, fueling their ship and stocking them with food for the long journey home.

When the day arrived for their departure, there were tears on both sides. They exchanged many thank yous for the help they found from the other side.

"Our journeys have led us to discover a great many things we would've been unable to find otherwise," Alex said to Mario. "And we believe each journey will teach us still more things."

"Do you ever feel fearful?" Mario asked.

"Jaxon does," Alex said with a grin. "But who could blame him?"

Jaxon threw a ball at him and everyone laughed.

The cadets suited up and got on board the spacecraft. They prepared for takeoff, adjusting the readings on their respective consoles. They sent one last message to their new friends, letting them know they were grateful for the experience.

Then they were off, heading back to their world to share this new experience with their friends at home.

# EPILOGUE

Yasu's alternate watched a clear night sky with a wistful expression. He missed Safira with everything he had in him. She wrote him a letter before she went into the other dimension to turn the computer off, leaving it with his alternate. He had read it several times, noting her fears and how she believed she would do everything wrong and fail.

One passage read:

*I've stopped dreaming of the Void's voice telling me it has to destroy everything. Now, all I dream of is going into the other universe and failing. Failure would mean the end of everything: your alternate and his friends who crossed space and time to find our world, our friends and loved ones. And you, taken away from me so soon. When I think of what failure means, I'm emboldened. I cannot afford to fail you. You must return. Even if not to me, you must return.*

*But what about you?* he wanted to ask. *Why can't you return too?*

He looked into the sky, trying to grapple with the knowledge of how he came to be with someone like her. The stories of her origin convinced him of the nature of destiny, of how a war in a distant system drove families to his sector. If not for the war, he might have never seen her.

He also considered the concept of alternate universes. The appearance of the cadets from another universe indicated that there might be a world where they were together, happy, and safe from prowling space oddities. Or was there? He didn't know.

He returned to his chamber, where his friends sat sharing stories of their adventures. The rest of the multiverse was yet a mystery, but perhaps one day, they'd unravel it. Then he could try again to find her and see she's living free and happy in a beautiful world.

**The End**

# THE NEBULA'S HEART

## A YA SPACE OPERA

# CHAPTER 1

ALEX RIVERA SAT in a shaded spot in the Academy's garden, completing a quantum physics assignment that was due that afternoon. The instructor said it contributed towards 10% of their final grade and Alex wanted to do it perfectly. He blocked out the sounds of the other students and officers milling about the Interstellar Academy campus as they discussed the latest discoveries in interstellar travel and the research on the multiverse.

"Alex!" a voice called.

Alex jumped at the sound of his name, recognizing the voice of his friend Jaxon Brooks.

Jaxon bounded up a short flight of stairs to the paved portion, where Alex sat on a wooden bench beneath a birch tree. In his grasp, he held a strange device tightly.

"What is that?" Alex asked, putting his tablet aside.

Jaxon sat next to him on the bench. "It's something I'm trying to work on — a zapping tool. But I'm trying to link it to the nerve endings in your hand, so you merely need to flinch, and it deploys a disorienting current." He tinkered with it a bit, and it made a buzzing sound. "It's not perfect yet," he said, shrugging and slipping it into his sleeve.

"Why are you here?" Alex asked. "I wanted to do this assignment without distraction. That's why I came here."

"Two things," Jaxon said, ignoring his previous statement. "One, I broke into something I shouldn't have."

"What?"

Jaxon ignored the question. "And found out that they're progressing with what causes the side effects on officers when they travel to other universes."

Alex's heart beat wildly. If they had made such strides with the older officers, they might begin to phase the cadets out of the multiversal research program. The program was the greatest source of excitement in his world. If he got removed, he would have to attend classes and regular activities like all the other cadets.

"Two, what's happening with Nia and that hockey player these days?"

Alex frowned at him. "Nia?" Nia Chen was their other friend and mother hen of their small group.

"She's been spending a lot of time with him." Jaxon made a show of picking at his fingernails. "I don't know his name. He's tall, blond, and has a strong accent."

Alex knew who he was speaking about, but couldn't tell why it mattered. "What's important right now is it might be safe for the officers to travel out soon."

Jaxon nodded. "Yes. And?"

"We'll get phased out."

For a moment, Alex hesitated. He had spent so much of his life imagining himself as indispensable to the program, yet here was the gnawing possibility of being left behind. It wasn't just the excitement of exploration he feared losing—it was the purpose it gave him.

Jaxon couldn't see the problem. Though he enjoyed the adventures and the exposure to the various technologies in other worlds, he wanted a break from the adrenaline. They were always running from something, fighting something, and destroying something whenever they crossed into a new world. He wanted to exist as a regular cadet in the Academy, learning at the same rate as his peers and not encountering anything life-threatening.

In their last journey into the multiverse, they battled a Void orchestrated by a rogue organic supercomputer. They had almost lost everything, but one of the crew members, a girl from that universe called Safira, had sacrificed herself to save them.

They hadn't been called on for another mission in the past few weeks, and Jaxon liked it that way. They engaged in various drills, going into space with smaller crafts and running simulations of the Quantum Leap Device. Those were good enough for him. But he knew his friend. Alex liked the thrill of entering a new world and going head-to-head with the wildest things that existed in the wilderness of space.

Alex leaned back on the bench, covering his face with his hands.

"You're smart," Jaxon said. "I doubt they'd phase you out. You're invaluable to the program. They'd keep you around."

Alex wasn't having it. "We have to find the others." He rose, gathering his things into his bag, his assignment forgotten. He figured Nia and Yasu would have the appropriate reactions and know what their chances of being removed from the program were like.

He headed towards the hockey rink, knowing he'd find Nia. Next to him, Jaxon walked, talking about Nia. "She's been unreachable lately, hasn't she? Usually, she studies in class, but now…"

They met Nia outside the rink, talking to the hockey player. He was a year older than them, so he was a 'regular' cadet. He attended all the usual classes and had enough time for extracurriculars like hockey. He and Nia were so deep in conversation that they didn't notice when Alex and Jaxon approached them.

"Nia," Alex said, announcing his presence next to her shoulder. "We have a problem." He glanced at the hockey player, expecting him to understand and leave them alone.

"We want to talk to her alone," Jaxon said, shooing with his hands. Jaxon's words pulled Alex back to the times they'd stood in situations like this before—first on Krissia, then the shadowed reaches of Orion. Every time, they had faced the unknown together, and yet he felt the weight of those memories hanging heavier than ever now.

"But we were already talking before you interrupted," the player said, his deep voice rumbling.

"It's okay, Kel. I'll catch you later." Nia waved at him shyly as he walked away.

"Has he always sounded like that, or did he go through a late puberty?" Jaxon asked, eyes wide as he watched the older boy's retreating form.

Nia wanted to counter Jaxon's assertion but thought better of it. "I was coming to look for you. It seems we might get a new mission soon. Earlier in the day, while Kel and I..."

"Oh. So, now you're 'Kel and I'?" Jaxon asked, raising his hands in mock shock.

Nia and Alex looked at him with mild confusion. "What is the matter with you today?" Alex asked, tempted to hit him with his bag.

"I'm sorry," Jaxon said, lowering his gaze in penitence. "Please carry on."

"Earlier in the day, Kel and I walked past one of the briefing rooms. It seems they were discussing us. I clearly heard them say 'team Alpha' in relation to a new mission. It seems they're reading some kind of anomaly in another universe and sending a team to check it out."

Alex stepped back. "Really?" Next to him, Jaxon had deflated, but he couldn't notice it over his excitement.

Nia shrugged. "That was all I heard. Why did you want to meet me?"

"Jaxon did some unauthorized digging again," he said, pointing at Jaxon's lowered head. In response, Nia snickered. "And he found they're making big strides with the older officers. Soon, they might travel across the multiverse."

Nia's face brightened in a wide grin. "That's great news! Why do you look so down?"

Alex's expression turned to one of horror. "Because if they figure it out, we might have to leave the program."

Their devices bleeped as one, interrupting the conversation. Nia pulled out her tablet to check it out, saying, "You think so? Perhaps they'll get some older officers for some missions, but they won't remove us completely. At least…" She paused, looking at her tablet screen. "We have a meeting with the commander tomorrow morning."

Alex was consumed by the thought of the meeting for the rest of the day. He rushed through the assignment, preparing it for the following lecture, but his mind kept drifting away. If indeed this was a mission briefing, they had to do their best to prove themselves invaluable to the program. They couldn't afford to be removed. *He* couldn't afford to be removed. He thought of all they had endured —the Empire's shadow, the rogue supercomputer, and now this anomaly. Each mission had brought them closer to something bigger, something that felt like the very edge of discovery itself. He wasn't ready to abandon that path now.

From his interactions with the others, he recognized that exploring the multiverse wasn't as important to them as it was to him. They loved the adventure, but were relatively content with whatever they met in their universe. He'd be the most badly affected if the program were taken away from them.

He could barely eat that evening. While the others chattered away, with Jaxon making snide comments about Kel and Nia, he considered what the best way to secure his future would be. He needed to show he was a powerful leader, but even if he couldn't lead a team, he was content to be an extra in someone else's team.

That night, he tossed and turned on his bed, annoying the boy in the bunk above his own. The boy banged his leg on the bed, saying, "If you can't sleep, maybe you should leave the room so I can sleep." Alex apologized and forced himself to lie still. Eventually, when he fell asleep, he dreamed of the collapsing supercomputer from his last mission. He saw Safira, and they talked about how little the world understood them and their desires.

Sweat covered every inch of him when he sprung up from the bed.

He glanced at his watch and, realizing he was late already, changed into this uniform and hurried to the meeting venue in dishevelment.

The others were seated and waiting when he came in. Jaxon and Nia were pointedly not speaking to each other, sitting with an uncomfortable Yasu between them. Yasu Garcia, the most quiet member of their small group, occasionally got caught in disagreements between group members. Alex sat next to Nia and lowered his head to ask for forgiveness.

"Your lateness is as much a part of you as your hair is brown. I doubt I can change it. Luckily for you, they haven't arrived yet. They were held up in another meeting."

Trying to change the topic, Alex asked why Nia and Jaxon weren't speaking. Yasu gestured to him to let it go, but Alex was desperate to take the heat off himself.

"Tell Jaxon we're no longer kids. His immaturity isn't very endearing," Nia said, scowling in his direction.

"Oh. Really?" Jaxon said, furrowing his brows. "Well, tell Nia she can't just abandon her team for an outsider."

Nia gasped in irritation. "I did not abandon…"

Just then, the commander walked in. Yasu gave silent thanks to whatever deity was in charge of near saves. The commander was with a few officials whose faces had become familiar to the cadets. Everyone greeted each other, and the room's lights dimmed.

"Once again, we have another mission for you, cadets. We've deliberated for a while on what team to send, and given your aptitude for problem-solving, curiosity, and quick thinking, we decided your team is the best suited for this mission."

The multiversal grid appeared over the table once more. A few more spots had been added since their last visit to the briefing room, showing the new universes visited by travelers from the Academy.

The commander pointed at a new spot, marked by a blinking red light, which expanded into a new window. There was some basic information on it, including the date they first located it and its energy signatures.

"This universe recently came to our attention," the commander said. "In your last mission, you visited another universe with much lower energy signatures. Here, however, we've recorded an unusual spike. We could identify occasional spikes in its signature from our research, and we wanted to investigate it."

Alex leaned forward, thankful for this opportunity. He didn't notice the looks of worry on his comrades' faces. His only thought was that this was an opportunity to prove his worth and show himself invaluable to the Academy's multiversal research program.

## CHAPTER 2

THEIR TRAINING BEGAN the following day. They had new instructors, and a new revised diet that miraculously tasted worse than the last one. They ate in the cafeteria with tired eyes, making postulations about the mission to keep their excitement up.

"The last time, the Void was sucking all the energy into a pseudo-universe of its making. Maybe this time, another Void is dumping the energy there," Jaxon said, spearing a lump of strangeness on his plate with his fork.

Alex shook his head. "That doesn't make sense."

Jaxon shrugged. "I'm not Yasu or Nia. I don't make the most educated guesses."

On the other side of the table, Nia rolled her eyes. "The higher-ups say it might also be the product of a rogue experiment. Something catastrophic might have happened in their world, leading to large energy fluctuations."

"I wish we got a preview of what's going on before we went in," Yasu said, looking at his nearly full plate of odd bits of nutrient-packed morsels. The cook walked past, wearing a scowl, and he quickly made a show of taking a bite.

"In a way, I like not knowing," Nia said, swallowing hard. "It feels like unwrapping a present. Even though the contents might be related to the Grim Reaper."

Alex motioned for them to finish their meal. They had a drill at the space lab in a few minutes. He was determined to be on time and ready for every activity this time around.

When takeoff day finally arrived, they proceeded with some apprehension. Alex kept the morale up by reminding them of their desire to be known in the Academy's history. "When other kids come here and dream of going far, they'll look at our photographs and stories in their history books and get inspired to work harder." The others would exchange glances behind him, mildly annoyed by his enthusiasm but encouraged to try for his sake.

A cloud had settled over the Academy, and a wild wind blew dust and icy rain about the place. The cadets walked to the strip with their eyes squinted against the splashing water. As they entered the craft, they noticed the higher-ups watching them from seats in the nearby control tower.

"This rain seems to be an omen," Nia said, keeping her tone light. "A darkness spread across our path."

"I agree," Jaxon said. "Is it too late to abort?"

Alex twisted in his chair to look at him. The expression baked into his features read, "Not on your life!"

After confirming that everyone was strapped in, Alex began the initialization process for takeoff. The others watched their consoles, ensuring that all the conditions were right. The spacecraft shot up into the rainy sky, the sound of water against the outer metal surface mingling with the beeps and squeaks of the various equipment aboard the craft.

Once outside the Earth's atmosphere, Alex started the Quantum Leap Device and called the command. Together, he and Jaxon worked to sync it to the right universe, and they initiated the jump. The spacecraft zipped through sound and light, heading towards their destination. The craft shuddered, and the cadets watched the changing colors and energy flow in awe.

They emerged on the other side, happy again for another successful trip.

"Everything seems in order," Nia said, looking at her console. The sky was regularly populated with stars and systems. What could cause the abnormal energy readings they registered at home wasn't quickly identifiable.

"Well, no," Yasu said quietly. He could see something in the distance. After taking a cursory look around, he noticed a gap where several systems should have been. Instead, there was a giant cloud of dust and gas in their place. It bore similarities to the cloud demon they encountered on Krissia, but this was more familiar. It was a nebula. "Around the Eos Sector," he said. "Look well."

Nia took a deep breath and adjusted her console to scan the surrounding regions. And there it was. "A nebula? Could that be it?"

"Should we head over there and investigate it ourselves?" Alex asked, staring at the images from his side.

"Absolutely not!" Jaxon yelled, finally waking up from his initial shock. "We'll land on this Earth, find out what we can about that thing, and zip back home. I think it's time we remind ourselves that we're explorers, not heroes."

Nia and Yasu agreed. Investigating what was wrong alone would be thrilling, but it was also a high-risk endeavor. They all decided it would be best to land their craft and learn what they could from the people.

"We could also find out if the space program there is sending out any officers to explore the nebula," Alex added. "Then we can go with them."

"Sure," Jaxon said. "Let's run along that bridge when we get to it, okay?"

They signaled Earth and got nothing in return. They began the landing sequence, their hearts in their throats as the new phase of their adventure kicked off.

As their ship descended through the unfamiliar clouds of this new Earth, they received a message from the natives of the planet. It read simply, "Welcome strangers. We trust you come in peace."

"So cryptic," Nia remarked when Alex read it.

"I agree," Jaxon said. "We should be on our guard."

Alex sent a message back to them, informing them of their purpose as explorers curious to learn of another world.

They brought the craft to rest on a tarred plane surface. They

204 / MARIE-HÉLÈNE LEBEAULT

could see a small town in the distance from the spacecraft, with houses very similar to those on their home planet. Evening was approaching, the sky awash in brilliant purples and oranges.

"I don't like this place," Nia said. "It feels empty."

"All of you are so negative," Alex huffed. Their behavior had become exhausting. "It just might be that we landed on a part of the planet where people migrated from."

"And what was the reason for their migration, commander?" Jaxon asked, his tone mocking. "Maybe the air smelled terrible?"

"Or their socks vanished from their closets at night?" Nia added. "Yasu, what do you think?"

Yasu merely laughed, also considering why their landing area was unpopulated. None of the reasons were good. In all the last universes they visited, they had landed in this location, and the Academy had been in the vicinity, too. As he watched the console, he noticed four hovercars speeding towards their ship from the deserted town in the distance.

"Okay. I understand," Alex said, "but we should at least try to find out…" He trailed off, his gaze trained on the hovercars racing towards them. "Hovercars?"

"Yes," Yasu said. "So, there are people here, but it could still mean trouble."

"Or it couldn't," Alex said, insistent.

"Okay, commander. What's the game plan?" Jaxon asked. "We can't just hop inside and expect things to fall into place."

"Let's step out of the craft, deploy our defense system, and wait for them. All we're here for is reconnaissance. We want to find out about the nebula and how it relates to the energy spikes. Perhaps we might learn something useful after speaking to the people here."

They exited the spacecraft and set up the force field around it. They had just completed that task when the last of the hovercars arrived, coming to rest on the tar beside the others. The cadets stood together, their hands at their laser guns on their belts. It was the first time they had brought weapons out in all their trips, but after much persuasion, the higher-ups agreed they could be beneficial.

The doors of the cars opened, and humans dressed in black from head to toe came out, holding hefty laser guns. Two strode to the front, and one pulled off his mask, revealing a shock of blue hair and a familiar face.

"Kel?" Jaxon swore under his breath, itching to shoot the fellow, even though he knew it would put them in a precarious position.

"Strangers," the young man who looked like Kel said. He had the same tall build, but his stance and aura differed. They could tell from his posture that this person was more cocky than the Kel they knew. "You come to our planet. And we hope you come in peace because –" he brandished his weapon, a lopsided grin contorting his features, "– we're ready to face you."

The cadets passed strained glances amongst themselves. The mission was already kicking off with a blast, and they were not entirely thrilled about their trajectory.

# CHAPTER 3

THIS KEL DIDN'T KNOW their alternate versions. He showed no hint of recognition as he instructed his men to search and take their weapons. "Necessary precaution," he said, still wearing his enormous grin. "We can't have you trying to take away our overlord now, can we?"

"Overlord?" Jaxon asked. "So, you're not the leader?"

Kel walked over to him, his head towering above him. From that height, he looked down at Jaxon, his stare growing more intense. "No. Just the leader of this unit."

Once his men were done searching, he gestured towards the cars. "Let's hurry. We have people to meet."

Alex tried to ask questions but was met with loud grunts and hushes. Eventually, he lapsed into silence, sitting quietly next to Nia in the car they were in. Nia tried to signal to him that things might turn out okay. She tried to mouth, "We just have to stay calm, meet the next in command, and ask to be allowed to return home." The driver caught her through the rearview mirror and threatened to gag her. Shocked by the brutality of his words, she swallowed the rest of her thoughts.

The other two rode in a different car with equally silent drivers. Yasu watched the day darken into night, thinking about all the ways to escape the situation. He thought their team had a knack for trouble. From the other reports he had read, most other teams encountered their alternate selves and learned about new cultures dominating the Academy. For some reason, they were the only ones who found themselves with hostile natives.

Jaxon was stewing over the turn of events. He hated that Kel's alternate was here, looking more confident and perhaps even more gorgeous than he had been in their world. His only consolation was that they hadn't taken the prototype of his zapping tool. It wasn't perfect yet, but it looked like scrap plastic to the untrained eye. And that's what he told them it was.

They passed through the town, and just as they thought, it was deserted. Some buildings had blackened exteriors, indicating the remains of a fire's ravage, while others were smashed as though a missile struck them. Though the cadets desired to ask questions, they knew they would be met with no answers. They saved their questions for later, when they'd meet Kel's alternate again. The hovercars wound around the deserted streets until they arrived at a large complex surrounded by high walls with electric wires.

The large black gates opened with a mild whine, lights blinking atop the spires and from the control tower to the side. Within the walls, a gray ten-storeyed building loomed, surrounded by parked hovercars and other roving vehicles. The cadets got out of the cars, huddling close and looking up at the building.

"Our eminent and most benevolent leader has graced us with his presence," Kel announced, spreading his arms towards the building. "We shall plead for an audience with him, and he shall meet us in due time."

"Who is this leader?" Alex asked.

Kel turned to them with a half-smile. "The savior of our realm. The one to rule all things."

They didn't understand what that meant, but they were in no position to ask more questions. They followed the trail of black-clad guards, looking at the other soldiers lounging around the complex's premises. They entered the building through a flight of steps and large wooden doors. Beyond the doors was a lobby with white and black floor tiles. A receptionist stand, equipped with a desk and dark wood shelf, stood in the corner. Kel's alternate strode towards it to speak to the blonde, fox-faced woman behind it.

"Hello," he said, leaning against the table with a sultry smile. "Guests for his eminence."

The woman cast a biting glance over the cadets, then turned around to make a call.

"Sit," she said when the call was over. "I'll let you know when to go in."

Kel's alternate waved them to a group of metal waiting chairs on the other side of the room. "Now we wait."

They sat there for some moments, listening to the light music streaming from hidden speakers.

"My name is Dorian," he said. Once again, the grin appeared.

"Not Kel?" Jaxon asked.

A strange look crossed Dorian's face, but Jaxon didn't notice it over the pain of Nia nudging him in the ribs.

"Not Kel," he said. "Dorian. I am a team leader. One of the Leader's prized fighters. I protect these parts from marauders."

"We're not marauders," Alex said. "We're mere explorers from another world."

Dorian nodded. "Yes. You've said." He crossed his legs, bouncing one over the other. "Very interesting, that." His smile vanished, almost like a light going off in the room.

"What?" Alex asked, ignoring the chill running down his spine.

"This crossing worlds. Crossing universes. One would think it was merely fiction."

Dorian turned away without saying another word. And though Alex had more questions, he was wary of asking them, unwilling to annoy the man. He nudged Nia, but she shook her head at him.

For the rest of the time, they sat in silence. Yasu observed the layout of the building, mentally mapping the potential escape routes. The place was a fortress, he noted. If things went south, they had no chance of getting out alive. They could try to run, but with all the men in black surrounding the perimeter, they would need to lose some of their corporealness to escape the shots from the lasers.

The woman at the desk gestured to them. "He wants to see you now."

"Perfect!" Dorian said, rising easily. "Come with me."

Only two of the other black-clad men followed them to the elevator. They piled inside, looking at their reflections on the silver surface of the walls, their hearts beating with mild panic. The door slid open silently, revealing an empty hallway.

Dorian strode ahead steadily, taking them to the door at the far end of the hallway. He knocked twice, then once, then twice again. Inside the room, someone coughed and said, "Come in."

The cadets went in with Dorian and the last of the black-clad men. Inside, one wall had floor-to-ceiling windows showing the peaceful night sky. The cadets breathed, thinking about how bleak the outside looked without any lights.

Within the room sat a long meeting table with chairs spread around it. At the head of the table, flanked by two more men dressed in black, was a man in a white suit.

The cadets looked at his face, feeling deflated again. They recognized him.

Colonel Klaus. In their world, he was one of the higher officials who antagonized them whenever they ran into issues in their missions. They wanted to say that he hated them, but they believed it was more about him not thinking they were capable yet.

"This day couldn't get any worse," Jaxon muttered.

"Travelers," Dorian said with a flourish, "Our Benevolent Overlord, Lord Kedron." He bowed his head, and awkwardly, the others followed suit.

Colonel Klaus' alternate, Lord Kedron, wore a thin-lipped smile. "Children," he said, his voice holding a hint of disdain. "From what parts have you come to us?"

Alex made to speak, trying to say the usual line about them coming as explorers from another world, but Dorian stepped forward to interrupt him.

"They come from a planet far, far away. They have journeyed

here, my lord, to behold your glorious visage for themselves. To see what so many have seen and fallen in love with."

Lord Kedron smiled, his eyes narrowing into mirth-filled slits. "You've always had a way with words, Dorian." He leaned back in his chair and clapped. "Let our guests sit."

The cadets, sending their confusion around with their wide-eyed gazes, sat next to each other on one side of the table. Dorian and the two guards sat opposite them. Dorian's smile gradually transitioned into a look of caution, akin to a hunter cautiously stalking its prey through a field

"You're here at the right time," the smiling Lord said. "I've come here to visit and see how my people in these parts fare. And here you are, too, auspicious travelers. I love the novelty of it all."

Unsure how to reply, the cadets stayed quiet. They watched him speak some more. He talked with great bravado, waving his hands with flamboyance. From his speech, they learned about the war that had torn through the region. He referenced a tyrannical government that had taken root, subjecting most parts of the universe to a strict dictatorship. Eventually, he worked his way up the chain and seized power. "I protected my people," he said, patting his chest. "I protected this region. They owe it all to me."

The guards and Dorian hailed him the more he spoke, and the cadets could swear that they noticed his head getting bigger and redder.

Alex raised a hand. "May we ask a question?"

The others leaned forward, eager to know what he had in mind. None of them had expected things to work out the way they had. The Leader seemed friendly enough, but something about the guards' behavior and Dorian's switching moods put them on high alert. They weren't safe.

"We noticed a brilliant cloud of dust and gas on our way. It looked dazzling, sprawling." Alex was seeking the best way to present the question. "And we wondered what it was."

Lord Kedron looked at him in silence for a moment. The other guards looked on, too, their faces hidden behind their masks. Then the leader burst into laughter, tipping his head back as though overcome with delight. The guards joined him, though theirs seemed forced and insincere.

"Why," he said, wiping a stray tear from the corner of his eye, "that is the aftermath of our influence. And the beginning of our dominance."

## CHAPTER 4

DORIAN ESCORTED the cadets to a room where they could spend the night. He asked repeatedly if Nia would like a separate room, but they told him they were fine sharing with her. Jaxon bristled the last time he asked, his eyes growing fiery as if itching for a fight. Nia had to speak up, placing a hand on his chest to calm him. "Whenever we go on missions, we usually share a room. They're like my brothers."

Once they were in the room, with a change of clothes available, Jaxon turned on her. "You didn't have to say we're like your brothers, " he said.

Nia looked at him, her eyes heavy with sleep. "Why not? But you are like my brothers. We spend so much time together…"

Jaxon placed a hand over his chest. "Like brothers?"

"We have bigger fish to fry, Jaxon," Alex said from the door. "The door is locked."

Jaxon shot one last look at Nia, as if to say the conversation wasn't over, and bounded over to the door. As Alex said, it was locked.

"So, we're trapped?" Jaxon said. "We're trapped?"

From her bed, Nia said, "At least it's not another sentient Void,' Nia muttered, though her voice wavered. 'Human villains are slightly less terrifying… right?"

"Not now, Nia."

"We should also be careful with what we say," Yasu said. "They might be listening in."

Alex scratched his head. "We could've headed straight for the nebula..."

Jaxon shuddered. "You heard what this strange Klaus said? That it's their influence and their dominance. That sounded like bad news from where I sat. Maybe we'd have met worse if we went to the nebula directly."

"Or maybe we'd have met better!"

Nia whistled through her fingers. "It's late," she said into the ensuing silence. "We're all weak and exhausted. I suggest we all head to bed and figure out what to do tomorrow."

Yasu let out an enormous yawn and flopped onto his bed as if on cue. He agreed with Nia. He had struggled to unravel their position all day, but he hadn't succeeded. Perhaps sleep would smooth the wrinkles in his thought process.

Reluctantly, Jaxon and Alex headed to their beds, too. They curled under the duvets, listening to the sound of nothing from outside.

"If murder ends up being our way out," Jaxon said sleepily, "allow me to do all the honors. So that I never have to come on another of these missions again."

The others laughed, but they were too sleepy to say anything more.

＝＝✒＝＝

Nia awoke to the feeling of someone's hand on her mouth. She immediately panicked, attempting to push them off, but she heard a familiar voice shushing her.

"It's me," the person whispered. "Kel."

Hearing the name weakened her resolve. She looked at his face in the dark, unsure what was happening and why he used that name.

Bringing his lips close to her ear again, he said, "You have to trust me."

She wasn't sure how to feel about this. The Kel she knew back home was different: quiet, determined, and somewhat shy. The idea of him breaking into her room to cover her mouth in the middle of the night was alien. But here he was, or at least, a version of him. And though his behavior had been unfamiliar, she trusted he wasn't a bad person.

"We're going to leave the room," Dorian said. "I've disabled many of the security systems in this place, but you have to be very quiet. If you make a sound, you wake the others and alert everyone about what's going on." He chuckled lightly. "You don't want that now, do you?"

She didn't, so she shook her head. Dorian took his hand away from her mouth, and she breathed a deep sigh.

Heart hammering in her chest, she rose and left the room with Dorian. She didn't know why she trusted him. It could be because he was Kel's alternate or because she wanted something good amid the chaos. She tightened her hands into fists by her side, moving with stealthy footsteps behind.

They went down the hallway, and he took her into another room. There was a single bed and a table in the corner. Nia guessed it must be the room he originally wanted her to stay in.

"What do you want?" she asked.

"I can help you escape," he said.

"What?"

"Yes. I can. I might be a monster, but I'm good at helping people, too."

Nia's eyes widened at the word 'monster,' a chill skimming down her spine.

"A monster?" she echoed, the word hanging heavily in the air between them. Her mind raced, trying to reconcile the person before her with the harshness of the label he had placed upon himself.

"Why would you call yourself that?" Her voice was a mix of wariness and an involuntary flicker of sympathy, searching his face for some hint of the darkness he claimed to own. Despite the fear that tethered her heart, her instinct to understand battled with her desire to flee.

"But why would you do that?" Something wasn't right, and Nia didn't know what it was. She didn't like how confusing everything was. As much as Jaxon hated the clouds, Voids, and other strange phenomena, she preferred those because those were things she could think her way out of. This situation, with this strange, unreadable version of Kel, floored her.

Dorian stepped closer to her, his expression blank. "Because you have something I want."

Dorian's jaw tightened as memories flashed before his eyes: Kedron's promises of salvation that twisted into demands for loyalty, the missions that left his comrades broken in spirit or dead, and the moment he realized he was simply another pawn. He couldn't let this cycle repeat, not with these cadets.

Nia's heart beat faster. "What do you want?"

"You came here with something. And you crossed the boundaries of our worlds to find us. What did you come with?"

"How does that matter?"

"If he gets his hand on the power at the center of the nebula, all our worlds will crumble," Dorian said. "Everything we know. He will take and take and take. His blood flows only for power. He discovered something."

At this point, Dorian stepped closer again. Too mesmerized by the fiery look in his eyes, Nia stood unmoving, pinned in place.

His voice dropping to a breathy whisper, Dorian said, "During the war, he crossed to another realm. No, not universe. Realm. A realm of higher energy and power, where cosmic deities and beings roam, sharing power amongst themselves. He wanted to share in the power, too. Believing he could end all suffering in the process."

"How did he go there?" Nia asked, unable to understand. Could they have devices capable of jumping universes in this world?

Dorian shook his head, impatient about her lack of understanding. "A portal formed during the war. He fell into it and returned a different man."

His speech was confusing. Nia needed him to slow down, though she understood he was probably speaking fast to reduce their chances of being caught.

"So, what stops him from entering the portal again?" Nia asked.

"He can't get into the nebula. He doesn't have the tools for it. But you do."

"We do?"

"Yes," Dorian said. "You came into this world somehow. Whatever allowed you to come in will allow you to enter the portal."

Unsure, Nia cocked her head to the side. Everything about this Kel was bizarre. She still needed to find out how he knew that name, but had to stay on topic. What mattered most now was this Overlord and his thirst for power.

Dorian came closer, leaning forward until his lips were next to her ear. "I want you and your friends to stop him."

Nia could barely breathe. As he broke into her inner space, she caught a whiff of him, and he smelled so similar to the version of him she knew. The similarities were unnerving.

Breathing sharply, she asked, "What if we can't?"

"Oh," Dorian said with deadly softness. "But you must. Or you'll never go home again."

## CHAPTER 5

NIA SLEPT FITFULLY the rest of the night. She might have found it strange how none of the others woke up all the time she was gone if Dorian hadn't told her he drugged them. She wanted to know how and what he used, but he was taking her back to her room at the time, and his demeanor had changed, reflecting his lack of interest in conversation.

The others woke up first and shook Nia awake.

"They brought us breakfast," Jaxon announced, his tone excited. "And it's real food."

The others laughed and sat with their trays on their beds.

Nia sat up and stared at her tray. Bits and pieces of her conversation from the previous night filtered in. "Did Dorian come here this morning?"

Jaxon glanced at her with some measure of irritation. "You just can't get enough of him, can you? Whether in this universe or ours."

Ignoring him, Alex said, "Yes. He came with the person who brought the food. Interestingly, he asked if you were awake."

Nia looked around the room, trying to figure out if anyone could be listening in. Dorian had told her the room would be safe from outside ears, but he never said if his ears were included in the package.

"I met him last night," she said.

Jaxon's face turned cloudy.

"What?" Alex asked, his fork stalling halfway to his mouth. "What did he want?"

"He wants us to help him take down Kedron."

Alex placed his fork on the plate and scratched his head. "Why would he want that?"

Nia shrugged. "Not every servant likes their master."

Jaxon looked around the room. "Hello. A big elephant is sitting in this room with us. Why would he meet Nia and not you? Or even all of us together?"

"He called himself Kel," she said, looking at Jaxon. "Perhaps he knows a version of me in this world. Or knew…"

"Did he hurt you?" Alex asked, his brow furrowing with discomfort. He couldn't help but blame himself for the wrong turn of events. If he had put his foot down and insisted they head straight to the nebula, they might have found out what they needed to find and headed home without a hitch. Now, they were stuck in a suspicious place with suspicious inhabitants and a ruler with unclear motivations. And now, one was sneaking into their room to talk to Nia. Jaxon crossed his arms, trying to quash the burning annoyance in his chest. He hated how the presence of Dorian—or Kel, whoever he was—unearthed emotions he'd been careful to suppress. What frustrated him most was the unspoken truth: he didn't just resent Dorian for his boldness; he envied it. He wasn't sure how he would take it if anything happened to any of his comrades.

"No." Nia shook her head. Dorian had been menacing, but some gentleness lay beneath the brash exterior. Or perhaps her brain was playing tricks on her. After all, he was Kel's alternate, and Kel was always gentle with her. "He told me he'll help us if we help him."

"But how?" Jaxon hated every part of this. He hated this blue-haired version of Kel even more than he hated the Klaus alternate who won a strange universal war. But even though he tried to focus on his priority—getting out of this planet—he kept returning to an image of Nia and Kel's alternate whispering to each other in the dark while he slept. His appetite was gone.

Nia lowered her voice, speaking to the plate. "That's why I asked if he came here. He said we'd disguise ourselves as guards and return to the craft."

"Does that mean we move this morning?" Alex asked.

"I should think so."

Jaxon didn't like how trusting everyone was of this blue-haired upstart. Emulating Nia, he dropped his voice to a whisper. "Let's all slow down the pace. How can we trust him?"

The position Alex was in left him unmoored. He had no clue how to escape this mess without a potential ally. Nia trusted Dorian, but he could also tell that her judgment might be clouded because of her relationship with his alternate.

"Yasu, if you've got a better idea, now's the time to say it," Alex snapped, the weight of their situation pressing heavily on his voice?" he asked. If anyone could be objective in the room, it would be Yasu. Yasu didn't have any outward feelings regarding Kel. He could assess the situation and give them the best way out.

Yasu's plate sat clean in front of him. While the others were deliberating, he had tucked in, wiping all the eggs, bacon, and toast from his plate. He let out a silent burp and mumbled an excuse me before proceeding with, "We have two options. Remain as sitting ducks here until we figure out another escape. Or ally with Dorian and see where it takes us." He held out both hands, each one representing a choice. "This place is a fortress. I've been analyzing it since we got in. Getting out will be nearly impossible. I say we take the chance."

Alex nodded. "All right. Everyone, finish your food. We'll work with Dorian."

＝◆＝

Dorian returned in fifteen minutes, accompanied by a black-clad guard pushing a covered cart. Smiling around the room, Dorian gestured towards the cart and said, "Uniforms. You must put them on in a hurry."

The cadets rushed to grab the black trousers, shirts, and masks from the cart. While they did that, the guard gathered their dirty dishes and placed them in the cart.

He stood beside his guard, letting them have space to change out of their previous clothes.

Unwilling to let him even glimpse Nia changing clothes, Jaxon coerced the others into holding up a duvet to cover for her. Dorian found it funny and let out loud laughter about it.

Once everyone was changed, Dorian led them out of the room, instructing the other guard to take the cart to the kitchen. The rest of them rode the elevator down to the first floor and met another guard waiting. The person joined them as they walked into the lobby.

The lobby was a different place in the morning light. It didn't have any of the coldness it had had the previous night. Warm sunlight streamed in from the windows, spilling gaily over the black-and-white tiles.

Another woman had replaced the fox-faced lady from the previous night. This one also had sharp features and keen eyes. She watched the cadets and Dorian cross the lobby's expanse to the door, her eyes following their every move. Dorian called to her, "Why, my darling? You look utterly divine today!"

She smiled back at him. "Where are you headed?"

"A perimeter sweep. I must see what the outside is like now that we've received guests from the outside world."

They descended the stairs and entered the complex's outer perimeter. "My friend, Laila, will drive," Dorian asked, still wearing his plastic smile.

Dorian tossed their silent guard a pair of keys, flashing a smile at another one, observing them from a distance. Through flashing teeth, he said, loud enough for only them to hear, "Act natural. And move fast. Lord Kedron planned to meet you this afternoon. If he finds you gone, they will come for us." To the guard, he said, "Davis, is that you?"

The guard, who must have been Davis, grunted. "Off to inspect?"

"Yes, Davis. I have to ensure the area is safe for Lord Kedron."

They piled into the hovercars. Dorian insisted on taking Nia, and Jaxon insisted on going with them. Laila took the two others into another hovercar with her.

Dorian's voice filled the car with Alex, Yasu, and Laila. "Are you ready, kids?"

Dorian's car took off, speeding through the gates and into the deserted town. Laila did her best to keep up, navigating the hovercar with fluidity.

"You kids are adorable," Dorian's voice called. "We have to hurry, though." His tone deepened in warning. "They've discovered you're missing."

Yasu glanced behind them, half expecting to see a bunch of hovercars heading their way, but there was nothing. Still, they had to move with more urgency. If their previous captors caught up to them, they could end up being trapped in a worse condition. They might get locked up, and then escape might be more daunting.

They sped past the charred buildings, winding along tight bends. Soon, they broke out of the town and found the expanse where they had landed the previous evening. They kept the cars going, Yasu looking behind them for signs of a pursuit. He eventually saw two cars coming for them at top speed.

"We've got company."

"Oh no," said Laila. "But we can make it!"

Yasu noticed the other cars trying to shoot at them. "Do we have weapons?" he asked, worry biting the back of his throat.

"I don't think so," Alex replied. He could only hope they made it in time.

Arriving at the craft, they hopped out of the still-levitating cars and raced to the spacecraft. Nia and Yasu disabled the defense field, and Alex rushed through the hatch to his seat.

"Everyone," he said, adjusting his seat and the settings on his console, "get to your places."

They hurried to their seats, quickly strapping in. There were a couple of extra seats, unconnected to any consoles. Nia directed Dorian and Laila to two of them, and they promptly strapped themselves in.

Outside the spacecraft, their predators had arrived on the scene. Alex watched them on his console as he initiated the takeoff process. He could hear the lasers pelting the craft's exterior, but it was too sturdy to be damaged. The spacecraft ascended, blowing out a cloud of fumes and smoke as it sped to break through the atmosphere, taking the cadets to safety.

# CHAPTER 6

THE CADETS LET OUT joyous cheers. Though they had survived multiple close calls, this one had seemed so close to killing them. They couldn't believe their luck at having escaped so quickly.

"Only one thing to do now," Alex said. "Return home."

"Not so fast."

They swiveled towards the sound of Dorian's voice. He held Nia against his chest, one hand covering her mouth, the other holding a steel blade against her throat. Laila stood behind him, holding two laser guns trained on Yasu and Alex.

Jaxon swallowed, his vision turning red.

Alex rose from his seat, attempting a diplomatic approach to the situation. "Dorian, what are you doing?"

"You want to renege on our deal." His smile was so unnerving, spreading his lips to his ears in what looked almost like a grimace. "We had a deal."

Alex shook his head. "No, we didn't."

"I told Nia I would save you if you agreed to save me and my people."

"We can't save you and your people," Alex said. "We're children."

"Who traveled across the boundaries of space?" Dorian said, his tone malicious. "You think I don't know all about the possibilities of travel? I was once at the stupid academy you and your friends probably attend. The same academy he blew up. All four of you; dead. Along with multiple other colleagues. I saw you yesterday, and I knew, in an instant, what was happening. We cannot let this man do as he wishes."

"But we're not equipped…"

"Stop saying that!"

Nia flinched in his grip, and he relaxed as if concerned he was squeezing her too hard. Seizing the opportunity, she shrugged him off. Jaxon sprang into action, deploying his zapping tool and lunging towards Dorian. Laila struck his arm from behind with a swift kick.

The two others scurried into the space, hoping to help restrain Dorian, but he was too fast and strong. He easily twisted Yasu's wrist and pushed him aside. He sidestepped Alex, watching him receive a sharp punch from Laila.

With little effort, Laila and Dorian subdued the cadets. Dorian grabbed Nia, holding her tight against his chest again. "I don't want to hurt anyone," he said.

Shocked at their speed, accuracy, and composure, the others took shaky breaths.

"We don't want to hurt you, either," Nia said.

Dorian laughed, the sound coming out with some strain.

"Guys," Nia said, her heart thumping, "let's cooperate."

"No!" Jaxon cried.

"We don't have a choice. Let's just see where this takes us. If he believes in us so…"

Jaxon didn't want to listen. "You only feel this way because he's Kel, and you're in love with him."

Nia blinked. Yasu coughed.

Alex was tired of the entire ordeal. "What do you want us to do?"

"We have wasted time," Dorian said. "I want you to hurry. We'll get to the outer edges of the nebula, and we can tap into it. Your device—the one you used for jumping—you should be able to use it to cross to the other side."

"What other side?" Alex asked, brows furrowing. He couldn't

deny the imperative pressure of curiosity weighing on him. Perhaps if they hadn't encountered the hostile natives of the planet, they could've journeyed to that nebula and found what Dorian referred to.

Dorian was calmer. Though his grip on Nia's form remained the same, his face had relaxed into his usual, amiable smile. "The nebula holds a portal to a cosmic realm bearing secrets about the very fabric of the universe. I told Nia about this last night. She didn't have the time to tell you about it."

"How do you know what secrets it holds?" Yasu asked. He had been quiet since nursing his hurt arm.

"We learned about it in the Academy. I'm almost surprised you didn't know about it." Using his knife, Dorian pointed at Alex. "You were obsessed with it back then, itching for an opportunity to explore it. That was after Lord Kedron first returned."

Jaxon groaned. There it was. More bait for Alex. Knowing that if Alex entertained even the slightest notion they might return home without ever discovering this place, he would be compelled to investigate it further. Jaxon took one glance at Alex and knew the war the boy was waging against his fiery, instinctual curiosity, knowing that it was one he'd eventually lose.

"Alex," he said, his voice soft. "Don't."

Alex gave him a blank stare and said, with a voice quite unlike his, "We're on the verge of something important."

Jaxon let out a guttural cry. "Always. Always!"

"Have I ever been wrong?" he asked, stepping closer to Jaxon.

"We can get out of this differently." Jaxon pointed at Yasu, who stood there, observing everything. "Tell him, Yasu."

"Time is ticking," Dorian called. "They'll be going to their ships. We had a head start. Let's not waste it."

Alex didn't want to risk losing Nia, and he also wanted to explore the nebula. The answer was obvious to him, but he needed the others on board. A trip that far away would take a couple of days, at least. Perhaps somewhere along the way, they could overpower Dorian and race home. But for now...

"Let's go," he said.

Ignoring the look on Jaxon's face, he hurried to his seat, strapping in. With a reluctant sigh, Jaxon and Yasu headed to their respective seats. Dorian kept his arm around Nia, and Laila remained behind, her guns steady.

As Alex sat at his console, he noticed an object approaching from the Earth. "Can any of you see that?" he asked.

"Yes," Nia said, with a soft gasp. "They're coming."

Alex instructed them on what they'd be doing next. Their craft had speed as an edge, but Alex couldn't risk getting caught.

"We'll be doing a light jump first," he said, adjusting the settings on the Quantum Leap Device. The device's controls were good enough to ensure an accurate arrival at farther destinations. The Quantum Leap Device functioned by creating temporary pathways between dimensional barriers, a feat that required precise calculations and enormous energy reserves. However, the closer they ventured to a high-energy anomaly like the nebula, the more unpredictable its calibration became. He was certain if they took that route, their risk of being caught would be much lower.

Reluctant and exhausted, the other three followed his instructions. A sigh spread across the craft, as if relieved for the change in direction. They sped into the temporary portal, linking two points in space. Their jump took them across space, and they re-emerged, several lightyears away.

Before them, the nebula loomed. A cloud of gas, dust, and sprinkles of light. Its appearance was glorious, and momentarily, the cadets watched it through the glass, their gazes awed. Relief washed over Alex as he scanned the console, the persistent red blips of their pursuers finally fading. "We're clear," he announced, but the tension in the cabin didn't dissipate. Jaxon slumped in his seat, his face pale. "Clear for now," he muttered. Nia leaned forward, her gaze locked on the nebula. "Whatever's in there, we need to be ready. If Kedron's forces could follow us this far, who knows what else we're dealing with?" Alex swallowed hard, gripping the controls tighter. "We've handled worse," he said, though his voice wavered just enough to betray his uncertainty.

"That was a long jump," Jaxon said. He had never expected they'd get so close to their destination so fast.

Alex couldn't believe it either. The Quantum Leap Device would have taken them close, but only close enough to journey for another few earth days before arriving at the nebula's borders. Either the device was stronger than he thought, or...

Dorian strode forward, his lackey behind with the laser guns. "Now we go in."

"Into what?"

"Your device will know. The cosmic energy here is unlike anything else. It called your craft."

Alex looked at him, wary. "Called it?"

"The cosmic force at the nebula's core latches onto the technology in your Leaping Device. The force called you."

"How do you know any of this?" Jaxon asked. "Is there a Quantum Leap Device on this side?"

Dorian shook his head. "Lord Kedron has been trying to create one. He knew that to pass into the core and gain the power he wanted, he needed to link a device capable of breaking through the fabric of space."

"And he couldn't make this device?" Alex cocked an eyebrow.

"It was in production before he destroyed the Academy."

Jaxon gestured with his hands. "And?"

"And nothing. He has some scientists working for him, and though they have made no significant breakthroughs yet, they might eventually."

"All right," Jaxon said. "I need us to backtrack. Who is this Kedron, and why does he want to gain this power?"

"Didn't Nia tell you?" Dorian glanced at Nia, crouched over a screen, observing the nebula.

"We didn't get the time," Alex said, impatient to get all the information he needed about everything out of Dorian.

"Lord Kedron was a high-ranking official at the Academy. He used to go by Klaus. He was the mastermind behind some missions during the war, to protect the Eos Sector and to infiltrate enemy defenses."

"What war?" Jaxon asked, placing his hands on his head. The more they learned, the more there was to learn. And this universe was so different from the others. In the last missions, there had always been enough time to ask questions and wait for answers. Now, they were rushing through decisions and learning entire histories in minutes. He needed a long break.

Dorian stared at all of them, his eyes going from one face to the other. "No wonder you're all so weak. There was no war on your side."

Nia looked at him, at the hardness in his eyes, and understood where the difference between the Kel she knew and this one came from. "What war?"

"The war against the Empire."

"The Empire?" The cadets said in unison. They recalled the Empire from their first mission. In that mission, they crashed into a universe where a shady Empire ruled parts of it. They had to destroy an essential artifact to cripple the Empire's power source.

"Don't tell me they rule on your side?"

"They don't," Jaxon said, "but we're familiar with them."

Dorian didn't look like he understood, but he didn't have the time to dwell on that.

"War broke Lord Kedron. The Empire had strange weapons and employed a large bomb to destroy entire systems in Eos; the force of which was incredible. It ripped a hole in the fabric of space, and Lord Kedron and his men were caught in it."

"But only Lord Kedron came out alive, alone in a ship, floating out of the brilliant debris left in Eos. He returned to the Academy, a shell of his former self. Initially, he merely spoke of another realm where the gods resided. We studied it at the Academy, hoping to go there one day and discover its secrets in person. But Lord Kedron grew more unhinged. He said he could steal the power from their hands and fix this world. He would be a god, all-powerful and benevolent."

"I suppose the others didn't agree," Nia said quietly.

"They didn't. So, he took over. He forced a coup and destroyed all the men in his path, moving so quickly and brashly that nobody ever saw him coming. He has been focused on returning to the other realm since, claiming he could take the power for himself."

"This is ridiculous," Jaxon said, leaning against a wall.

"Truly."

"No, Dorian. I mean, you think it's possible for him to do it. That's ridiculous."

Dorian fixed a glare on his face. "We didn't think he could win the war either, but he has. We can't leave this up to chance, either."

Alex shut his eyes, thinking about everything. Another realm with gods? Cosmic beings of power? This was beyond everything he could ever dream up. He could stop here, but he didn't want to.

"How do we stop it?" he asked, eyes still closed.

He could hear Dorian let out a deep sigh. "I was hoping you'd know."

## CHAPTER 7

THOUGH DORIAN INSISTED they enter the other realm immediately, Alex decided they should sleep on it. The other cadets raised their voices in argument. Nia argued they had no plans and couldn't just rush in, but she agreed it was worth a try. If the production of a Quantum Leap Device was underway, there was no telling how quickly it would be done.

"We can see this other realm," she said. "I want to see this other realm."

Jaxon sulked about it. The others, though not as enthused as Alex, still wanted to try. He didn't like the uncertainty. What if in that new world, they found something more perilous? He went to sleep before the others, eyeing Laila.

Alex awoke while the others slept, heading to the kitchen area to grab something to drink. He found Dorian there, staring out of the glass at the distant stars.

"You can't sleep?" Dorian asked without turning.

"I was just thirsty," Alex replied.

"You used to be so restless then. Just another cadet on a team to research multiversal jumps. You'd be walking past classrooms with your hair mussed up and your nose in a book where you were calculating oddities."

Alex had never quite spoken to Kel before. He knew he was one of the few students in the Academy who got in because his father made a big donation. Perhaps he'd have never noticed him if Jaxon wasn't so obsessed with Nia's friendship with him.

"So, you believe I can do this because my alternate was intelligent?"

Dorian turned to look at him, shrugging. "Of course. If anyone can do this, it's the four of you. Of course, there were other fiery-brained older officers, but we don't have them now, do we?" He wore a sad smile; a smile which carried a weariness that belied his age. "You can do it. And if somehow we can't, you can let me die there and return home."

Dorian's words pressed upon Alex as he lay in his sleep station. It seemed his responsibility had built up, and though it should have been a source of encouragement, Alex took it as a challenge.

When they woke up several hours later, Alex was resolute about what came next.

"We'll go to the other side," he said, facing his comrades. The silence that followed Alex's words was heavier than the air in the nebula. Jaxon looked away first, his jaw tightening as he muttered, "You never know when to quit, do you?" Nia touched his arm lightly, her gaze steady. "It's not about quitting, Jaxon. It's about finishing what we started." Yasu stood, folding his arms. "We've come this far. Turning back now won't undo what we've seen." Alex nodded, the flicker of resolve in their eyes mirroring his own. "Then let's finish it together."

"And if we can't come back out?" Jaxon asked.

"We will."

Jaxon released an exasperated breath. "When will it be enough for you? At what point will you just stop?" He whirled around to look at the rest of them. "You too! We can't keep on enabling his behavior."

But the other two shared some of Alex's curiosity. Something like this was indeed dangerous, but abandoning the mission at this point, after getting so far, would be worse. The thought of returning home and handing the mission over to some other cadets or even higher officials was too much for them.

Yasu and Nia were apprehensive, regardless. From their observations, so much could go wrong, but they were determined to power through, riding on the coattails of Alex's optimism.

Alex deployed instructions to everyone, sending them to their various stations. Dorian and his silent guard strapped themselves in at the back, watching the unfolding tension.

As Dorian had said, the cosmic force was calling their craft with the Quantum Leap Device. The Device had unfamiliar settings, allowing Alex to link into a space he never would have imagined existed.

"Initiating leap in 3, 2, 1..." Alex gripped the console, his fingers trembling. This wasn't just another jump—this was a leap into the unknown, a decision that could define their place in the Academy's history. The cadets exchanged glances, the weight of unspoken fears evident in their expressions. Jaxon clenched his jaw, his reluctance barely masked, while Nia's hands hovered over her console, her lips moving in a silent prayer. Even Yasu, the calmest among them, had his shoulders squared as if bracing for impact.

He pulled the lever and braced against the impact, expecting the usual flow of their spacecraft through various energy layers. Instead, the craft seemed to coast through something like a shower of glimmering lights, the glare almost blinding. The cadets covered their eyes, hoping for it to pass. The sensation was familiar, reminding them of their experience with the Quantum Key's portal. Somewhere in Alex's mind, he wondered if they were made from the same material, with technology forged from this bizarre plane.

The cadets noticed the lights fading from behind their eyelids and gloved fingers. They raised their heads and observed their surroundings.

"What is this?" Yasu asked, his voice awed. The whiteness around them seemed to stretch into eternity, pressing on their senses with its weightlessness. Alex couldn't help but feel as though they were walking through the pages of a myth, their actions being written into some universal ledger. He glanced at his friends—Jaxon, still gripping his seat as if he could force himself to stay grounded; Nia, her gaze distant, lost in thoughts she hadn't yet shared; and Yasu, his usual stoicism cracking as he whispered, "It's like we're not meant to be here." In a way, it seemed like he had seen it before. His brain was split, fragments of memories he shouldn't have access to coming to him. He tried to push them aside, so he could drink in the view.

The world was white around them, as though the spacecraft was journeying within soft clouds. There were no other beings in sight, just whiteness, with streaks of bright light, and occasional streaks of darkness.

The others waged a war against their bizarre memories, too. Voices clamored for attention in their heads, and they couldn't select what to listen to. But behind the noise, there was a serenity that flooded them, filling every cell with peace.

"I feel like I could sleep here forever," Alex murmured.

The others mumbled in agreement. This place seemed like the end of everything, the point where all energies converged and canceled and peace found them.

"But..." Dorian shook the fogginess out of his head, a strange memory of Nia asking him how classes went, of him telling his father he didn't need handouts from them, and of him rescuing a kid from a racing stream. "We have to focus."

They all nodded.

"Perhaps we should keep moving the spacecraft?" Alex asked.

The others agreed.

Alex navigated the spacecraft through the strange terrain. None of their consoles worked, so they had to do the navigation blind. But the craft seemed to favor one direction, its body shaking as Alex tipped it one way. So, he followed the craft's will.

They journeyed in one direction for what could've been several days. They met nothing of note, just more whiteness, and the inundation of strange memories.

"Does anyone else feel these could be our other lives?" Alex asked, wishing he could bleed out the image of himself getting into a fight with a bigger boy on an unknown campus, while other boys surrounded them chanting.

"I do," Jaxon said. One particular memory delighted him. He

and Nia together, looking at the brass miniature of the solar system. There was a tenderness between them which their current relationship dynamic lacked.

They discussed this as their craft moved through the blankness. Each person mentioned some of the standout memories for them.

Nia talked about being back home, to see her astronomist parents again. She described the pride in their faces and the love they poured on her in the moments they spent together.

"Something is wrong," Jaxon said suddenly, interrupting Yasu's memory of working for a shipping company. "It seems we're taking hits from something."

"Hits?"

The others rushed to their frozen consoles, attempting to pick up some images from the cameras on the craft's perimeter. Dorian ran into the back of the spacecraft and peered out through one of the windows there.

Nia succeeded in getting imagery. "We have company," she said. On her screen was the large ship they had seen before they made the light jump. It didn't make any sense that they were here. They weren't supposed to have access to this realm, unless… Her head cleared immediately. "It seems they might have perfected their Quantum Leap Device. They're here too."

# CHAPTER 8

THERE WAS no time to consider what to do next. Alex shouted instructions for everyone to buckle in, and after confirming they were all strapped in, he accelerated.

A hot chase began, with the larger ship moving much faster than he could ever expect it could. Alex would have preferred all the other memories to depart, leaving him with a clear mind for navigation, but he could see overlaps of himself in pursuit. Vaguely, he wondered if they weren't things that had happened and were things happening at the time, different versions of him being chased by different enemies.

He dodged the shots fired from the larger ship, taking instructions from Yasu and Jaxon. He kept heading in the direction the ship had always wanted to go, allowing it to snap back in that direction after each dodge.

"Can we lose them?" Nia asked. This was not how she expected things would turn out, but she realized having expectations was delusional. Nothing about multiversal travel for them had ever been as expected.

"I'll try my best," Alex said with a grunt.

The spacecraft lurched through a gap, flying into a new space. Here, the whiteness was gone, replaced by a large body of water and sturdy, enormous columns reaching up into nothing. The columns looked to be made of mirrors or a similar reflective surface. The surface reflected the eerie glow filling the environment, the water, and their craft.

They moved the craft into the center of the water body, looking through their windows at the new, marvelous sight.

"Where could we be now?" Jaxon asked, his mouth slightly agape.

"Any ideas, Dorian?" Nia glanced in his direction. He was leaning against a window, staring out with all focus.

"I've never been here before," Dorian said.

Alex was watching the water, unwilling to bring their spacecraft into what might be a hole or another portal. And yet, they had pursuers. If they remained in the wrong place, they could get caught.

Before he could decide, something rose out of the water. The cadets, Dorian, and Laila scrambled to the window at the front. Before them was a dark gray sphere, rising higher and higher. The sphere had no drop of water on it, as though what it had risen from wasn't capable of leaving wetness behind.

"What is that?"

"Travelers," a voice boomed, reverberating in their bones, echoing in their minds. The sound of the voice was layered, as though a crowd spoke as one. The travelers reeled under the weight of it, unable to comprehend how it cut through the fog in their minds. "You're at the end and the beginning. The point where all time, space, and energy converge. Welcome."

The sound splintered their minds. Everyone held their heads, trying to hold the fragmented parts together, but the force was stronger.

They spun in an endless sea of images; people talking, walking, fighting, eating, living. The worlds merged, split apart, repeatedly, all the sounds crashing together and splitting.

Alex could sense it; the frightful moment when his sanity was about to slip away. Bits of his consciousness were eroding at the influence of the prevailing forces. *This is it*, he thought, *the power that*

*Kedron saw.* The end and beginning of everything that could ruin a mind.

Vaguely, he wondered about his comrades. If any of them were unraveling over what they were seeing, too. He could not think for too long.

They crashed through the fuzz and landed in a vacant hall. It didn't immediately look like a hall. The floor was white, lustrous material, which they thought looked similar to marble. High above their heads, almost too far away to see, was a gray ceiling. They couldn't see any columns in the vicinity holding up the ceiling.

They huddled together, taking in the environment. Their previous clothes were gone, replaced with sleeveless, white, flowing robes. The starkness should have brought a chill, but the temperature was perfect. Not too warm, not too cold.

"Where are we?" Nia asked, her voice echoing eerily.

"No idea," Dorian said. "Lord Kedron hasn't ever told me about his journey; where he landed or what he saw. He simply referred to the experience in grandiose terms, referencing the purity of the energy flowing in the realm."

Dorian could feel an energy. He could sense all the possibilities of holding such energy in one's grasp, and he understood Kedron. Energy of this kind could right the world, set all the crooked places straight and relieve the burden of wars, loss, and pain. Why would these beings hold such power and not use it for the right purpose?

The others were discussing the next moves. There was nowhere to walk towards, but they wanted to try. In this place, they had nothing. No tools, no direction.

Their discussion was interrupted by a loud crash to their side. The sound echoed around the space, and they turned towards the source.

Kedron and eight of his men stood there, trying to get their bearings. In the white robe, Kedron looked less menacing than he previously had. But when he turned towards them, setting his eyes on them where they huddled together, his terrifying aura returned.

"You little rascals," he said, stomping in their direction. The cadets instinctively took a step back, their training kicking in despite the surreal circumstances. Alex's mind raced, each step Kedron took ringing like a countdown. The man was unarmed, yet his presence filled the space with a suffocating energy, a dark storm coiled within him. Jaxon shifted on his feet, his fingers twitching toward the hidden prototype in his sleeve, while Nia whispered, "Stay calm," though her voice betrayed her own rising panic.

"Especially you, Dorian! I took you in. And after everything, you turn around and betray me with strangers. And look at that! You brought Laila with you."

"You're dangerous," Dorian said, his voice wobbling a bit. "You're harmful to this world and all other worlds."

Kedron stopped before them, squaring his shoulders. "I am salvation."

"You're a man. You cannot handle a power of this caliber."

Kedron's voice lowered to a murderous growl. "I eliminated all the rest. I will eliminate you, too. Guards!"

The cadets spun around to run, hoping for a chance to get a head start. They didn't know where to run, but it was better than fighting.

The same voice from before cut through the air. "Silence!"

Everyone froze in place. The cadets struggled to continue their movement, but they couldn't move.

They heard footsteps echoing in the hall as a being approached. The being stopped, and they all flew around it in a circle.

The being was a shroud of black and white, faceless, and almost formless. Like a black and white cloth thrown over a human form.

"Insolent children," the being said, its voice filling everyone's souls with sinking dread. The voice wasn't the same anymore. It was a single strain of crisp sound, as opposed to the layering from before. "You come into our home and desecrate the place with your mindless squabbles."

There was something boundless about its form, like it stretched into the past and future, existing here and now, there and then, all at once. It was beautiful in a sickly way, like if they knew it fully, their minds could not hold the information properly.

Another voice called in the distance. "Those ones are so young," it said. It was a clear sound, like sweet music spilling out of a talented singer's mouth. "Let us show them mercy."

A new voice rumbled from another direction, a clap of thunder. "They seem innocent, but that one, that one we know. One of his threads is trouble."

The cadets wondered who they were referring to. Most of them thought it might be Kedron, so their heads swung in his direction.

The being seemed to read their minds. He stepped to Yasu, touching his chin with a phantom hand and lifting his face.

"Guileless," it announced. "Free of blame and stain. And the strings of his destiny are fruitful."

Yasu didn't understand. He tried to speak, but couldn't. Somewhere in his mind, he could see a crowd below him, awed faces gazing up at him in reverence. The vision unnerved him, setting an icy hand crawling up the ridge of his spine.

Somehow, of everyone there, Alex found his voice first. "Who are you?"

Laughter tinkered out from various parts of the hall. The being didn't find it amusing. It floated away from Yasu and gravitated towards Alex.

"I remember this one," it said. "Inquisitive in every iteration. It doesn't matter if he's digging dirt to find food, or born in the lap of luxury, his brain remains bright with the desire to know. An optimism filling his form, sharp like a knife, and edging into the arms of folly."

Alex struggled to breathe. In the being's form, he saw various versions of himself reflected, his eyes bright and shining, his soul spilling out with fullness. He could also see his deaths; gutted with blades, explosions, betrayal. A tear rolled down his cheek, and a cold phantom hand brushed it away.

"I will tell you. In simple terms, we are everything. The beginning. The end. The guides. The guardians. The compass. Justice. Power. Creation." It leaned over Alex's face, its breath a frightening chill. "We've had many names, but the concept is the same. We are god. Once, men knew us. Knew how to reach us and revered us, but now…"

Alex swallowed, disliking the silence that ensued. He couldn't see any of the others and didn't know if they were watching. "But now?" he offered.

"They seek to be us. But to wield our power is to unravel oneself," the entity continued. "Even the mightiest of beings cannot contain the infinite without fracturing. Your Kedron's folly is not ambition—it is hubris." The entity shifted, a ripple of energy echoing through the room. "Yet, like moths to flame, they always return.They ruin the order of things, and instead of remaining content to leave them the way they are, they seek to exploit them further. They crawl into our home, hoping to taste our power. Hoping to become us."

More silence. The being moved away, sweeping across the floor. It didn't have feet, but they heard footsteps still.

"Always fighting. Always destroying. Always wanting what is not yours."

"But you could've just closed the portal," Dorian said. He had found his voice too, tucked somewhere at the base of his stomach. "You could've closed it and saved us from men who would take your power for themselves."

"But now," a fourth voice said, peaceful like water running over smooth rocks in a pleasant spring, "what's the fun in that?"

Laughter tinkled around the room, the sound of it equally haunting and humorous.

The cadets drank in the situation, how dire it was and how low their chances of escape were.

Jaxon wished he could look Alex in the eye one last time, hoping to communicate that this time, his inquisitiveness and optimism hadn't saved them. They were going to die facing a creator or guardian of realms. Perhaps this meeting would've been perfect if people back home knew. But their journey had no trace. People would think of him and only recall that he went missing on a mission and never returned.

Nia thought of her family and wanted to cry. Her parents, renowned astronomists, had always trusted her to make the right decisions. Now, she had failed them and was going to die for it. Here, in this perplexing other reality.

Yasu's distress was two-fold. He was worried about the images of his alternate's subjugation of an entire world. But he also hated that this place could be the end for him. There was so much he wanted to do. And now, all of it would end here. He couldn't help but blame himself. Perhaps if he had listened to Jaxon and persuaded Alex to change his mind, they could've figured out a way to save Nia, overpower Dorian and Laila, and return home.

"They are children, though," the singing voice returned. "Let's give them a chance."

The being tilted what might have been its head, as though thinking.

"Just the infants," it said. "The rest will leave to roam this space forever."

Everyone struggled to see themselves. Who were the infants? And who were the ones to roam forever? They didn't get an answer. The ground opened up beneath them, and they dropped, falling through a void, the being's voice echoing around them: "Now, a test."

# CHAPTER 9

ALEX CAME TO AN EMPTY ROOM. He was now in a shirt and shorts, similar to the kind he wore as a kid on his parents' farm. He had come a long way from those humble origins. He couldn't remember the last time he had visited the farm, and inhaled the stench of organic matter, hay, and sweaty animals. He missed it.

He walked around the empty room, looking through the windows. In all directions, a grassy field stretched into the distance. The sky was a pure blue, with soft clouds scudding past. But there was no sun.

Alex leaned against the frame of one window, absorbing the cool breeze, and drinking in the serene view.

"Isn't it gorgeous?" A woman materialized and walked up to the window, bearing an empty bowl. She wore the face of his mother; striking blue eyes and a strong jawline. Many people in their home-town had said he looked exactly like her. He recalled one neighbor telling him that if he was a girl, he could've been her clone.

Alex opened and closed his mouth. "How?"

"I'm not her. I'm the Guide. I bring you through the Tribunal's quest to see if you're worthy."

"Worthy?"

"Of return. You've found many things on your journey here.

You might have become corrupted." She wore a sweet smile. "We can't let you leave if you've become corrupted."

Alex gulped and nodded. "Where are the others?" He needed to know his friends were safe.

The being wearing his mother's face shapeshifted, going across various iterations of herself, perhaps representing people familiar to his friends. "With me."

Taking her answer to mean they were safe, Alex said, "What's the quest?"

The house around him vanished and he was left in the open field, watching the brilliant sky above him. He smelled his mother's apple pie, and his nerves relaxed somewhat.

"This is the battlefield," the being said. "Your will to respect the natural order of things will be tested here. Then you can go home."

Alex couldn't see what the test could be. He stared at the field; the grass leaning in the wind, the light without a source, and felt some fear.

"It's simple," the being said. It placed the bowl in his hands, and Alex immediately felt the rush of power it contained. It was charged with the same cosmic energy he had felt prevalent at the start of the journey. "You're not to use the power."

That's all?

"Yes." The being smiled brightly. "That's all."

"And the others?" Alex asked aloud, embarrassed that it had heard his thoughts.

"The same test."

Alex nodded, ready.

The being brushed his hair out of his eyes. "We're not supposed to be picky, but you're my favorite. I trust you to win. There's much work to be done in the coming days as well."

The being walked away from him, and just like that, it vanished.

Alex stood for several moments in that land, holding the bowl filled with profound cosmic energy. Her last words haunted him. *What work?* he thought. But he knew that wasn't as important as the present task. He was thinking of calling to someone, anyone watching, to request what came next when the scene changed.

He could see it then: the farm. He heard the cows bellowing in their pens, saw the guard dogs running around with dripping tongues, and watched one of his brothers shovel hay while whistling a gay tune. It was gorgeous and serene. Alex sought to go towards him, asking about the farm and their parents, uncles, and aunts, but he worried he'd be invisible, a shroud, an unknown.

"Alex!" his brother called.

Alex raised a hand to wave. The bowl disappeared from his other hand, but he still sensed it hovering in the vicinity, waiting for his call. "Alfie!"

They ran towards each other and flung their arms around one another. Alfie smelled of sun, grass, and hard work. It was a comforting smell, the smell of home.

"Where is everyone?" Alex asked, his cheeks hurting from smiling. Seeing Alfie again was emotional. He had missed his older brother's loud voice and kindness.

Alfie brushed Alex's hair away from his face. "Everyone is inside. Mama is making pie."

Alex followed him in. He met everyone there: his parents, uncles, aunts, cousins, and other relatives. It was like he had never left. Everyone asked him about his time at the Academy. "We saw you on the news," one uncle said, beaming with pride. "You were one of the first humans to make a trip across worlds successfully."

His mum held him against her side. She smelled of apples, cinnamon, and nutmeg. "Yes. That's my boy!"

They ate together and laughed about the farm. Alex didn't know what occasion brought everyone together like this, but he tried to believe it was all for him. Perhaps they heard he was returning from the Interstellar Academy and wanted to see him again.

As the meal wound down, the wind picked up speed outside.

"A storm is coming," one of his uncles said, scratching his bald head.

They scrambled around the house and outside, setting things right, herding the animals into the barn, and calling instructions to one another. Alex, unsure of how to help, watched the events unfold through the window. His mom met him there and told him to stay calm. "It's just a storm. It'll pass soon." Her voice was steady, carrying the assurance of someone who had seen this happen repeatedly.

Alex remained inside, calm as a stagnant pond. His mom wrapped his shoulders in a blanket, and he stayed next to the window, watching the sky grow darker and waiting for the rain.

But the rain never came.

Rather, the wind picked up, blowing dust, dirt, leaves, and hay into the air. The house shook, the joints creaking beneath the influence of the surrounding forces. Everyone grew more panicked, worrying about what was going on.

Alex remained at the window, watching the now dark sky. He saw a ship materialize in its midst; large, silver and black, and shaped like a saucer. It lowered until it hovered just above the farm.

"Aliens," his dad said, staring out in awe.

Alex wanted to correct him. They had been told the term 'alien' was derogatory in the Academy. The acceptable term was foreigners or travelers. However, it was not the time.

Alex recognized the symbol on the ship from a memory he knew could not be his own. They were soldiers of the Empire.

"We need to get out of here," he cried. But where would they go? The ship was too large and fast for them to escape.

Alex knew this would be the end of his family. His heart ached deeply, twisting, hurting. He tried to gather everyone together, wondering about the safety systems on the farmhouse, but there was no time.

Soon, the soldiers had descended from the ship. They were at the door, knock-knocking on the wood, bang-banging their way inside. They were dressed in blue, silver, and black spacesuits, their faces hidden behind breathing masks. Their leader, a human with salt-and-pepper hair, instructed everyone to get down on their knees.

Alex did so immediately, watching for a way out. The other soldiers gathered around and put them in cuffs.

The human leader paced before them. He spoke of something

hidden in their house, an instrumental tool for the Empire. "We know it's buried here. We want it back."

"We have no idea what you're speaking of," Alex's father roared. "We're honest folk. We don't have any such thing in this house."

Time dragged on as the human asked more questions. Growing weary of the back and forth, he pulled Alex's father to the front and fired a shot into his head. After the shot, he asked for another weapon. He selected another family member, a young cousin with toothless patches at the front of her mouth. He killed her, too.

Alex could feel his body growing colder. He could sense the call of the power in the bowl, a desire to stretch reality into something else, to save his family. He could do anything with the power. He could kill these people and resurrect his family, but he knew he couldn't touch it.

He watched the light leave each person's eyes, sweat covering him in a glossy sheen.

His mom was the last, her face troubled and snot spilling from her nose. "Please, please," she cried. "We're innocent."

But that wasn't enough. Soon, she was slumped on the carpet, her blank eyes staring into nothing.

"Why did you have to do that?" Alex said, his voice broken, his heart empty. He hated the human with a fury. He wanted to hurt him, pull his limbs out, and parade them around the farm. He wanted his family back, whole and alive, like before these Empire fighters arrived. He wanted peace and wholeness.

He knew he could have it. And yet...

The human pulled him to the front, wearing a mild smile. "So foolish, sometimes," he said, pressing the barrel of his gun against Alex's head. "So, so foolish."

Alex heard a bang, and the lights went out.

# CHAPTER 10

ALEX OPENED his eyes to find himself in a classroom at the Academy. He was wearing his cadet uniform, but it sat differently on his body, like Nia had arranged it. He looked around the classroom, wondering about the others.

Jaxon materialized next to him first, settled on his hands and knees, breathing deeply through his mouth. He rose slowly and narrowed his gaze at Alex. "Where are the others?"

"On their way," Alex said.

Jaxon forced a smile to his lips. "Right. On their way."

"I said everything would work out well, and I wasn't wrong."

Jaxon waved his hands at the space to the side. "Of course. That's why Nia and Yasu are right here."

Nia materialized next to him then, her eyes wide with shock. She took in the classroom, Alex, and turned to look at Jaxon's stunned face. With a small squeak, she leaped into Jaxon's arms, burying her nose in the space between his neck and shoulder. "I thought I'd lose all of you," she said. "I was so terrified."

The tension bled out of Jaxon, his shoulders loosening up and dropping. He squeezed Nia against him, feeling the beat of her heart, and hoping she was real, really real. After everything he had seen in the last few hours, reality seemed so flimsy. "Yes," he said, voice breaking. "I was scared too."

They stood that way for a little too long. Alex looked on, realizing what their relationship truly meant for the first time. He was thinking: I hope this marks the end of their squabbles now when Yasu materialized close to the back of the classroom.

Yasu was silent.

The huggers pulled apart, heads turned to him.

"Hey Yasu," Jaxon called, "what's happening?"

Yasu swiped a hand beneath his right eye and gazed at the dampness on his palm. His chest hurt, a tight, twisting pinch. He didn't know what the others had seen, but what he had seen troubled him.

What kind of test was that? Who was the other him he had had to fight to the death? And why? Why was that so emotionally draining?

"It's not over," Yasu said.

"What's not over?" Nia stepped away from Jaxon, mildly uncomfortable now that a new issue had taken priority.

"Everything," Yasu said, his voice foreign and deadly.

"You're not making sense," Jaxon said. He willed his heart to stop pounding. If it wasn't over, did that mean that this wasn't the Academy? Were they still in a trance in the other realm?

"We joked about me being an overlord," Yasu said, walking to the front of the classroom where the others stood. "A joke. A very dumb joke. But what if I told you it's real?"

The other three stared at him with open mouths. "One of your alternates?" Jaxon asked, a headache spreading from the back of his head.

"Yes," Yasu said, forcing on a wobbly smile.

"Oh no," Jaxon said.

"Oh no," Nia echoed.

Alex drank in the information, observing the falling moods of his comrades. This moment seemed crucial. At least they were on this side while they figured it out.

"Let's meet the commander," he said.

"What?" the other three shouted.

Alex shrugged. "Yes. Let's do that. We're young, we're not so experienced. This seems like a job for the higher-ups."

Jaxon looked at Alex with some admiration. "Don't you want to find out more about this?"

"I do, but... we could've lost someone today. Perhaps it wasn't mere luck and we're really impressive to those beings. But we can't let such events repeat themselves. Let's take this to the right authorities now." He also thought about the 'work' the celestial being had referenced before the test. If something of that nature could spring up, they had to tell someone more competent about it.

Everyone nodded, agreeing with Alex's conclusion. They huddled together for one last hug before they went to the commander's office. They knew that losing the craft and falling into a strange reality wasn't part of the job description. In their first mission, though they had returned without their craft, they had gotten away with it because the Quantum Leap Device had failed, causing the crash. This time around, they were older and had gone on more trips. Returning without their craft was heinous. But they were all together, and that mattered more.

## *EPILOGUE*

When Dorian opened his eyes to find himself back on Earth with Laila, silent tears streamed from his eyes. The test had stretched him, his hands itching as he watched the soldiers drag his comrades out of the Academy and fire blasts into their heads. He shouted *No, no!* countless times, but his words were swallowed up in a haze.

Laila came to him, crawling on her hands and knees through the loose sand and dust of the abandoned town. She took him in her arms, patting his back and stroking his blue hair.

"So much we can't change," he said, his voice hoarse. "We're so powerless. So fragile. And even in the face of power, we can't wield it."

He understood Lord Kedron more than he ever had before. After losing so many people to the war, perhaps the losses broke something in his mind. He needed to get everyone back, no matter the cost, even if it meant breaking something sacred.

Kedron was gone, he knew. There was no way he could've survived the test. He wasn't an infant.

The cadets were gone, too. He missed them.

He had wanted to tell Nia and Jaxon to not miss the chance to be together. In his world, they had skirted around their relationship, squabbling incessantly in every classroom and in the cafeteria during meals. But he remembered Nia being the one to shed the most tears when Jaxon died. He wanted to tell Alex to stay curious, to keep his mind constantly seeking information and ways to find novelty, no matter the odds. He wanted to tell Yasu he was quiet, but he had so much to say, and that he should say everything.

But they weren't there anymore.

"Do you think they made it?" he mumbled into Laila's shoulder.

Laila shrugged.

Dorian decided they did. They had to. If not, the mission wouldn't be fully successful, and he couldn't live with that.

**The End**

# THE STARBORNE PARADOX

## A YA SPACE OPERA

## PROLOGUE

THE BOY LOOKED at the slate gray sky, tears blurring his vision. His world, as he knew it, was gone. Somewhere, in the rubble of his home, the bodies of his parents and siblings lay still now. He wouldn't hear his mother laugh again. He wouldn't hear his father tell the same joke about broccoli and carrots going to the market. His siblings wouldn't ask him to help them take the kites outside anymore.

Rain began to fall. He remained seated in the middle of the deserted streets, staring at the bleak sky.

Someone was wailing nearby. He thought it might be his neighbor, Mrs. Yamamoto. The voice sounded familiar. Some part of him wanted to go to her, to pat her curved back and tell her things would be fine. "We'll gather the rubble, Yamamoto-san. We'll rebuild. Everything will be OK." But he couldn't move. He wanted to lie in the middle of the road and get washed away by the rain.

The voice quieted to wails as night fell, and then there was silence. He rose, his limbs aching. In his chest, his heart had hopped out and run away, leaving him hollow. He could sense the pain of his loss, of the devastation, but he couldn't sense it as he should. A veil stood between him and the full extent of his grief.

He walked into the distance, passing destroyed buildings, wondering how he had survived. It seemed better to have gone with everyone else. His parents wouldn't have to weep any more, and his siblings wouldn't have to carry the weight of being here while everyone else wasn't. This was rubbish. He shouldn't be here, he thought.

He found lights in the distance and, without thinking, walked towards them. Some people were swaddled in blankets, their faces full of anguish. Others talked animatedly to the white-clothed personnel tending to them.

Before he could drink in the scene properly, someone ran up to him, gripping his arm. "Kid, where are your parents?"

The person could've been sixteen years old, barely a child. A sparse mustache covered his upper lip, his jaw set with determination, and his eyes blazed.

The boy stared, momentarily too stunned to speak, and then, sluggishly said, "With the ancestors. Dead."

The mustache boy patted his head awkwardly, noting the boy's lethargy. "How old are you?" he asked.

Somewhere in his head, the boy searched for the number. It was nestled in a dark place he was already trying to bury, where all his other memories had gone for safekeeping. "Nine," he said, finally, with a soft exhale.

The older boy nodded. "Come with me."

They wove through the crowd of distressed people, sidestepping the heaviness of their emotions, and soon they reached the end. A few lorries stood there, with a few young boys and girls standing around.

"I brought a new one," the mustache boy said.

Someone called from the back. "Bring the child to me."

The people around politely parted for them to meet the unknown speaker. Holding the young boy's upper arm, the mustache boy escorted him there. The speaker sat on a tall metal stool. He was much older, a salt-and-pepper beard covering his chin and his hair shorn close to the scalp.

For a moment, he observed the boy as he wiped his gun with a cloth. Then, with a nod, he beckoned the boy forward.

The boy flinched when his icy hands grabbed his chin and turned his face from side to side.

"So young," the man said, his voice like gravel. "But I like his eyes. They're fiery." He released the boy's face. "What's your name, kid?"

Once more, the memory was lost. It slipped further away, and the boy reached into his mind to pull it out of the hidden place. "Yasu Garcia," the boy wanted to say, but it was too late.

The man had dismissed him. "It doesn't matter, anyway. All of you will get a code number. That's your new identification from now on."

The boy's number was 10-819. He never used the name Yasu ever again.

# CHAPTER 1

IT WAS a chilly day at the Interstellar Academy. A dry wind swept through the campus, leaving all the cadets, officers, and officials shivering. The sky overhead was overcast, the sun occasionally peeking through the swollen clouds.

In an empty classroom in the main building, four cadets huddled together, looking at the dark clouds beyond the window. Their books sat unattended before them.

"So what are these dreams like?" Jaxon Brooks asked, leaning back in his chair.

Yasu Garcia shrugged. "I wouldn't call them dreams; they don't happen at night. They might occur in the middle of the day. I could be walking down the hallway to class and get this flash, like a memory."

Alex Rivera stared out of the window. "Could it be residuals from what we went through?"

Yasu shrugged. "I have no idea. Do the rest of you have that?"

Everyone shook their heads.

It had been a few weeks since their last mission. On that mission, they traveled to a planet dominated by a strange nebula. Soon, they discovered that the nebula held a portal to another realm. Their journey through the portal took them to a world filled with celestial beings with access to all the universes spread across the multiverse.

While in that realm, they had access to memories from their other versions. Knowing what was happening was challenging, as their minds struggled to handle the strange new information. But soon, it became clear that they were experiencing memories from their alternates.

However, Yasu hadn't stopped seeing those memories. One alternate's memories continued to haunt him. He saw this strangely powerful and domineering version of himself, who had built an empire and had taken over everything in his world.

Yasu saw everything through that version's eyes: a bleak world and a heavy burden upon his shoulders. Whenever the memories subsided, he'd be left with a sinking feeling of dread, as though something terrible was coming their way.

"In everything we've encountered," Nia Chen said, "this might be the most unprecedented. Who knew you'd have these burdens to bear now?"

"Should we tell the commander about it, though?" Jaxon asked. This new turn of events displeased him. He had thought that their last mission marked the end of their adventures for a time. Even if it meant that for the next few years, he wouldn't go on any missions. He was content to stay in the Academy, in their universe, and go on tamer adventures.

After their return, they spoke to the commander about the dangers they faced. It seemed the commander and other officials agreed with Jaxon's sentiments. If potential dangers of this caliber existed in other universes, it was unwise to keep sending cadets on missions. At that meeting, they heard about their new strides for the older officers.

"Perhaps soon," the commander had said, "that program will be well-developed, and we can partner our cadets with our more experienced officers. That way, there'll be an even better flow of knowledge."

In the present, Alex said, "I don't know if we should. This might not be such a big deal."

Jaxon shook his head. "It very well could be. When Yasu returned, he talked about how that other version of himself was on his way. Suddenly, we've forgotten about that. Maybe these visions he sees are a sign. Evil Yasu could get closer."

Alex chuckled. "Evil Yasu? Is that what we're going for? Evil Yasu?"

"Do you have a better name in mind?" Jaxon asked, cocking an eyebrow. "And now isn't the time to wait for names and all that. We have to be proactive. You usually are. What's happening to you?"

"I just don't think we should bother the commander with this," Alex replied. Secretly, he wanted them to figure it out more before they took it to the authorities. Now that his travel opportunities had been stripped away until further notice, he needed something else to hold on to. Working at this provided him with some excitement. If they took it to the commander, there was no telling how he or any higher officials would react.

"I think we should," Nia said. "I agree with Jaxon. It could be serious. But ultimately, the choice is up to you, Yasu. What do you want to do?"

Yasu pointed at himself. "Me?"

Nia nodded.

"I don't know."

Yasu didn't want to admit it, but he was terrified. The ominous sensation of being watched had clung to him since he returned from the test at the end of the mission. He hadn't asked the others how their tests went, but his had left him hollow.

Stuck in a room similar to the one he had grown up in, he had struggled to find a way out. The walls seemed to close in on him, the anime posters on the wall getting distorted and grotesque. The power he wasn't supposed to touch lingered somewhere, lapping at the edge of his consciousness.

Soon, a version of himself appeared, standing taller and prouder than ever. His gaze was sharp and pierced Yasu's very core.

"Who are you?" he'd asked, taking a frightened step back.

"I can't tell you that. But ..." he assumed a fighting stance, "you cannot leave here without defeating me."

They fought for what seemed like hours. The test made little sense to Yasu. Why did he have to battle this equally skilled version of himself to prove his worth to some strange celestial beings? But soon, he understood. He hated being stuck in a situation that had no way out. This was an everlasting loop, this fight. He wouldn't get out without using the powers he couldn't touch.

But, but, but, he reminded himself. I must not touch it!

Yasu was sure he didn't pass the test. The pull of the orb of power the being gave him was too much. He reached for it. And that's when things went awry.

The room darkened, and his opponent's eyes filled with ink.

"You," his chilling voice said, "and your nasty little friends. You went poking where you shouldn't poke."

Yasu tried to scramble backward and away, but his opponent had him pinned to the room's wooden floor. "What do you mean?" he asked, voice taut with fear.

"You destroyed what you shouldn't," his opponent said. "Twice! And you destabilized the balance in my world."

"What are you talking about?"

The opponent pressed his hands firmly against the floor. "You'll know. Soon."

"Yasu!" Nia snapped in front of his face.

Yasu moved with some discomfort. "Sorry. I was thinking."

Nia's gaze softened, and she patted his arm. "I'm sorry to have interrupted your thoughts. But we'd like to know what you want to do next."

Letting out a soft sigh, Yasu shrugged. "I think we should go to class."

The others looked at the time, realizing their class was in a few minutes. They gathered their books into their bags and hurried down the hallway to their lecture theater. Many of the students were already seated, discussing amongst themselves in low voices.

The cadets found seats for themselves in the middle of the class and adjusted their tablets to begin work when the instructor arrived.

The instructor came in a few minutes later, wiping his forehead with a towel. He dropped his books on the podium and waited for the buzz to quiet down.

"We have a very exciting topic for you today!" He walked to the board and scrawled 'Advanced Orbital Calculations.' He dropped his marker and clapped. "All right then! Who did the last class assignment?"

The class began in earnest. Everyone listened with rapt attention, looking through their notes and jotting down the new formula the instructor listed on the board.

Yasu was so engrossed in the lecture, he didn't notice when his consciousness slid from him.

He fell out of the classroom and into a new, stark white chamber. The sensation reminded him of the other realm they entered on their last mission. Light energy buzzed in the air as though another kind energy of was contained there.

"Yasu," a voice called.

Goosebumps sprung over Yasu's body. He didn't need to turn to know who stood behind him.

His alternate was dressed in all black, a floor-length cape draped about his broad shoulders. Beneath one eye, a scar ran down his cheek to the corner of his lip. Everything about his bearing screamed danger. Oddly, he seemed way older, too.

The alternate walked up to him, the heels of his black boots making a terrifying clicking sound. He stopped in front of Yasu, his gaze boring into him.

"I've found you," he said. "I'll be there very soon. Just wait for me."

Stunned by the revelation, Yasu couldn't draw a breath or access his thoughts. He remained frozen in place. When he returned to the class, his head banged on the desk.

His friends glanced at him, expressions shocked and worried. Nia, who sat next to him, grabbed his arm.

From the front, the instructor called, "Is there a problem over there?"

"No," Nia said, hearing Yasu's groaned No. "Everything is fine."

But she and her friends didn't know then the extent to which things were not fine.

## CHAPTER 2

JAXON GRIPPED his fork with a shaky hand. "We have to tell the commander."

Yasu sat quietly in the cafeteria as his friends discussed the next steps. His body was icy, and his forehead hurt where he had banged it. Thinking was proving difficult. It was as though this last vision had scrambled his thoughts.

"What if he's on his way as we speak?" Nia was worried, her food abandoned before her.

"He most likely is," Alex said. "We should meet the commander. Let's eat."

"Yasu," Nia's voice turned gentle. "Eat."

Yasu stared at her, but he wasn't quite seeing her. His gaze pierced into the distance. "How did this happen, though? How could there be an evil version of me?"

"I'm sure there are evil versions of all of us," Jaxon said, shrugging. "There might be a tech-wiz version of me completely gifted at tearing planets apart from their core."

"But none of your versions are doing this. Mine is. Mine is coming here. We don't even know what he's coming for and why." Yasu lowered his chin to the cool table. "Besides, when they spoke about evil in the God Realm, they only looked at me. Not at any of you."

Jaxon began again. "Maybe our versions aren't so evil …" He quieted at the look on Yasu's face.

"Let's eat," Alex said. "The commander will know what to do." Alex wasn't so sure the commander and higher officials could handle this, but neither could he and his friends. He believed it was time for them to relinquish control to their superiors, though the thought killed him.

They rushed through their meal and left the cafeteria for the commander's office. On the way, they met Tom, an older cadet who led another multiversal travel team.

"I heard," he said softly, his eyes glinting.

Alex cocked an eyebrow. "You heard what?"

Tom stepped closer, his eyes darting around the cafeteria. "About Yasu's incident in class. Everyone is talking."

Alex took a cursory glance around the hall where the members of the Academy had their meals. Many cadets were glancing in their direction, wearing looks of thinly-veiled suspicion and annoyance. The news of the halt in multiversal travel spread like wildfire after their last mission. Many of the cadets around the school didn't care much for the program, as they hadn't been included to begin with. But those who did bore some resentment towards Alex and his friends. After all, the program only ended after their last mission. Additionally, because of the peculiar nature of their discoveries, the higher-ups had filed the related information as classified. Nobody even knew what they had encountered and why they were being punished.

Yasu stepped closer to Tom. "It wasn't a big deal."

Tom chuckled. "That's not what everyone else is saying, though. They said you slammed your head against the table like a lunatic."

"That's way too harsh," Nia muttered.

Alex had had enough. Gossip might be damaging, but they had larger fish to fry. "We'll see you later, Tom."

They exited the building and crossed the courtyard to the main building, where the commander's office was. The walk was tense and quiet, and the cadets considered what their position here meant.

Alex recalled something and tried to smother it before giving up. "The gods," he began as they entered the elevator, "or the god, the one who guided us through the test."

Jaxon recalled his test guide. The being had appeared as the science teacher at his middle school, a dark-skinned man with a bushy mustache and eyebrows. The being never told him about itself. It merely pointed out what he had to do, whispered that he should not fear death so much, and left. "I remember the one," Jaxon said.

"Well, I remember something she told me."

"She?" Jaxon scratched his head.

"The god appeared as my mum."

"Oh."

"What did she tell you?" Nia asked.

"She said there's lots of work left to be done. Or something along those lines. Could this be the work? Dealing with this evil Yasu?"

Nia pondered it. "The god didn't tell me any such thing, though."

Yasu and Jaxon shrugged in agreement.

"Oh well."

They met the commander on the way out of the elevator. He stood there with a technician they knew from their training, waiting to ride the elevator down.

"We were coming to see you," Alex said.

The commander's expression was grim. "Really?"

The cadets nodded. "It's important."

After passing a few instructions to the technician, he led them to a conference room down the hallway. He sat at the head of the table and steepled his fingers. "I'm waiting."

"Yasu has visions," Alex blurted.

"When you put it that way," Jaxon said, with a slight growl, "you make it sound less important than it is."

The commander watched them with mild amusement. "What are these visions, Yasu?"

Yasu drew a deep breath. "On our last mission, we encountered a world between worlds. And we got access to memories - of our other lives. The lives our other versions were living." He stared at the commander, gauging how to offer the rest of the information. "One memory lingered."

The commander's eyebrows raised. "Lingered?"

"Yes," Yasu said. "Lingered. I get these residues of his life. Of him fighting. Of him traveling the galaxies. Of him becoming triumphant."

"Yes," the commander said, nodding. "I remember that from your mission report. You mentioned some memories you all encountered. But why is this more important?"

Gesturing to the others, Yasu said, "None of the others see any memories from any one particular alternate. In fact, none of the others can remember much from any of their alternates."

The commander's brow furrowed. "Perhaps you're more sensitive than the others?"

"No," Yasu said. "That's not the problem. Today, I had a lapse during class, and I saw my alternate. He said he was coming for us."

The commander leaned back in his chair. Perhaps the absurdity of it had drained him of energy. His expression was strained. For a time, he remained silent, watching a spot on the ceiling. "Could it be, Yasu, that you're merely scared of your alternate version?"

"Scared? How?"

"Well, you might find it hard to come to terms with the information you encountered in the other realm, and now your mind is making things up."

Yasu narrowed his eyes. "How does that make sense?"

Casting a glance at the other cadets, the commander scratched his chin. "I'm trying to explore other options here. If this other version of you comes, as you say, what will he do?"

"I wrote about him in my report."

"The warlord?"

Yasu nodded.

"But isn't he like you? A child?"

Alex couldn't bear it. "Sir, you sent children to explore other universes. Maybe in some universes, they crown cadets as emperors."

Something was different about the commander, the cadets noted. Usually, he was more upbeat. On that day, he seemed demoralized. They decided he might be facing other things they knew nothing about. After all, being one of the most important personnel at a prestigious institution came with its low points.

"It just seems rather absurd," the commander said. "How is he communicating with you in dreams?"

Exasperated, Yasu threw his hands in the air. "They aren't dreams!"

"What are they?"

"Visions! Or memories." Yasu breathed heavily. "I don't know." Everything about this was sapping all his energy. He missed who he was several weeks ago. This realization that he could be so power-hungry in one iteration and be regarded as trouble by celestial beings chilled him. He wanted to have a sane conversation with that kid and ask why.

"Also absurd," the commander said. "However, much of our missions have dealt with absurdity. So, I can't entirely discount Yasu's claims yet. We'll reconvene with the council. Perhaps we'll need to run other tests —"

"Or tighten security," Alex said, his jaw set.

The commander looked at Alex like he hadn't seen the boy before. "Or tighten security. Yes."

⸺⸺⸺⸺⸺

In a bid to lighten the tension in the group, Jaxon talked about other things during dinner. Trying for a nonchalant tone, he asked Nia about Kel and when they last saw each other. Nia told him Kel and the rest of the hockey team had gone to another country for a tournament. When Nia didn't gush about Kel, Jaxon was relieved and steered the conversation in another direction by asking everyone about their favorite sports.

"I loved to play soccer in the garden at home with my older brothers," Alex said, chuckling.

Nia looked at him in amusement. "I've never played that before."

"Me neither," Jaxon said. "We played basketball and baseball in my school." He turned to the silent Yasu. "What about you, man?"

Yasu was usually quiet, but his expression would hold an inviting openness. Now, his stare was distant, his lips pressed together as though his mouth was clamped shut.

"I played baseball," he said softly. "My siblings and I. With the neighbors' kids. Until my parents figured I might be a genius. Then they kept moving me up in my classes. And the workload increased." He paused. "Could that have been it? Could the work-load have made my alternate snap?"

Nia glanced around the table at Jaxon and Alex. "Who could blame him? When my parents discovered I had this natural aptitude for numbers and science, they wanted to bleed me dry, too. I had to attend one class after another."

"Very little time to sleep and play," Alex said, shaking his head.

"So little. You become a robot for them. Classes. Assignments. And more classes."

"And then the Academy swoops in like a hawk." Jaxon mimicked the sound of a bird of prey.

Laughter rippled across the table. Even Yasu cracked a small smile.

"We can only hope the commander might be right," Nia said eventually, reaching across the table to squeeze Yasu's icy hand.

Yasu appreciated the warmth of her touch. "What if he ..."

They heard a loud boom outside. The edges of their vision blurred, as though they all experienced a sudden drop in blood pressure. Everyone sat at their tables, their eyes hazy and their expressions befuddled. Then, they snapped out of it and ran to the windows to look.

Yasu turned ashen. "Could it be?"

"I hope not," Nia replied. "I sincerely hope not."

But by the time they rushed to the window, they knew it could be. The darkening sky was obscured by a large black ship. A disembodied and toneless voice drifted out from the ship, striking the air like a solid surface.

"Greetings, people of this prestigious institution. We do not come in peace. But you shall have peace if peace is what you want. Bring me the one called Yasu Garcia, along with his meddling friends. Or face the consequences."

## CHAPTER 3

ALL THE EYES in the room found Yasu and his friends standing behind a small cluster of people at one window. Jaxon offered a small wave with a thin-lipped smile and muttered, "I think we should run."

"I don't think we should," Alex said. "That will make us look —"

"We don't want to die," a kid said, his voice sharp in the silence. "Shouldn't we just offer them up?"

"We can't just do that. Even if nobody likes them," someone else retorted.

"Isn't that why we should do this?" a third kid shouted, her voice like a shrill instrument. "Because nobody likes them? They'll be gone, and whenever any of the programs are reopened, the school can send cadets who are less adventure-hungry."

Nia found the entire situation unnerving. Why was everyone acting like they weren't standing right there? She moved closer to Jaxon, grabbing his hand, hoping he might interpret the concern in the squeeze she gave him.

Alex bristled. He was adventure-hungry, but hearing someone else say that about him, especially while he was standing right there, was incensing. "Since when has curiosity become a crime?"

"Curiosity?" The girl who spoke stepped forward. She had small features set in a pale face and waist-length blonde hair. "You call what you do curiosity?"

"It is more than anyone else here has ever done," Alex said, itching for a fight. If she weren't a girl, he would have marched over there and challenged her.

"Enough!" An officer stood at the hall's door, his bearing stiff and his eyes blazing. "What is the commotion for?"

The cadets all fell silent, watching the officer approach, flanked by two well-built and heavily armed soldiers.

"Yasu Garcia," the officer said. Exhaustion was etched into his features as though he had spent the earlier portion of the day training and found the new turn of events a frightful bore. "Come forward."

An icy hand traced the ridges of Yasu's spine as he stepped forward. He could sense all the cadets staring in his direction, their judgment washing off them in waves. "Yes, sir," he mumbled.

"Where are your friends?"

Yasu turned to look at his friends, beckoning them forward with a wave.

The three other members of Team Alpha came forward. They wore identical expressions of wariness, a chill running along their skin.

"You're not in trouble," the officer said, crossing his beefy arms over his chest. "But, come with me." He raised his voice, sweeping his piercing gaze around the hall. "The rest of you, stay calm. Our soldiers should begin the evacuation process soon. Stay calm!"

The four cadet friends were anything but calm as they proceeded from the cafeteria behind the officer and in front of the soldiers.

"Where are we going?" Alex asked.

"Alex Rivera, was it?" The officer didn't deign to turn around and spare him a glance. "Your reputation precedes you. Quite the questioner."

Alex detested the man's patronizing tone. "Well?"

"A hasty tribunal," the officer said. "One or all of you might have the key to averting this crisis."

"In what way?" Nia asked.

"We'll find out when we get there, won't we?"

They lapsed into silence.

Yasu contemplated what came next. It seemed his evil alternate had a vendetta against him, but why was he dragging his friends into it, too? Could they have harmed him in some way in the other universe? It seemed unlikely all this was happening because of some bullying, but he couldn't find any other reasons his alternate would want to involve his friends.

They filed into a room on the highest floor of the building. A few higher officials were seated in waiting, the commander in their midst. They also recognized Colonel Klaus, the official who seemed like their mortal enemy.

"Please, cadets, sit."

The cadets sat close to each other, staring at the other faces in the room.

"It seems I was wrong, and you were right," the commander said, his expression grim. "But now isn't the time for us to discuss who was right or wrong. We have to find a way out. And fast." His eyes glided to Yasu's face. "What can you tell us about this version of yourself?"

"Not a lot," Yasu said with a shrug. "And it doesn't matter."

Colonel Klaus grunted at the other side of the table. "These children. It never matters to them."

The commander held up a hand to silence him. "Let's hear why, at least."

Shutting his eyes and picturing the crowd of followers he had once seen clamoring for his alternate's affection, Yasu considered who his opponent was. The people didn't seem oppressed. They seemed to have a genuine love for their leader. "I want to meet him myself."

"Oh, my!" Jaxon raised his hands in exasperation. "Yourself?"

Yasu met his gaze with steadiness. "Yes. By myself."

"What about the rest of us? I thought we're a team?"

The commander waved his hands, dismissing Jaxon's words. "You might be a team, but that is irrelevant, there's …"

The toneless voice called out again. "Time is no man's friend. I might be tempted to begin a search by myself." The voice changed then, bearing the quality of a disgruntled young man. "And if I do that, you won't like me very much."

"A search?" one official said. "How does he intend to cross the protective force field?"

The commander turned to look through the window behind him. There was nothing noteworthy to see. The sky was dark, and light spilled, cold and lonely, from open windows in the nearby buildings and the perimeter lamps. "I don't think we should wait to find out," he said. Looking at Yasu and his friends, he asked, "What do you think he wants from you?"

"I can merely guess. I think we destroyed something important to him."

The other three swung their heads at him in surprise. This was the first time he mentioned it. So far, all they had known was that he saw visions of his alternate.

"Something like what?" the commander asked.

"I don't know. Whatever it was, it destabilized the balance in his world. And he wants revenge."

For a moment, there was only silence. Then Colonel Klaus looked at the commander, and said, "Haven't they destroyed a few important artifacts in their trips out?"

The commander ran a hand over the rough salt-and-pepper beard on his face. "Define a few, Colonel."

"Well, two. The Quantum Key and the organic computer that developed a Void."

Behind his ribcage, Yasu's heart beat violently. Those could be it. But how were they connected to this evil version of himself? Unless …

"But wouldn't that mean he's somehow connected to those phenomena?" Alex asked, looking around the room. "Does that mean he's been jumping between universes before now?"

"Is that so hard to believe?" the commander asked.

The voice boomed again, this time full of agitation. "I am giving you a minute. I want my quarry, or I will destroy everything!"

Though he was afraid, Yasu rose and straightened his back, wearing a bold expression. "I have to go."

"What if …"

"We'll come with you," Alex said, rising too.

"Sit down," the commander said. "It's much too dangerous. We have our watch towers with orders to shoot him down if he tries anything he shouldn't. And the force field should hold."

"And what's the guarantee that your towers will work against him? What if his weapons damage the force field you've set up?" Yasu's voice wobbled a little, and he hated it. "What if he's stronger? Let's employ diplomacy first."

The commander shifted with discomfort. "You'll go with some guards," he said. He pointed to the officer who brought them there. "Officer Alexeev, you'll accompany them. The watchtowers are also on standby. Let's hope it doesn't come to that."

The cadets left the room with two guards and met a retinue of six more outside the door. They shuffled towards the elevator and rode it down to the ground floor. The hallways were deserted, red lights blinking at intervals. They guessed the other cadets had now been ushered to a safer location.

It was cold outside. The wind howled like a banshee, buffeting the metal surfaces of the buildings and whipping through the trees. The sky was dark, but they could see the clear outline of their enemy's black, saucer-shaped ship, a perimeter of white lights glowing on its body.

Once in the courtyard, Officer Alexeev grabbed a microphone from one guard. He tapped on it and heard the sound echo around the Academy's public address system.

"Foreigner, we don't want a fight. We've brought Yasu Garcia as you've requested. However …"

"Splendid!" the voice replied.

A hatch opened at the bottom of the ship, and brilliant light streamed out. Light typically filtered through force fields as though it was encountering a translucent surface. This light fell to the Academy's courtyard as though there was nothing there. Whatever was in the light or the energy from the ship, it cut through the Academy's defenses with terrifying ease.

They watched, awed, as a caped figure dressed in all black descended downwards. He landed softly on the courtyard's concrete and brushed jet-black hair away from his face, a smirk dancing on his lips. He looked exactly like Yasu, but his presence had a different effect, a chilling one.

"Why are you so afraid?" he said, tilting his head. "I don't mean any harm. I merely want to talk."

There were about fifteen paces between them. Yet, the young man struck fear into them.

Yasu pushed between the guards and stepped forward, ignoring his friend's cries of protest. "What do you want to talk about?"

A ghostly smile touched the alternate's lips.

"You and your friends, of course. You meddle. A lot!"

Ten's smirk faltered, just for a moment. "Do you think I wanted this?" he asked, his voice low but filled with an undercurrent of rage. "Do you think I asked to shoulder the weight of an entire universe? To play god while my people begged for salvation? You broke what little balance I had left, and now I'm here to fix it."

Yasu wanted to sound bolder, to have a stronger counter, but no words formed. He could sense the soldiers stepping around him to pull him back.

And then he couldn't sense them again. They were gone. The Academy's courtyard was gone. His alternate. The black saucer ship and its blinking lights. Gone.

He stood in the hall from their last mission. The place where they met the shrouded guardian in their last mission. The floor was white, and the ceiling, almost too far above his head to be seen, was gray.

## CHAPTER 4

MOMENTARILY, Yasu Garcia drank in the space, stunned. He imagined he might have slipped into another memory or a trance. But why now? He had had nothing to say to his alternate, but leaving this way made him seem weak.

"Yasu!"

It was Nia's voice, and it came from behind him. The others were with her, too.

"Guys!" he called, mildly out of breath. "Is this real? Are you real?"

They came towards him, their expressions concerned. "What do you mean?" Jaxon asked. "Of course we're real. And disgruntled."

"Speak for yourself," Alex said.

"I could speak for Yasu, too. This isn't how he thought his day would go. Neither did Nia."

"I don't know why you're always so negative!"

Jaxon lifted his hands in mock surrender. "I am not."

Yasu shook his head. "Let's calm down. How real is this?"

"Would you like us to punch you?" Jaxon asked.

Nia let out an exasperated sigh. "It's a pinch, Jaxon. Nobody asks for a punch to check the validity of their reality."

"Well, maybe he wanted a …"

"But if this is real, why are we here?" Yasu looked worried. "How are we here?"

Alex ran a hand through his hair. "Remember, before my test, the being said there was still work to be done. Maybe this is what she was referring to. Maybe they'd explain."

"'They' being the beings in this realm, yes?" Nia asked.

"Yes."

"But if we're here, what's happening back home?" Jaxon asked.

They lapsed into silence, wondering. They didn't have long to talk with the evil Yasu. Their interaction had been so sparse they couldn't judge if their departure would send him into an Academy-destroying rage. He had sounded unhinged, but only mildly.

"How long are we going to remain here, though?" Nia asked.

"Not long."

A stranger stood in their midst, dressed in the same white robes as them. The stranger had no face. Where their face should have been, there was only an unnerving smoothness. The stranger's hair was a dazzling mix of brown, gray, red, sliver, and blonde that fell in curly locks down to their feet.

Terrified, the cadets shifted away from the being. They noted the aura spilling from it, believing it bore similarities to that of the being from the test, but were unsure.

"I am Peace," it said, tilting its head. Slowly, its appearance changed. First, it became Nia's father, bald with a thick black beard. Then it became Alex's mother, Uncle Koike, and Jaxon's elementary school science teacher. "I was your guide through the test. Now, I'm your guide through this mission."

"I thought we had the test because we weren't supposed to be here," Alex asked. "Now we have another test?"

"This time, you're here by our choosing. That's not the same."

"Why are we here?" Yasu asked.

"Because of Ten."

"Ten?"

"Yes. The Yasu Garcia version from Earth-3446."

Jaxon thought his head might explode. "Earth-3446? How many Earths are there?"

"They are innumerable. Reality is infinite."

That was important, but not so important to Yasu. Right now, all he cared about was – "Why Ten?"

The being swung its blank face at him. "It's the start of his code number. It's the name he went by in his formative years."

Yasu didn't understand.

Perhaps if the being had a face, its features would have softened. "You will understand fully soon."

It stepped into their midst, brushed them aside, and formed a black circle on the white floor. Stepping away from the circle, the cadets noticed colors forming on it as though it were a monitor or television screen.

They saw images of a war, explosions, destruction, and frightened people. "Not all universes are like yours: peaceful. Some live beneath the shadow of the Empire, bearing the heavy burden of a frightful dictatorship."

They watched as the scenes changed to a peaceful neighborhood. Yasu recognized the white walls, red roofs, and well-manicured gardens. "I grew up there!" he said, mildly excited. He hadn't visited there in ages. He missed everyone back home.

"Ten grew up there, too. That is until his home was destroyed."

Missiles landed in the neighborhood, turning everything into burning scraps. Some people sat amid the devastation, mourning their losses. A version of Yasu, Ten, several years younger, walked with one bare foot and a torn sandal on the other foot. A soldier brandishing a sleek black gun took him in.

The scene changed to a slightly older Ten, now dressed in a gray and navy blue uniform, fighting with a creature covered in fur.

"Ten fought many years for the Resistance," the being said softly.

"The Resistance?" Alex asked.

"Yes. Against the Empire's forces. They wanted peace in their region and valiantly battled daily to reduce their influence."

The scene kept changing; showing Ten in various battle positions. He flew ships, worked with knives, and was adept at using guns.

"Did it work?" Nia asked.

The being looked at her. "What?"

"Sometimes, some of these fights are pointless. Did their efforts work?"

Tilting its head, the being said, "It depends on your perspective. You could say accepting the Empire's rule was the best way to approach the situation. After all, though some people will die, still many others will live in relative prosperity. Regardless, people will always fight for freedom. It is their nature."

When the scene changed next, a nebula similar to the kind the cadets encountered in their last mission floated in the vastness of space. Ten's spacecraft hovered at its perimeter, and he flew in. His ship navigated between flying rubble, dust, and clumps of charged particles. At the core, there was a dark hole, which seemed to suck in all the energy in the vicinity.

Ten's face was resolute. He adjusted his settings and flew the craft in.

Alex swallowed. "Is that …"

"A portal to our realm, yes."

"So, Ten was here?" Nia asked.

"For us, it seems like mere minutes ago. But it has been some time. He was here."

The images at this point were distorted, fluctuating stills that showed Ten entering one strange hall after another, wading through water, floating through clouds, and slipping through a bed of shiny balls. He emerged in the hall where they stood with an orb.

"What just happened?" Alex asked.

The being didn't speak for a time.

Ten fiddled with the orb, and his brow furrowed as his form flickered and scrambled. Eventually, it appeared he was satisfied with what he had created. Energy burst forth from the orb, covering the hall in blinding light.

"Order made a deal with him," the being said.

Jaxon scratched his head. "What?"

"We don't know the details. But it wanted freedom. And in exchange, it split some of our power with Ten."

"Freedom?" Alex asked. "Freedom from what?"

"From here. This place is our home. But this place is also our prison. We watched the world form at the dawn of reality, but we can never leave here. We don't have the power to."

Nia attempted to piece it together. "So, right now, Order is on the loose?" If Order was running around the multiverse, released from its previous shackles, why was the world still so messed up?

"No. Ten didn't release it. Ten took the power and manipulated it himself. He returned to his home and made a universe on his own terms."

The circle showed energy rippling across space, cutting through their realm and spilling into other realms.

"The thing is, Ten was smarter than any other who has ever found our home."

"How?" Though it was unreasonable, Yasu felt jealous. Not only was there a rogue version of himself on the loose, but this version was also so much better than many other intelligent sapient life-forms to waltz into the realm of gods. That made him think of himself as a piece of gum stuck beneath someone's shoe.

The being shook its head. "Contrary to what the Guardian told you the last time, we are not creators. We don't claim to know everything. Occasionally, something spills out of the randomness of life and outsmarts us. Ten was one such phenomenon."

The scene changed to Ten returning to his world, power lying latent in the orb he grasped. His face was set with a wry expression.

Alex knelt beside the circle and watched Ten's progress back home. His world slowly bloomed, the fires going out and the chaos retreating to the edges, until the vision faded, and the circle went back to black. "But how does this relate to us? What did we destroy? Ten said we destroyed something."

The being sounded like it was smiling. "You did." It made an upward gesture with its long-fingered hands, and the circle on the ground split into six smaller circles. The smaller circles floated upwards, miniature 3-D images forming on them.

"Isn't that the organic computer?" Jaxon remarked, recognizing the portal Safira, a cadet from one of their missions, helped them to destroy.

"And the Quantum Key," Nia said, pointing at the Quantum Key from their first mission floating on an upraised surface.

There were other things in the other floating black circles. A jagged, glittering knife. Something that looked like a crystalized eyeball. A mountain covered in purple plants.

"There were many other effects of Ten's manipulation. His effects cut across time, as he didn't know how to use the power adequately. What he did transplanted some of the power into artifacts across various universes. Some effects we have yet to see. However, these are some effects from universes close to yours."

Alex looked at the being's faceless face. "So…"

"When you destroyed the Quantum Key and the rogue supercomputer, you caused a destabilization in his world. The artifacts, though scattered across the multiverse, were bound by the same threads of power Ten had woven into his world. Destroying one was like pulling a thread from a tapestry—it weakened the whole. Ten's universe, already fragile, had begun to fray at the edges."

Jaxon shut his open mouth. "What?"

"He might have split the power, but all the powers were still connected. All the artifacts are still linked back to what he had in his universe."

"And that's why he's after us?" Alex found the whole thing incredulous.

The being nodded. "Yes. That is why."

"But what does he want to do to us?" Nia asked. "There's no way we could've known our actions would affect his world. Besides, if he left your power alone as he was supposed to, none of this would be happening."

"Regardless of what was supposed to be and not supposed to be, we are here now. Your actions have tied your destiny with Ten's."

Jaxon could see another dangerous mission before him and didn't like it. "I hate how you speak in riddles. What do you want? Why are we here?"

The being stood taller. Its voice changed then, layering with several other voices, as though the other beings in the realm were speaking through its nonexistent lips. "We want you to help us defeat Ten."

Jaxon laughed, doubling over and then squatting when the sound refused to stop leaving him. "How?"

"We will help you. We will give you guidance."

Alex patted Jaxon's shoulder to calm him. "But why us? You could have chosen anyone else?"

"Everyone has a role to play. Your actions sent ripples across time and space, most of which you couldn't properly grasp even if you were given the opportunity to confront them. This is your chance to right your wrongs."

"So, what you're telling us is our actions led to other instabilities beyond Ten's universe?"

Jaxon barked out bitter laughter. "What if we don't want to? What if we decide to take the power for ourselves?"

The being turned its head to him, and though no face lay there, Jaxon could have sworn it gave him a pitying look. "You passed the test. You won't take the power."

# CHAPTER 5

WITHOUT WAITING to get confirmation from them, the being detailed the plans for their departure. Its voice returned to normal, a single strain of calm sound.

"Ten used a fragment of the orb to journey to your world. But he keeps most of the orb in his universe. The fragment wasn't just a tool—it was a piece of the realm's very fabric, imbued with the ability to manipulate time and space. But with power came chaos, and Ten's inability to fully control it had left fractures across his universe. Every action rippled outward, threatening to unravel not just his world but others connected to it."

"So, you just want us to go there and find it?" Alex asked, following the being as it walked away from them.

"Yes. And return with it. We'll take it from there."

Jaxon lay on the white floor, groaning in irritation at the turn of events. Nia knelt beside him to pat his shoulder and calm him down. "It'll be fine," she said, though her chest felt tight.

Yasu didn't know how to feel about any of it. "But do you at least know where in his universe it is?" he asked.

"We can't access his universe. That's the problem. We can see everywhere else but not his universe. It's like a black hole in our consciousness."

"That makes everything a lot better," Jaxon cried.

The being ignored him. It waved, and a golden ship, shaped like a saucer, like Ten's, appeared before them.

Jaxon sat up, staring at the shiny surface. Next to him, Nia let out a soft gasp.

"It's gorgeous," she breathed.

"Yes," Jaxon said in agreement. "But gold? Won't that make us obvious?"

Yasu nodded. A plan was forming in his head. "If we were going to search his planet, we would want a ship that looked more similar to his. Black."

The being nodded, as if impressed. "You'd need that. You'd need to think like him if you want to capture him." It waved, and the ship turned black. The cadets stared at it in awe.

Alex looked at him with a furrowed brow. "What else are you thinking, Yasu?"

"I'm thinking that I should impersonate him," he said. "We go to his universe and I act like I'm him."

Nia figured it might be a good plan. "But how well will that work? We can't access their communication channels. How will they know it's their Ten? Besides, we don't know what mission he said he was leaving home for. We can't just show up with holes in our memory."

"Or maybe we won't have to," Yasu said. "Maybe with some power from you ..." he cast a pointed glance at the being, "I can access his memories and see what we need to be successful."

The being spun on its heels, its curly mane swishing. "Is that so?"

Yasu could sense his nerve slipping away, but he forced himself to say, "Yes. That is so."

The being watched him, and the others watched the two of them. To further redeem himself, Yasu added, "And you can kill me if I try anything funny."

Nodding, the being conjured up a small hovering orb of light. It walked over to Yasu and thrust it into his skull without hesitation. Yasu let out a pained grunt, his head tilting upwards, his eyes, mouth, and ears emitting light.

Nia's heart beat fast, worried about her friend. "Now what?"

"We wait. And see."

Alex was consumed by many questions about this realm and its others. "Who are the others?" he blurted, while Nia asked, "Can you tell what's going on back home?"

The being turned its face to Alex but answered Nia. "Yes. Nothing."

Alex swallowed. "What does that mean?"

"Time doesn't flow the same way here than it does over there. Here, we can create time bubbles. In all our interactions, not a moment has passed since you left. Ten is frozen in the middle of his laughter. The guards are watching with rapt attention. When you're ready to move, everything will reset."

That sounded unsavory. Nia was disturbed afresh. "Won't he just come after us first?"

"Exactly," Jaxon said. "And imagine trying to run from someone with godly powers who commands an entire universe!"

"Sapiens are so stressful," the being said. "The ship is cloaked. When Ten discovers you're gone, he'll come here first. He won't notice you've entered his world. And while he's here, we'll hold him as long as we can until you return."

"And if you can't?" Jaxon asked.

"You underestimate us."

Jaxon raised his hands in mock surrender. "No, I don't. You underestimate yourselves. You said you can't leave here. You said a human came here and outsmarted you. But suddenly, I underestimate you. Right."

"Uphold your end of the bargain. We'll uphold ours."

Alex was more concerned about Yasu now. Blood dripped from his orifices, staining the white of his robes. "Will he be …"

The orb floated out of his forehead, and Yasu collapsed, gasping. His friends rushed to his side, Nia wiping his bloody cheeks with the hem of her robe.

His breathing steadied eventually, and in a low voice, he said, "I've got it now."

Alex and Jaxon sat at the controls in the ship, marveling at the bizarre technology contained within. Jaxon had some time to familiarize himself with it, and soon, he had gotten the hang of it enough to attempt flight.

Yasu sat at the navigation console with Nia, still wiping blood from his nose. He had acquired a fake scar, a simple gift from Peace. It ran along one cheek, similar to Ten's.

On the ship, they had a small army of robot soldiers burdened with various tasks for the ship's well-being. They moved about the ship, attuned to Yasu's commands.

"Do you feel okay?" Nia asked.

Yasu didn't know. "I feel responsible. Does that make sense?"

As she wasn't in his shoes, Nia couldn't tell if he felt the same sense of responsibility as she did. "I don't know. I feel slightly responsible as well. I want to make things better. I just wish we had more time."

"We don't though." Yasu's voice was almost mournful. "We barely have any time. If we don't move quickly and decisively, we could lose everything. Seeing his memories made me realize that …"

Nia waited for him to complete the thought. But he merely sat there, staring into space. "Realize what?"

"That I might be mildly incompetent." He looked at her, at her wide eyes. "Is everyone ready?" he called.

"Yes, Lord Ten," Jaxon said.

Yasu shook his head, zooming out on the console. "It's just Ten."

"What?"

"It's not Lord Ten. His people call him Ten."

Jaxon looked like he didn't understand, but he merely nodded and went with it. "What comes next?"

"We're ready!" Alex called. The being stood in front of the ship, watching them. It nodded at Alex's signal.

"Farewell, Team Alpha. May you succeed."

The being gestured above, and a portal opened above the ship. They craned their necks to see it and saw only blackness.

"You'll find Ten's world if you pass through there," it said. "Travel safe."

Alex adjusted the controls. "All right, team. Let's do this!"

# CHAPTER 6

THERE WAS NOT much to note on the other side. Ten's universe could have been theirs. The sky was populated with the right number of stars, and their consoles calibrated with the available information.

"Where to?" Jaxon asked, staring at his console. The ship's operation was unlike anything he had enjoyed working with. It was like cutting through butter with a heated knife.

Yasu studied his console. "We're currently somewhere close to the Orion Sector. We have to head to the Gaia Sector. His hideout is on planet Amateru, on the inner ring of the Gaia Sector. And we have to hurry. How quickly can we make it?"

"It depends on this ship. How far are the light jumps? And how many can it do at a time?" Jaxon worked through some calculations with Alex.

Nia and Yasu worked on some, too.

"Are you all right?" Nia asked, watching another drop of blood fall from his nose.

"I'm fine," he said, swiping a hand across his face and leaving a faint bloody streak. "A little tired."

"We can handle it. You should sleep."

"No, I can't."

"Listen to Nia," Alex said, rising with his notepad. "You've done a lot so far. You should rest. Or you'll collapse."

Now that they had spoken of sleep, Yasu felt the full weight of his tiredness descend. His eyes drooped. "What about the robots?"

Alex waved at Jaxon. "He has them under control. They take some instruction from you, but Jaxon can bypass that to give you a break."

Jaxon saluted him. "Yes, Ten. It's all under control. Sleep."

Yasu found his chambers and clambered onto the bed without changing out of his black robes. His eyes shut, and he drifted away as soon as his head hit the pillow.

For a time, his consciousness drifted in nothingness. Then he found himself in his neighborhood, with the white houses and red roofs. He walked down the street, naming the members of the houses he saw there. At the end of the street, he found himself as a child.

This boyish version of himself held his gaze for what seemed like hours. Eventually, he said, "This is where it started. This was the diversion point."

"What does that mean?" Yasu asked, stepping closer.

"You ask so many questions. But you don't have so many answers."

Yasu looked around. The neighborhood was empty, as though everyone had moved out and away.

"He went to buy eggs that day. And he returned, and they were dead." The kid kept staring. "The power can manipulate the past, present, and future."

Yasu could see where this was going, but he didn't like it. "You want me to…"

The child smiled. "I don't want you to. You want you to. Choose wisely. This option can reset everything. Other options …"

The child turned and walked away. Yasu kept calling for him, but the distance between them kept increasing, more houses sprouting up along the side of the street.

The dream turned to other unintelligible things. He chased a squid at the beach. He ran after a dog in the park. He played with his friends at school.

He woke up to Jaxon shaking his arm, holding a bowl of soup in his hand. "You need to eat, too."

Yasu sat up, leaning his weary head against the wall behind the bed.

"How's everyone?" he asked, shutting his eyes.

"Good. Worried about you. How are you?"

"Better," he lied. He wasn't sure if his current state could be deemed better. It was as though a storm waged a war in his head. "How long do we have before we arrive?"

"About two days and a few hours."

"Can I speak to the others?"

Jaxon's eyebrow cocked. "Are you strong enough?"

"Strong enough."

Yasu stumbled out of the room and went to the control room with Jaxon. The others looked happy to see him.

"Did you eat the soup?" Nia asked, clutching her tablet to her chest.

"I'll eat it later. I just …" Yasu breathed heavily. "I had a strange dream."

"Eat your soup first!" Nia pointed at Jaxon. "Give him the bowl."

Jaxon was upset at her tone. "I tried. He didn't want it."

"Yasu, sit and eat. Now!"

Yasu wanted to protest, but he was much too weak. His vision blurred at the edges, and his knees got weaker. He found a seat and lowered himself onto it. Jaxon brought the bowl to him, and he tucked in. The soup had little flavor, but he figured if that were all he had to eat, he would manage it.

When he was done, Nia took the empty bowl from him, patting his head as she walked away.

"So," Alex began, "what's so important you had to rush here like you saw a spirit?"

Keeping his eyes shut, Yasu relayed his dream to them, laying down the facts as plainly as possible. "I think that kid was a part of my subconscious mind. And I think a part of me just wants to kill this version of me, to put an end to everything."

Alex sat quietly, stroking his chin. This revelation added a new twist to the mission, but he wasn't sure he liked it much. Besides, Yasu wasn't usually the one suggesting detours of this nature. This seemed like a lot coming from him. "If we get rid of him, we could reset everything. But I don't think that's what the gods want us to do."

Next to Jaxon, Nia nodded, the empty soup bowl still in her hand. "I agree. Our instructions were to bring Ten to that realm, and they'd handle him. We can't be making our own decisions and trying to handle him by ourselves. What if we mess something else up again?"

Alex nodded. "Exactly. And then we'd have to deal with new consequences. I say we stick to the original plan."

Yasu turned to Jaxon, expecting an answer from him. "You?"

"Sorry, Ten."

"Please don't call me Ten."

"Sorry, Yasu. I don't think your dream is the ultimate wisdom. I agree with the others."

Yasu's eyes drifted shut again. "I'm like him," he said softly. he words hung in the air, heavier than he intended. He saw his friends exchange worried glances, but Yasu's thoughts were elsewhere. How many small decisions had shaped Ten into the warlord he'd become? Could those same choices turn him down a similar path? He clenched his fists, trying to dispel the chilling thought. He had to believe he was different—didn't he?

Not liking the sound of that, Alex strode over to him, tapping his shoulder. "What does that mean?"

"Why did I think of something like that? None of you thought of it, but I did. He seized the power for himself because he thought he could fix the world. He might've created a kind of utopia, but he didn't do it well enough. Just a couple of actions from us and the balance he created was ruined. I was about to do something similar. Why would I think such a reset would be wise?"

"I don't think you're like him at all," Alex said, a little more forcefully than he intended. "You're willing to ask for help. You're willing to gain other opinions."

"I agree." Nia's voice was shrill, but she got the words out somehow. "We're all struggling to understand the full dynamics of this mission. The good thing is you didn't think all of this by yourself and keep it to your chest."

Alex clamped a hand on his shoulder. "You're not a bad person, Yasu."

Yasu didn't say the other thoughts he had about himself. He merely shut his eyes, allowing the rest of their words to wash over him. Though his fear of the last portion of the mission remained, he was a little more resolute now. With his friends, he could succeed.

# CHAPTER 7

THE CADETS WATCHED as the planet Amateru got closer.

"Now, we land, follow Yasu or Ten, grab the orb, and leave," Alex said.

Nia chuckled, recalling all the other plans they had had for travel over the years and how none of them had completely worked out. "It might not work out that way."

"Or it might. For once, let's be positive."

Yasu needed Alex's positivity. Perhaps it was the one portion of Alex's personality he loved the most. All he felt at the moment was dread.

A message reached their ship from the planet's security squad. It was a scrambled, garbled mix of numbers and figures. The cadets gazed at the screen, trying to decipher it.

"Is this familiar to you?" Alex asked Yasu.

Though he wanted to immediately dismiss it as utter gibberish, something about it looked familiar. He grabbed a notepad off one surface and scribbled it out. "I've got it," he mumbled.

"You have?" None of it made any sense to Jaxon.

"It's something my uncle used to play with me as a kid. It's just… I can't explain it." He sat before the console, his fingers flying over the keyboard, typing a response.

From behind his shoulders, the others watched in confusion.

"That makes no sense." Jaxon shook his head, deciding this was something he would never piece together.

Something about this new turn of events brought joy to Yasu. He chuckled, looking at the others. "It probably looks that way. But to me, it makes a lot of sense." He hit send.

A message returned. "Welcome back, Ten."

The cadets let out cheers. One portion of their infiltration was over. But now that they were in...

"I don't mean to be the storm cloud over our sunny day, but how do we land?" Jaxon asked amid the laughter.

His words were a storm cloud, though. Everyone quieted and stared at one another.

"I'm sure we can figure it out," Yasu said, searching his memory for anything related to that.

"But we have to land soon. In minutes. Where do we land?"

Jaxon's insistence mildly irritated Yasu. "We'll figure it out!"

Jaxon lifted his hands. "All right then. Go ahead."

While forcing his breathing to slow down, Yasu sat next to Alex at the control desk. He opened the navigator on the panel and took in the planet's layout. "It's here," he said, pointing at a portion of the planet. "That's where we land."

"How do you know?" Jaxon asked behind him.

"I just do. It stands out in the memories I recovered."

The spaceport highlighted on the navigator was massive, covering an area much larger than their academy. Alex zoomed in to look at the buildings, control towers, and landing strips. "But where is the orb itself?"

"It's not far. Ten built the port so that he has easy access to the orb. It's in a secret lair underground."

Satisfied with Yasu's explanation, Alex clapped, ready to begin the landing sequence. "Let's do this. Strap in everyone."

The cadets braced themselves for the landing, watching the spaceport get closer and closer. The buildings were varied and unique, with gleaming steel alloys and flexible transparent composites. Lights sparkled from various lamps, adequately illuminating all the surfaces. Even the landing strip was lit with brilliant white lights, casting a cold glow on their ship.

They emerged from the ship through a descending staircase. Outside, a small audience of multiple species waited, bearing flowers, food, and high-pitched tinkling music.

One man in front, a creature Yasu recognized from the Orion Sector, bowed low. His skin was a scaly textured deep blue that was almost black, and he wore a white uniform with a purple cape. "Welcome home, Ten."

Yasu straightened his spine and strolled towards the man. As he walked, he tried to recall his name, but couldn't. Awkwardly, he arrived by the man's side, bowed back, and said, "Thank you!"

The man gave him a curious glance, surprised by his behavior, but he said nothing else. He watched the other cadets dressed in white, capeless uniforms and passive expressions trailing behind him.

"You've returned with new friends, I see," he said, his voice grating. "How was your trip, Ten?"

Without slowing his pace, Yasu waved the man towards him and gave a casual reply. "Unexpected. This journey was unlike any other. And yes. I did return with new friends. These are the friends of my alternate."

Boots clicking, the man hurried over to walk beside him. The music kept tinkling around them, and they proceeded to the main building with an entourage of welcoming officials.

"We've prepared a feast for your return, Ten," the man said, and hearing the pleading tone in his voice, Yasu immediately latched onto it.

"Do you think me displeased?" he asked, halting and spinning to look at the man. The name returned then, Kaida.

A lump went down in Kaida's throat. "Yes, Ten. You seem… different. Cold. Was the mission unsuccessful? You did destroy the boy's planet, did you not?"

Yasu waved at the cadets with an assumed dismissive air. "Why, yes. It did. But I worry."

Kaida forced a smile. "What about, Ten?"

"The orb."

Kaida's brow furrowed. "Oh, dear."

"In my wrath, I fear I may have overdone it. It seems I damaged something."

"Oh, my."

Yasu lowered his eyes, hating how pretentious he sounded. "I must check if what I have here is all right."

"Certainly, Ten! Right this way!"

Kaida picked up the pace and took the lead. He passed greetings to the security detail at the gate, who also bowed low to Yasu and stared curiously at his friends. As they entered the building, their footsteps echoing around, Kaida asked, "Will you bring his friends with you, Ten?"

"Certainly! They must see what else I plan to do before I get rid of them."

Their journey continued down a sterile white hallway lit by fluorescent tubes lining the ceilings. Several members of their entourage broke off from the group, entering different rooms on the side. The cadets drank in the place's organization, marveling at the diversity of the members of the building and their cohesion as they went about their duties.

Alex wanted to work here. This port, with its bustling activities and the diverse cultures colliding there, seemed to be an exciting environment.

"Now that the journey is over, Ten," Kaida resumed as they rounded a bend and only two extra guards remained in their retinue, "would you be able to solve the anomalies?"

Yasu remained silent, and they kept walking.

"Ten?"

"That, I do not know. It seems I've finally found something capable of overthrowing me."

"Surely not, Ten!" Kaida cried. "I am certain, as the wise and peaceful leader you are, you shall find the way out of this. Soon."

Though Yasu would have liked to know what anomalies their actions caused in this universe, he could merely nod. It was something he could find out in the realm of the gods. And only after their mission had ended. After all, the gods previously had no access to this world because of Ten's protection.

Presently, they arrived at a secret door. Kaida pressed his thumb onto the biometric scanner at the door, and the door slid open with a hiss.

"Let's go in," Yasu said, waving everyone in.

They entered and proceeded to another door at the other end. Kaida pressed his thumb against the scanner there again. Mist poured out from behind the door when it opened. When the mist cleared, a small chamber was revealed.

Yasu looked at it with mild confusion.

"Ten, is everything okay? Go in."

Yasu glanced at him, his brow furrowing. "I was merely recalling some parts of my journey. Let's go in."

They filed into the chamber, and Yasu recognized it as an elevator. He also recalled something crucial. His thumbprint was the only one that could get it to start. He stepped to the biometric scanner, slipped off his glove, and pressed his thumb against the scanner. The door hissed shut, and the elevator descended.

They rode it in silence, and at the bottom, it opened again, showing a long, dark hallway. Yasu walked into the hallway ahead of the others, clapped, and called, "Raito!" The lights flashed on, filling the hallway with a yellowish-orange glow.

For some odd reason, he had this urgency to move faster. He walked ahead, speeding towards the chamber at the end. It seemed like he could hear the questions in his friends' footsteps.

"Why are you in a hurry, Ten?" Kaida asked, almost out of breath.

Yasu ignored the question and ran the last few steps towards the chamber. He pressed his thumb into the biometric scanner and lowered his eyes for a retinal scan. The heavy locks on the door undid themselves, turning with loud whines and clicks. Then silence.

The door opened, a soft, cold mist pouring out from within. Dull red lights illuminated the stark settings, showing the orb in its protective case at the center. Energy hummed around the chamber, indicating the presence of a higher power.

Yasu walked in, stepping with care, as though scared the ground might be laced with booby traps. He touched the protective case with reverence, full of respect for his alternate.

Behind him, his friends filed in, their eyes darting around the dark room. The high ceiling was lined with blinking sensors, and on the ground, a cold mist swirled. They soaked in the energy in the room, thinking of all the possibilities an artifact of this magnitude could open to them.

Full of reverence, Yasu pressed his palms against the scanners at the sides of the protective case. The case slid upwards and away without a sound. Yasu touched the orb, shutting his eyes to steel himself against the energy surge that slammed into him.

A loud boom erupted outside the chamber behind them.

Everyone except Yasu, who was still reeling under the power's influence, turned to look.

Ten stood there, his upper half bare and an ethereal glow surrounding him. His laughter traveled down the hall, sounding like something out of a nightmare, sending a smattering of goosebumps along their skin.

Confused, Kaida stood there, swinging his head from the cadets in the chamber to the Ten heading down the hall.

"Yasu!" Alex shouted. "Now is a good time to snap out of whatever it is you're in at the moment."

The words reached Yasu through a thick fog. He understood the urgency but couldn't find it in him to hurry. If he had to face this version of himself in a fight, he would do so. And he would win.

He split a portion of the power, wrapped it around his friends like wily tethers, and flung them through a portal of his making. He pictured the place they had emerged from, the white halls and the white robes, and shot them right into the arms of Peace.

Comfortable now, he turned and faced Ten.

His voice surprised him as it came out. "Let's go play somewhere nobody can stop us."

## CHAPTER 8

THE POWER WAS STRANGE. Yasu should have been terrified, but he had a sudden sense of calm. This version of him was full of energy, bubbling with a celestial ability he shouldn't have access to, but Yasu wasn't frightened. The energy filled every cell in his body, making him hyper-aware of his surroundings. He could see the particles floating in the air with clarity, hear the equipment's distant workings above ground, and sense sweat emerging from a pore on Kaida's dark skin.

Mostly, he was full of an almost unnatural confidence. He could win this. He needed his friends to work with the gods to grab hold of Ten at the right time, and he trusted they would not disappoint him.

Ten stalked down the hallway to him. The guards and Kaida pushed themselves against the wall to escape the heat rolling off his body.

When Ten was close enough to the door, Yasu opened a portal on the ground and jumped in. Ten came along.

Alex, Nia, and Jaxon crashed onto the cold, white ground of the grand celestial hall. They were back in the flowing robes, their minds breaking over the knowledge of what they just witnessed. If Ten had shown up in their universe, then…?

"He escaped," a voice said. It was Peace. It looked the same, calm and unbothered by the current change in events.

"How did that happen?" Alex asked, throwing his hands up in the air.

"He outsmarted us."

Jaxon barked out harsh laughter. "Very nice cop-out. He outsmarted you. What if we died? We were vulnerable out there!"

Alex walked towards the being, all caution thrown away. "We met our own end of the bargain. You were supposed to ensure we stayed safe. And you didn't."

The being's chest heaved as though it was taking a deep breath. "But you're safe now, aren't you?"

With a peal of nervous and anguished laughter, Jaxon gestured in front of him. "That's why we can see Yasu right here. Standing here. Looking at us. Very safe."

"All right, guys." Nia's voice trembled, but she powered through it. "Let's calm down."

"Calm down? This situation is dire!"

"This time, I'm with Jaxon. I can't see a way out of this."

Nia rubbed her nose and bounced her weight between her two feet. "Well, I can't either. But let's work with Peace to see…"

Nia stepped forward, her voice steady despite the tremble in her hands. "We need a plan," she said firmly, her gaze locking with each of her friends. "Panicking won't help Yasu. He trusted us to finish this mission, and I refuse to let him down." Her conviction cut through the rising tension, grounding them all in the moment.

Jaxon waved her words away with a vigorous shake of his head. "No more! Look how they fumbled their end of the bargain. We trusted them!"

"And maybe a mistake happened." Nia's heart was hammering fast.

Alex cocked an eyebrow. "What mistake and how? We didn't

make any mistakes. Even Yasu didn't make any mistakes. Why did they?"

With her hands flattened against her ears, Nia screamed, "Let's. All. Calm. Down. Now."

The other two looked at her with identical expressions of concern. Peace tipped its head her way as though impressed by the shrillness of her scream.

"Yasu is trying his best to stop what's happening. Let's not mess up on our end. We have to find out what we can do on this side." Nia looked at Peace, tears brimming in her eyes. "What can we do to help?"

Again, the being's chest moved like it was taking a deep breath. "There isn't a lot. We have to focus or we may never get another chance."

---

Yasu rifled through the memories of a million alternates, even zipping into universes further along on the timeline. There, he was older and more sure of himself. He wrapped his energy around Ten, pulling him along. He could hear Ten's distress, his irritation at being thwarted by one he thought less capable than himself.

A universe stood out to Yasu. It was further back in the past, with a version of Yasu walking around in his shorts around the neighborhood. Yasu latched onto it and pulled Ten with him.

---

Unable to stay still, Jaxon paced as Peace explained what they had to do. He couldn't see the tethers Yasu had attached to them, but Peace said all the celestials could.

"So, it leads to Yasu?"

The being nodded. "And when Ten's guard is down, he'll give the signal."

Nia searched her body for the tethers but found nothing. "That sounds like a plan."

"Who will pull him in, though?" Alex asked, his arms folded across his chest.

Peace's voice turned layered again, all the other gods speaking at once. "We will."

Yasu and Ten crashed out of the vortex of memories Yasu had created and fell into a room. Yasu landed easily on the wooden floor, and Ten fell on the bed and rose, disgruntled. His eyes blazed, blood dripping from them.

"You," Ten growled.

"Me," Yasu said, sounding almost bored. He didn't know why he had ever feared Ten. Here and now, his alternate looked almost pitiful, red-eyed and exhausted by the strain.

"Why? Why couldn't you just stay still?" Ten almost looked like he was pleading, however, the fire burning in his eyes told another story.

"Stay still?"

"I wasn't hurting anyone. I only wanted my people to be safe."

"You took power that didn't belong to you."

Ten's laughter was cold and derisive. "As if you wouldn't have."

"If I had, I would also be hunted down and face the consequences." Now Yasu's confidence was fading. Holding so much energy within himself was sapping his own strength. He knew if he didn't finish this soon, he would lose consciousness. And lose everything.

Ten continued laughing, tipping his head backward. "You still have time. Surrender my power back to me and I will let you off with a mild punishment."

Yasu cocked an eyebrow. "Your power?"

Ten lunged for him, heat pouring out of his pores. Anticipating his attack, Yasu stepped away, allowing him to run into the wall. But just before he could crash, Yasu threw up an energy cushion, changing the impact to a dull thud. Strong enough to have a debilitating impact on Ten, but muted enough to reduce the sound.

Yasu held his breath, waiting.

Uncle Koike opened the room door, holding a baseball bat tight in his grip. He stood at the door, his expression confused. "Who are you?" he asked in Japanese.

The moment had arrived. Yasu was right. Seeing Uncle Koike was enough. Ten stood momentarily, his guard lowered, his eyes misting with tears. Yasu latched onto him then, twisting his essence into Ten's mind and crawling under his skin to lay him bare.

He opened another portal on the floor, grabbed Ten's hand, and fell through it into blackness.

———————⌄———————

"What will the signal be?" Jaxon asked, looking at the dark circle of murkiness on the hall's floor. Surrounding them were unfamiliar energies. Jaxon figured it was the other celestials, coming to sit around, waiting for the time they'd be needed.

"No idea," Nia said. "But I'm sure they'll know."

"But is Yasu okay? I think that's more important." Alex was focused on the makeshift circle screen, but he couldn't see Yasu or tell if he was okay.

"It's time," Peace said.

The cadets felt a tug around their cores. Their eyes rolled back in their heads and they levitated above the white floor.

———————⌄———————

Ten's head was a muddle of screaming, emotionally charged thoughts locked behind cages. It was like he noticed a thought leading to some emotion he was unwilling to confront, and he bound it in chains to keep it hidden.

His memories of Uncle Koike were treated much the same way. Yasu struggled to find the man's face, his voice, and the feeling of his hand brushing over Ten's silky hair. It was like a corrupted file, made up of splintering images and jagged pixels.

So too were the memories of the rest of his family. His mother, father, and sisters. There was barely anything of them left, and what was left was sullied, like he had gone into his brain to rewrite the memories over and over until there was nothing decipherable left.

Ten hated the intrusion. As Yasu uncovered a memory, he sensed Ten's irritation, his struggle to scramble the memories and leave them in a worse state than they were before. But Yasu was unrelenting.

Yasu burrowed down, deep within him, finding the day his parents died. He watched through Ten's eyes as he went to buy eggs. Through the windows, they saw the missiles fall from the sky and knew where they had fallen. They dropped the eggs and raced home, not minding the sandal that slipped off their foot. They ran, ran, and ran.

"I hated myself so much," Ten said, his voice small. "I should've been home. My heart... I felt I could rip it out. I wanted to rip it out."

Yasu understood. In a way, it felt like he had experienced the loss, too.

"I wanted a world where this never had to happen. Where everyone could be safe. Where everyone would be peaceful. Of course, I would be god, but I was willing to bear that burden. I knew it was wrong, but I was willing to bear it."

"I understand," Yasu said softly.

He reached for Ten, and Ten didn't pull back. He wrapped the energy around him, tugged on the tether he placed around his friends, and waited to be pulled out of this reality.

## CHAPTER 9

ALEX WOKE up on a soft white bed in a white room with three large windows looking out into nothing. Three other beds were in the room, and his friends lay peacefully on them. They were all snoring, their mouths slightly apart.

"It's peaceful, isn't it?" Peace was his mother again. She wore a floral-patterned dress with puff sleeves, her hair packed up high.

Alex nodded, looking at the whiteness beyond the windows. "Peaceful. Calm." He looked at his slumbering friends. "What happened? I'm hoping we were successful."

The being walked into the room, its bare feet slapping on the tiles. "We were. We've imprisoned Ten."

Alex let out a soft sigh, quickly followed by a loud yawn. "That's good. That's very good."

Peace nodded.

"What happens next? Will you send us home?"

The being laughed, its eyes crinkling. "You're already home. This is a dream. A dream you're all having."

Alex looked at the others in confusion. He tried to pinch himself and felt even more confused when he couldn't grab his flesh.

"See," Peace laughed, "a dream."

"So, where are our bodies?"

"In your world. In your Academy's infirmary." It turned to look at Yasu. "It might be awhile before that one gets up again. What he did took a toll on him."

Alex nodded. He tried to imagine how Yasu coped with so much pressure only on him, but he couldn't think too far. He was overjoyed it was all over.

"No more multiversal missions," he said, letting out another sigh. "I think we've had our fair share of otherworldly adventures for a lifetime."

The being laughed, turning around to walk away. "I don't know about that." Its voice echoed around the room, filling Alex's consciousness with a strange and pleasant airiness. His eyes opened, and he found himself in the infirmary.

Jaxon was sitting in the bed opposite his, wearing a hospital gown, his face crumpled in displeasure. "You're up," he said.

"Why are you so grumpy?" Alex asked. "We're back home. Everyone is safe. Isn't that a good thing?"

Jaxon scratched his head. "I don't know about that. I asked about Yasu when I woke up. And they said he's in critical condition."

A sharp pain shot through Alex's heart. "You can't be serious. The god said…"

"That he was stressed, but fine. That's what they told me, too. But I got here and…"

Alex's brow furrowed. "Let's hope he'll be okay, then."

They sat in silence. Alex soon noticed Nia's bed next to his. She lay on her back; her face peaceful in her repose.

"She looks so beautiful when she's asleep, doesn't she?" A small smile lit up Jaxon's face as he watched her sleep.

"Maybe when she wakes up, you can finally ask her out," Alex said.

"Absolutely not!"

"Why not? A few months ago, you were worried about her and Kel. You should ask her out before she starts hanging out with someone else and you get worried again."

Jaxon opened and shut his mouth in disbelief. "Shouldn't you be more focused on your books? Why are you concerning yourself with mine and Nia's personal lives?"

Alex laughed long and loud. Jaxon kept asking him what was funny, but Alex had no answers. He was merely giddy about everything that had happened. Naturally, he was worried about Yasu, too, and perhaps that anxiety lay beneath the laughter, waiting to turn him into a jittery mess later. For now though, he was more pleased that they had returned home. He couldn't have imagined they would go through any of the things they went through after their first mission. They had battled rogue leaders and rogue interstellar phenomena, and still, they lived. He didn't know what would come in the future, but he knew they were wiser now, and better equipped to face it.

# EPILOGUE

For weeks, Yasu didn't wake up. The other cadets went to his room daily, taking flowers and their notes with them. They talked about school and the progress being made with the research. Multiversal travel was still halted, though the scientists were making significant progress in ensuring the older officers could make it in future journeys. They were also still pariahs of sorts at the Academy. Some cadets thought they were brave for facing an otherworldly villain and returning, while others didn't care.

"What if he dies?" Jaxon asked. They were going from his room to a class.

Nia stopped in the middle of the hallway and smacked his shoulder. "Don't you dare think that!"

"Ouch."

Nia's eyes were misty. "He cannot die."

Jaxon shook his head vigorously. "No, he can't."

"This isn't a joke, Jaxon. If he dies, that's just terrible."

"I know, Nia," he said. "I'm sorry." He opened his arms for a hug and she stepped into his embrace, sniffling.

Alex watched them with a knowing look.

They went to class, concentrating as well as they could on the quantum mechanics topic before them. It was in the middle of that class when an attendant rushed into the lecture theater, his face shining.

"Yasu Garcia has woken up!" he cried.

The cadets didn't wait for permission to leave. They left their books on the desks and flew out of the theater, sped down the hall to the elevator, rode it to the ground floor, and raced out of the building to the infirmary.

Yasu was lying on the bed, his eyes fixed on a single spot in a corner of the ceiling. He heard the footsteps and looked to the door before it opened. "Hello," he said, his voice a weak croak.

"Yasu!" they all called, flocking around his bed in tearful happiness. "We thought we lost you," said Jaxon.

Yasu laughed weakly. "Unfortunately, you'd need more than that to be rid of me."

Jaxon awkwardly brushed his soft, black hair from his face. Alex adjusted his blanket. Nia asked, softly holding his hand, "How are you feeling?"

"Tired," Yasu said. "Let's never do this again."

Everyone began to laugh. They didn't know why, but it seemed to be all they could do. Tears streamed down their faces, and they thought about the stress they had encountered in the past few weeks. They hoped they were entering a calmer period in their lives, filled with mathematical calculations and leisurely walks around the campus.

**The End**

Did you enjoy *The Chronicles of the Starborne Cadets, Volume 1*?
Please consider rating or reviewing it on Goodreads, Bookbub, or
your favorite retailer.
Reviews help me reach new readers.

Want more stories in the ***The Chronicles of the Starborne
Cadets*** series? As soon as I have over 20 reviews, I'll publish the
next 5!

Join my newsletter for writing updates, sneak peaks, review copies,
sales, and giveaways! www.mhlebeault.com

## ABOUT THE AUTHOR

Positive, uplifting books and stories.

Marie-Hélène Lebeault is the author of *The Evers Series, Clarity Castle, What Happens Next? Readers Decide Which Story Becomes a Book, the Blood Magick Trilogy, Holiday Shifters, Ghost Stories, Defenders of the Realm, Utopia, Chronicles of the Starborne Cadets, Legends Reborn,* as well as a series of picture books called Fairy Grandmother. She lives in Canada with her grown children.

www.mhlebeault.com

Follow on Social Media, she'd love to hear from you!

facebook.com/mhlebeaultauthor

x.com/mhlebeault

instagram.com/mhlebeault

amazon.com/author/mhlebeault

bookbub.com/authors/marie-helene-lebeault

goodreads.com/mhlebeault

linkedin.com/in/mhlebeault

tiktok.com/@mhlebeaultauthor

## ALSO BY THE AUTHOR

### Legends Reborn (Fairytale Retellings)

A Curse of Snow and Ash

A Curse of Thorns and Slumber

A Curse of Glass and Shadows

A Curse of Scars and Silver

### The Chronicles of the Starborne Cadets

Confluence of Destinies (Prequel)

Stars Beyond Realms

Shadows of Orion

Echoes of the Void

The Nebula's Heart

The Starborne Paradox

### Defenders of the Realm

A Journey to Power

The Quest for the Emerald Rattleback

A Summer of Discovery

The Quest for the Sacred Tree

A Summer of Opposites

The Quest for the Phantom Feather

A Summer of Courage

The Quest for the Kraken's Ink

A Summer of Destiny

The Quest for the Cursed Mirrors

A Summer of Unity

Defenders of the Realm - Special Edition Hardcover Set

**The Evers Series**

The Ancestors' Key

The Academy

The Time Walker

The World Jumper

5th Anniversary Edition Omnibus

The Traveler's Handbook

The Lost Key

**Blood Magick Trilogy**

The Blood Mage

Blood Magick

Blood Legacy

Extended Edition Omnibus

**Standalones**

Clarity Castle

What Happens Next?

Ghost Stories

Holiday Shifters

Echoes of Tomorrow

Utopia

**Picture Books**

Fairy Grandmother: Millie Goes to Antarctica

Fairy Grandmother: Millie Goes to the North Pole

Fairy Grandmother: Millie Goes to China

Fairy Grandmother: Millie Goes to Africa

(Also available in French, Spanish, German, and Italian)